# THE BODY UNDER THE STAGE

---

KATE HARDY

## Storm

PUBLISHING

Ebook ISBN: 978-1-80508-384-9
Paperback ISBN: 978-1-80508-386-3

Cover design by: Dissect Designs
Cover images by: Shutterstock, Adobe Stock

Published by Storm Publishing.
For further information, visit:
www.stormpublishing.co

## ALSO BY KATE HARDY

### A Georgina Drake Mystery

*For Fi and Phil – here's to all the wonderful performances we've seen together since our student days :)*

# ONE

Irene Taylor didn't *look* like a murderer.

Then again, the two murderers Georgina had already met hadn't looked like murderers, either. Nor had the one she hadn't met but whose actions had rippled out to affect Georgina's life.

Irene sat in a high-backed easy chair by the window overlooking the garden, a blanket over her lap, her hands in a soft muffler and her fine white hair cropped short for easy management. She was wearing a cardigan that was way too big for her and clashed with her sweater, and her face was completely bare of make-up. Her blue eyes were watery. Instead of being the haughty, immaculately groomed woman that Georgina had been expecting from Doris's description, Irene looked small, wrinkled and lost.

For a moment, Georgina thought of her own mother and felt a wave of pity for Irene.

But then she thought of Doris, and her heart hardened again. This woman had got away with murder – or, at the very least, had caused a fatal accident and done nothing to help the victim – for half a century. She'd continue to get away with it, too, because Georgina had no proof that would stand up in a court of law. There had been nobody to witness Irene Taylor pushing ten-weeks-pregnant Doris Beauchamp down the stairs – at least, nobody who could be heard by anyone other than Georgina, through her hearing aids.

The evidence was circumstantial. And, even if Irene admitted the truth, she couldn't be tried in a court of law. Her diagnosis of dementia meant that she didn't legally have the mental capacity to answer questions in court.

In some respects, this visit was pointless. But, if Irene told the truth, it would at least give Doris closure. Georgina was the only one who could find out what had really happened to the young woman who haunted her house and had become her friend. Had it been an unfortunate accident, or had Doris been deliberately pushed? And had Irene been the one to deliver the fatal shove – or had it been Trevor, the love of Doris's life and the father of her unborn baby, who now seemed to have disappeared?

'Someone to see you, Mrs Taylor,' the care assistant said chirpily. 'And, look, she's brought you some lovely bright flowers.'

Orange lilies. Lovely and bright, indeed: but, in the language of flowers, they signified contempt, which Georgina thought made them the perfect gift for a woman who'd been steeped in unkindness. *Lilies that fester smell far worse than weeds*, Georgina quoted in her head, stiffening her resolve with Shakespeare.

'Mrs Taylor. Thank you so much for agreeing to see me,' she said.

'It'll be nice for her to have a visitor for once,' the care assistant murmured. 'She's been here for three years and not had a single visitor in all that time apart from the social worker, the poor love.'

She's not a 'love' at all – she's the epitome of a difficult mother-in-law, Georgina thought, but managed an innocuous, 'How sad.'

'Her son lives abroad,' the care assistant continued. 'He sends her flowers once a month, but it's not the same as a visit, is it?'

And now Georgina felt really guilty. It must be a month since she'd seen her own mother in person. They spoke every day on a video call, but the care assistant was right: it wasn't the same as a visit. You couldn't hold someone's hand or give them a proper hug over the phone.

'That summer cold really took it out of her,' the care assistant continued.

Georgina had had a similar virus at the end of July. Knowing how quickly a simple cold could turn to pneumonia in the elderly, and not wanting to risk passing it on to anyone vulnerable, she'd rescheduled her original planned visit to Irene's nursing home. The virus had spread through the residents anyway, and Irene had been too poorly with pneumonia to see Georgina for the following month. But now the nursing team had said she was fine to have visitors again.

The care assistant checked the temperature of Irene's hands, tucked the blanket a little more closely round her, assessed how much of the water Irene had actually drunk from the lidded beaker, made a couple of notes on her tablet, and smiled. 'I'll go and put these in a vase for you, Mrs Taylor. And you can have a nice chat with Georgina, can't you?' She looked at Georgina. 'Can I get you a cup of tea or anything, love?'

'No, but thank you for asking,' Georgina said, smiling back.

And then, once the carer had closed the door, it was just her and Irene.

Time for the truth.

'Hello, Irene,' Georgina said.

Irene's pale blue eyes narrowed. 'Why are you calling me by my first name? I don't know you.'

All right. She'd play it Irene's way. 'No, you don't know me, Mrs Taylor. But my name's Georgina Drake and I live in Little Wenborough. I'm looking into the history of my house' – and the murder of my friend, she thought but didn't say – 'and you told the staff here you'd be happy to share your memories with me.'

Irene simply stared at her.

Had that dose of pneumonia taken out another layer of Irene's memories? Was Georgina too late to find out the truth? 'Do you remember Little Wenborough?' Georgina asked, keeping her voice rather more gentle than she felt.

'Of course I do. I used to live there.'

That curl of Irene's lip, and the little tinge of contempt in her voice, exactly chimed with what Doris had told her. Irene had clearly decided that Georgina was her social inferior, too. Georgina didn't react to Irene's snootiness; instead, she talked to the older woman about the village and the people who lived there. They touched on Irene's late husband, Howard ('dead'), the Red Lion ('the Fulchers are no better than they should be'), and Little Wenborough Manor ('terrible snobs' – which, to Georgina, sounded like a cover-up for the fact the Walters family hadn't let her into their social circle. Knowing Sybbie and Bernard, Georgina was absolutely sure it had had nothing to do with Irene's social class and everything to do with the fact that Irene was utterly poisonous).

Georgina hadn't known Howard Taylor, but in her view the Fulchers were kind and generous, particularly Jodie who cleaned the barn for her; and, in the two years since she'd moved to Little Wenborough, Lady Sybbie from the Manor had become one of her dearest friends. And how could Irene be so dismissive about her husband's death? OK, so Irene had been a widow for much longer than Georgina, but Georgina couldn't imagine ever being so blasé about Stephen. Irene's sniffy, dismissive attitude took away the remaining shreds of guilt

Georgina felt at tackling an elderly, sick woman about a diffi-cult subject and she flicked into her phone. 'I thought you might like to see my house.' She showed Irene a picture of Rookery Farm.

Was it her imagination, or had Irene's face lost a little colour?

'It used to be a dairy farm. Back in the 1970s, the Beauchamp family lived there. Do you remember them?' Georgina asked.

'I didn't have much to do with them,' Irene muttered.

Because her husband was an accountant and she thought that made her so much better socially than a dairy farmer? Georgina thought. Or had Irene reinvented the past, and was pretending that her son had never dated Doris? 'Trevor liked Lizzy and Albert,' she said quietly. 'Very much.'

Irene said nothing.

'And he loved Doris.'

'That little red-haired *tart*. She set her cap at him,' Irene hissed, her face creased with spite. 'She was only after our money.'

Georgina was really glad that she'd refused to let Doris join her today. No way did she want her friend hearing venom like this. Despite Doris protesting that Irene couldn't do any more to hurt her, Georgina knew that words could wound as deeply as physical weapons. Even after all these years since Doris's death, Irene clearly still bore a grudge. And the saddest thing was that it wasn't true. Doris was all about love, not money.

'Trevor loved Doris,' Georgina repeated. 'And Doris loved him.'

'He had a bright future. He had a guaranteed job as an accountant, working with his father. She would have just dragged him down,' Irene said, her lip wrinkling into a sneer.

An *accountant*? According to Doris, Trevor had wanted to play his guitar and teach music. Georgina held her breath. Was

Irene about to admit to what she'd done? 'So you made sure she didn't get the chance?' she asked, very quietly.

'I know what I know,' Irene said, lifting her chin and looking away.

Georgina had a feeling that Irene was the sort to play power games. No doubt if she'd realised Georgina was deaf, she would've mumbled too low for Georgina's hearing aids to pick up the words, and sat with her face turned away so that Georgina couldn't even lip-read. 'I know about the baby,' Georgina said. 'And what happened on Valentine's night.' That last bit wasn't strictly true, but she hoped it might loosen Irene's tongue enough for the truth to come out at last.

'She was going to trap my son,' Irene said, turning back to face Georgina. 'I had to do *something*.'

'So you made her drink gin and pushed her down the stairs?' Georgina asked.

Irene frowned, and said nothing. Just as Georgina was about to rephrase her question, Irene asked, 'Who?'

She suddenly seemed confused. But was that really the case, Georgina wondered, or was she pretending not to know? There was something belligerent in the set of Irene's jaw.

Georgina knew from the staff at her mother's sheltered accommodation that music often sparked memories for patients who suffered dementia. Maybe that would help. Or, if Irene was shamming, maybe the musical connection to Doris would annoy Irene enough to make her drop her guard and tell the truth. 'Remember their favourite song?' she asked, and sang a little of 'My Sweet Lord'.

'I hate that song,' Irene said. 'He's a scruffy man who needs a good wash and a haircut. I like Perry Como.' She sang a quavery snatch of 'Magic Moments'.

'What about a bit of Doris Day?' Georgina asked, remembering what Doris's ghost had sung to her on the day they'd 'met' and she'd heard Doris's voice through her hearing aids. She sang the chorus of 'Que Sera Sera'.

Irene's lip curled. '*Doris*,' she said, angry spittle flying from her mouth. 'She wanted to take my son away. I couldn't have that.'

'So you killed her,' Georgina said softly. 'And you got away with it for all these years.'

Although – in some ways, Irene *hadn't* got away with it. It sounded as if she'd pushed Doris down the stairs to make sure Trevor couldn't go to London with his girlfriend; but Trevor had left Little Wenborough anyway. And he hadn't visited Irene for at least the last three years, probably longer than that. Irene's plan to keep her son right by her side clearly hadn't worked.

'You saw Trevor with the gin; then you realised what had happened and what the doctor would've told them to do,' Georgina said. 'You made Doris have a hot bath, you made her drink the gin... and then you pushed her down the stairs.'

'I had to make her get rid of it,' Irene said through clenched teeth. 'I had to.'

'You didn't need to push her down the stairs,' Georgina said. 'She hit her head. You must've seen it happen. You could've called the ambulance and saved her. But you didn't. You deliberately left her to die – because you wanted to get rid of her as well as the baby. You killed her, Irene.'

'I did what I had to do,' Irene said. 'And it's not my fault that Trevor did what he did. It's *not*.'

Georgina caught her breath. What was Irene trying to say? That it wasn't her fault he'd got Doris pregnant? Or was it something more sinister, and Irene was trying to say that *Trevor* had pushed Doris down the stairs, not her? But Trevor had loved Doris... Hadn't he? 'Did what?' she asked.

'I can't talk about it.'

Which didn't help. Back in those days, being unmarried and pregnant had been seen as shameful. Then again, pushing someone to their death was also something you wouldn't want to talk about.

Georgina decided to go for the blunt approach. 'Did Trevor push Doris down the stairs?'

The pale blue eyes turned on her, along with a snooty expression. 'Who?'

It was clear to Georgina that she wasn't going to get any further with Irene. Either the older woman was clever enough to know when to pretend to be confused, or she had the Lewy Bodies type of dementia that made her confusion levels vary from hour to hour and she really *was* confused. And if she did know what she was saying, she wouldn't incriminate her son. 'Never mind,' Georgina said. She couldn't stay one more minute in this woman's poisonous presence. Irene made her feel sick to her stomach. 'Goodbye, Irene.'

She closed the door behind her and headed back out to the reception area.

'How did you get on?' the receptionist asked with a smile. 'Did she remember anything that helped you?'

'Some things,' Georgina said, returning the smile. She didn't want to burn her bridges by admitting what she'd really wanted to know. 'I believe her son lives in America?'

The receptionist looked awkward. 'Sorry. With Data Protection regulations and what have you, I can't really say anything.'

'Would you be able to pass my details to him and ask him to contact me, please?' Georgina asked.

The receptionist's face cleared. 'Yes, I can do that. Though obviously I can't promise he'll get in touch. That'll be up to him.'

'Hopefully he'll call me.' Georgina took a business card from her bag and gave it to her. 'Thank you so much.'

The care assistant who'd taken her to Irene's room came

into the reception area, and said, 'I'll come and let you out of the front door.'

Georgina smiled her thanks.

The care assistant looked over her shoulder at the reception desk, then tapped the code into the panel by the door to release the catch. 'I know Khaj on reception can't tell you anything, but I hate to see these poor old dears never having any company,' she said in a low voice. 'He works in LA. He's got a recording studio. It's called Dorian or something like that – I remember that because my gran's name was Doreen and it reminded me of her. You should be able to find a website.' She gave a cross nod. 'And you tell that Harrison Taylor he needs to get his backside over here to see his mum, before it's too late.'

'Harrison?' Georgina hadn't expected that. 'I thought he was called Trevor?' Had she got the wrong Irene Taylor? But Irene had known people in Little Wenborough. She'd known Doris. This couldn't be a case of mistaken identity – could it?

The care assistant shrugged. 'Mrs Taylor calls him Trevor, but there was a problem with the flowers one time, and when we rang the florist she said his name was Harrison, not Trevor.' She shrugged again. 'Or maybe he just calls himself that in LA to make himself sound like a film star.'

'Harrison Ford?' Georgina said. 'Maybe he's a big *Star Wars* fan.' Or perhaps he'd adopted the name from his and Doris's favourite musician.

No wonder she hadn't been able to find Trevor Taylor. She should've been looking for Harrison Taylor all along.

And his company was called Dorian. After Doris? It was far more likely that he'd called it after the woman he'd loved than after the woman he'd killed, Georgina thought. Which still left his mother as the number one suspect for pushing Doris down the stairs. 'Thank you. I'll look them up. And I'll pass on your message.'

'Good,' the care assistant said.

Back at the farmhouse, she fielded Doris's questions about Irene and Trevor, stonewalling Doris until she gave up and went off in a huff, then looked up Harrison Taylor of Dorian Studios in LA.

There was a phone number. Georgina glanced at her watch. Four pm UK time would be around eight am LA time, she calculated. Even if Trevor – or Harrison, as he was now – was the sort who'd stay up all night with music and roll into the studios in the middle of the afternoon, someone in his office was bound to be a health nut who did a workout before breakfast and would be at their desk early, sipping green tea.

She rang the number.

'Dorian Recording Studios, Marcia speaking. How can I help?' a West-Coast accent asked her.

'Hi, my name's Georgina Drake. I'm from England and I'm researching the history of my house. I'd like to talk to Mr Taylor, please,' Georgina explained.

'You live in his old house? How cool! His village had such a quaint name – Little...' Marcia paused. 'Something or other. I can't remember.'

'Little Wenborough,' Georgina said.

'That's it! So cute,' Marcia said.

'And it looks even cuter than it sounds,' Georgina said. 'I was wondering, would it be possible to speak to Mr Taylor, or leave a message, please?'

'I'm so sorry, Ms Drake. He left here three years ago,' Marcia said.

One step forward and two steps back, Georgina thought. 'May I ask, do you know where he went?'

'Back to England because his mom was ill,' Marcia said. 'It was only supposed to be for a couple of weeks, but he never came back. His partner, Todd, bought him out.'

That was odd. Irene had moved to Lake View Nursing Home three years ago. Trevor – or Harrison – definitely didn't live in Little Wenborough, and the nursing home staff were convinced that he still lived in LA. Why did his colleagues in LA think he was in England? 'You don't happen to have any contact details for him, by any chance? Or would Todd?' Georgina checked.

'No. The last few emails he sent bounced, and his cellphone number was unobtainable. Todd sent a letter, but it came back marked "return to sender", so I guess Harrison must've moved. Maybe with the worry of his mom, it slipped his mind to pass on his new number and address. I'm so sorry.'

This sounded as if he hadn't wanted to be traced. 'Well, thanks for your help,' Georgina said.

'Good luck. I hope you find him,' Marcia said, and ended the call.

Georgina was still brooding about it later that evening, when Colin Bradshaw dropped in. Since Colin had investigated the death of Roland Garnett in her holiday cottage some months before, they'd become friends. More than friends; neither of them was quite ready to define their relationship, but on days when they didn't see each other they usually phoned or texted.

'It's really odd,' Georgina said, filling him in on the way she'd failed to find the boyfriend of the young woman who'd died at Rookery Farm fifty-two years ago. 'He changed his name from Trevor to Harrison, but nobody in Little Wenborough seemed to know about that. And he left his recording studios in LA three years ago, when his mother went to Lake View Nursing Home. In LA, they think he left America to come back here to take care of his mother, but in England they all think he's still in LA. He sends Irene flowers every month, but he never visits her.'

'Plenty of people change their name,' Colin said. 'As for not visiting her – some people don't get on with their parents and it's easier to keep a bit of distance.'

She recalled what he'd told her a couple of months ago about his parents not approving of his job – or his sister's. He'd given her the impression he wasn't close to them. But she rather thought that if his parents needed nursing care, Colin would sort it out. And he'd visit them, even if the visits were brief and not very frequent.

'There must be some way of tracking him down.'

Colin raised an eyebrow. 'I hope you know better than to ask me to find him.'

'Because it's against the rules for you to use the police computer to find out his details. Don't worry. I understand that.' She paused. 'Though Irene said something odd. She said what Trevor did wasn't her fault. So was *he* the one who pushed Doris down the stairs?'

Colin looked shocked. 'Are you telling me you asked her straight out if she killed Doris?'

Georgina rubbed a hand across her face. 'Not *quite*. I asked her if she pushed Doris down the stairs. She said she did what she had to do. Which makes it sound as if she was the murderer, except then she appeared to be blaming Trevor.'

'Georgie, I really think you should leave this,' Colin said quietly. 'The woman has dementia. She probably isn't aware of half of what she's saying. Even if she *was* the one who pushed Doris down the stairs, she'll never stand trial for it because she doesn't have the mental capacity to answer questions in court. And if Trevor – or Harrison – was the one who killed her, then I'd say that living with fifty years of guilt will have made him dangerous. Ask the wrong questions, and you could end up getting hurt. Please don't put yourself at risk.'

'I won't put myself at risk,' Georgina said. 'But I need to know the truth, Colin. It's important.'

He looked at her for a long, long moment, assessing her, then sighed. 'If you find him, then I'd like to be with you when you talk to him. Firstly to make sure he doesn't lash out at you, and secondly to support you in asking the right questions to help you get to the truth.'

'I'm fifty-two, Colin. I'm old enough not to need babysitting,' she said, rolling her eyes.

'True, but during the last six months you've also been poisoned, had a stone finial pushed from a roof onto the place where you were standing seconds before, and been driven down a hill in a car which had the brakes cut,' he reminded her.

'I'm guessing you've been shot at, stabbed and hit with a variety of things yourself,' she countered.

'Which is part of my job, and I'm prepared for it,' he said. He folded his arms and stared at her. 'Of course, if you refuse to take me with you, I'll see it as my duty to warn Bea, Will and Sybbie what you plan to do.'

'That's blackmail,' she said. If he told them her plan, her children and her closest local friend would nag her about it.

'I promised them I'd keep you safe,' he said. 'And I keep my promises, Georgie. So. Your choice. You agree to take me with you, or I grass you up to them.'

'Oh, you *canary*,' she said, huffing. 'All right. If I find him, I'll tell you.' She paused. 'Actually, I'm going to London to stay with Bea for a few days, next week. I promised to take the Regency Theatre's promo shots for *Macbeth*. If you've got some leave, maybe you'd like to join me?'

'I'd like that,' he said. 'So I'll get to see you work?'

'Pretty much,' she said. 'Though you can earn your dinner by sitting with Bert while I'm working.'

'Sounds good to me,' he said. 'It's a date.'

'Yes.' She stole a kiss. 'It is.'

# TWO

'I'm only sorry it's not the West End,' Georgina said as they walked through Islington from the Tube station. Plenty of people in the city used an earpiece with their phone; anyone overhearing her in the street would assume she was on her phone and ignore what she was saying. And they certainly wouldn't think she was chatting to a ghost.

'Are you *kidding?*' Doris sounded as if she was nearly weeping with joy. 'I get to see the dress rehearsal of a play I know and love *in London*, just as I would've done if I'd been a student. I've walked down the King's Road with you and Bea, and it doesn't matter that the Biba shop isn't there anymore – I finally got to walk past where it *was* and I can imagine what I would've bought from it. And we walked up Primrose Hill, a path Sylvia Plath would've walked along, and we saw Shakespeare's tree. I've been on the Tube. We're going to the British Museum to see the mummies and the Natural History Museum to see the dinosaurs and the British Library to see the First Folio. You're making so many of my old dreams come true, Georgie. I can't thank you enough.'

'My pleasure,' Georgina said, meaning it. And, in a way, it

was useful that Colin had become involved in a case at the last minute and couldn't come to London, because it meant that she could share London with Doris without having to explain anything to him. Knowing his views on the paranormal, she was pretty sure he wouldn't believe her if she told him about Doris. Sometimes even Georgina struggled to believe she was talking to the ghost of an eighteen-year-old who had died in the house Georgina moved to after her husband's death. Georgina's new hearing aids had picked up Doris's voice and, once they'd got over the shock of actually being able to communicate with each other, the two women had become firm friends.

'The only things missing,' Doris said, 'are Trev and George Harrison.'

Georgina winced. 'Sadly, George Harrison didn't play in London when you would've been a student here, so you wouldn't have seen him play,' she said. 'And I'm still trying to track down Trev.' Or Harrison. She hadn't quite been able to bring herself to explain that to Doris yet. How did you tell someone that the person they'd loved for more than half a century might have been involved in their death?

'I know,' Doris said. 'I wasn't having a go.'

'I know,' Georgina echoed. 'I'm just grumpy because I should've been able to find him by now.' She'd called the nursing home and ended up speaking to the care assistant who'd helped her before, explained that Irene's son had moved on from the recording studio without a forwarding address, and asked if she could pass on a message via the florist.

'You're trying. And I appreciate that,' Doris said. 'Just as I appreciate you bringing me to London. How amazing, to be going to an original Regency theatre.'

'Not *quite* original. It was repaired in the 1960s,' Georgina reminded her, 'after being bombed during the Blitz, and then about twenty years ago Peter Newton – who leases the theatre as well as being the director – restored it back to how it was in

Regency times. His team used copies of etchings, plus accounts of the theatre in letters and newspapers, to help with the restoration.'

'So it's going to be just like seeing Shakespeare as they would've done two hundred years ago,' Doris said gleefully. 'With a dress circle, a gallery and a pit.'

'Except with much more comfortable seating, proper toilets and electric lighting,' Georgina added. She groaned. 'I don't think I would've enjoyed a Regency performance. Imagine how hot it would've been, all those people squashed into a small space for five hours while they watched a couple of plays, jugglers and tightrope walkers and singers.'

'And the smells – people overheating, drinking beer, and not being able to go out to the toilet,' Doris agreed. 'What's the plan for today?'

'I'm meeting Peter for a chat, and then I'm going to take the promo pics of the cast. I'll shoot them in costume, first, and take a few action shots during the dress rehearsal; and then I'll do some more headshots when they're out of costume. Meanwhile, you can sit wherever you like and just enjoy the play. Bert will follow me.'

'I still can't believe I'm actually going to see *Macbeth* performed in a London theatre,' Doris said. 'And Islington is so much grander than I expected.'

'The architecture round here is lovely,' Georgina agreed.

'Do you know Peter Newton well?' Doris asked.

'Yes. I've known him for years. He's a family friend and he even directed Stephen in a few shows,' Georgina said. 'But that isn't why Bea got the part of Lady Macbeth. She got it because she was the right person for it.'

'Duh. That's *obvious*,' Doris said. 'If there's no chemistry between your leads, the play won't work and the reviews will all be terrible.'

Georgina gave a wry chuckle. 'Sorry. Of course you get that.'

'If you want the audience to buy tickets and tell everyone they enjoyed the show, you hire the best actors,' Doris said. 'And I've heard Bea practising her lines in the garden at Rookery Farm. She's *good*.'

'Thank you. And, even if you take out maternal bias, I agree,' Georgina said.

They stopped in front of the Regency Theatre; it was built of rich, honey-coloured stone, with a triangular pediment. There were flat pilasters between the windows, with ornately scrolled capitals and bases; carved swags of flowers draped between them, over the tops of the large windows with their ornate tympanums containing theatrical masks. The whole thing was beautifully dramatic and exactly what a Regency theatre should look like.

Inside, the foyer was more understated, with recessed lighting and two very large ferns in duck-egg-blue pots. There were plenty of photographs on the walls of famous actors who'd played on the stage over the years – including, to Georgina's delight, one of Stephen.

Peter Newton came out of the box office and into the foyer, greeting Georgina with a hug. 'Good to see you, Georgie. You're looking well.'

'You, too, Pete.' Though it wasn't strictly true; his face was etched with strain, he was noticeably thinner than the last time she'd seen him, and his hair had gone wispy. It was worrying to see an old friend change so much in a couple of years. Was he ill, perhaps? And then an unsettling thought struck her: or had something gone wrong at the theatre where her daughter had just got her dream job?

'So this is the dog Bea's been telling me about.' Peter bent down to scratch the top of Bert's head. 'Hello. You're a lovely boy, aren't you?'

Bert wagged his tail and sat very nicely, clearly hoping for a treat as well as a fuss.

Peter smiled up at Georgina. 'Stephen would've liked him. Though I think he might've chosen a more Shakespearean name.'

Georgina laughed. 'I certainly wouldn't have let him change Bert's name to Crab!'

'Ah, the naughtiest dog in Shakespeare,' Peter said, standing up and accepting the dog biscuit she gave him. 'He pinches a chicken leg and pees on a woman's skirt. Would *you* do anything so naughty, Bert?'

Bert wagged his tail again, clearly recognising the word 'chicken', and lifted a paw politely. Peter chuckled and fed him the biscuit.

'Stealing chicken, probably, if he couldn't charm it out of you in the first place; peeing on a skirt, no.' Georgina smiled at him. 'I take it the cast's ready for me to take the headshots?'

'Nearly. And then you can take whatever shots you like during the rehearsal,' Peter said. 'I know you won't distract them. Come and have a coffee before you start.' He led her through to the theatre kitchen and made them both a coffee before shepherding her through to his office.

Bert curled up next to Georgina's feet while she sipped her coffee.

'You're looking a bit worried, Pete,' she said quietly. 'What's wrong?'

He wrinkled his nose. 'You know how it is with the Scottish Play. A few little things go wrong, and you try to brush them off – just as you would if it was any other play – but in your head they start to add up to rather more than the sum of the parts. And then you wonder if the old story about the curse on the play really *is* true.'

Starting with the very first performance of the play where Lady Macbeth had died suddenly and unexpectedly, and

Shakespeare himself had had to step in and play the part – even though that particular anecdote had been completely made up by the nineteenth-century cartoonist Max Beerbohm, people still believed it. Georgina suppressed a shiver. Bea hadn't mentioned any problems with the play. Although Georgina had been horrified when her daughter had called, three weeks ago, with the news that she'd broken her wrist, Bea had made light of it, saying it was her own fault for being 'in the zone' for the sleepwalking scene, not noticing that the edge of the stage was so close, and falling. 'What's happened? Apart from Bea's wrist, that is?'

'What hasn't happened?' Peter asked, rolling his eyes. 'The first day we were building the set, some of the scenery collapsed on one of the carpenters, hurting his shoulder and putting him out of action for a couple of days. Then Bea fell off stage and fractured her wrist – luckily it wasn't a bad break, she doesn't have to lift anything with her left hand and the costumes for both her roles hide her cast. We've had lights breaking – expensive ones – and it's been a hassle to replace them. Rebekah, our First Murderer, had food poisoning. A weight from the flies fell and narrowly missed Elias – he plays Macbeth,' he added, in case Georgina wasn't completely familiar with the cast. 'Taken singly, they're nothing unusual. But, put together, they feel *unlucky*. And half the cast are spooked, saying they've heard weird noises and seen shadows where there shouldn't be any.'

'*Life's but a walking shadow*,' Georgina quoted.

His answering smile at the appropriateness of Macbeth's most famous soliloquy was only momentary. 'You know how jumpy actors can be. It's starting to rub off on me. Ignore me. I'm being ridiculous. Overdramatic.'

'Which is what a director is supposed to be,' Georgina teased. He didn't laugh. Seeing the worry in his eyes, she asked gently, 'But?'

'I need this show to be a hit,' Peter admitted.

Georgina knew that the arts sector had been struggling for a while, and Covid had made things harder. 'Pete, you know as well as I do that this play will bring the schools in,' she reassured him. 'If the play's not on the syllabus for GCSE or A level, it'll be used as an introduction to Shakespeare for the Year Nines. You'll be able to fill up matinees easily – and maybe get schools in for special workshops, if you want to run them.'

'It's on the syllabus and I've got a couple of workshops booked,' he said. 'Rebekah – the First Murderer – her sister-in-law teaches English at one of the local schools. Her class is coming in for a workshop.'

'That's good,' Georgina said. 'And you know as well as I do that the ridiculous superstition about *M*— the Scottish Play,' she corrected herself swiftly, not wanting to make him feel even more twitchy, 'being unlucky only started because it was the play a company would put on if the run was going badly and they needed to pay the bills – it's popular and almost guaranteed to sell out.'

'Even so. I kind of wish I'd picked a different play,' Peter said. 'Some of the crew have been muttering about the theatre being haunted.'

'Any old building in London worth its salt will have a ghost story attached to it,' Georgina said, ignoring the wry chuckle from Doris. 'What's the story with the ghost here?'

'No idea. Probably something to do with the Blitz, seeing as this place was pretty much gutted back then,' he said. 'We're lucky that the local heritage group bought the site just after the war and made what was left of it watertight. It took fifteen years or so for the legal wrangles to be sorted and it was made usable again, and then when I took over the lease I decided to restore it to how it was in Regency times.'

'You did a great job. Stephen loved it here,' Georgina said.

'And he was good with the younger actors. He always

brought them on instead of –' Peter wrinkled his nose. 'Sorry. Some days I have less patience with actors' egos than others.'

'Stephen always put the egomaniacs on the "Wannabe Nick" list,' Georgina said with a grin. Peter, as an old friend and colleague, would know exactly what she meant.

'Except you'd have to be good for Stephen to actually cast you as Nick Bottom,' Peter agreed ruefully. 'Maybe I ought to make my own "Wannabe Nick" list.'

'Talking of lists, I need to work through mine. Do I need to shoot the actors in any particular order, to make your life easier?' Georgina asked.

'No. I've done more than enough pandering to egos, this week,' Peter said. 'You're the photographer. You do it how it suits *you*. And if N— *anyone*,' he corrected himself quickly, 'gives you a hard time, refer them to me.'

'Thanks.' Georgina smiled. 'I'd better get started.' She headed for the green room, and took her headshots of the cast in strict alphabetical order.

'One would have *thought* the photographer would do the shoot in descending order of cast seniority,' Neil Faulkner drawled when it was his turn.

You and your over-whitened teeth are definitely on the 'Wannabe Nick' list, Georgina thought. Clearly you're the 'N' Peter was about to tell me was likely to kick up a fuss. But she gave him a bland smile. 'Alphabetical order makes it easy for me to tick off names and make sure I don't miss anyone,' she said sweetly.

Bert gave the tiniest growl, and she looked at him in surprise; he was usually the sweetest-natured dog, keen to make friends with everyone he met. He'd definitely taken to Jake, the young boy who played the roles of Fleance, Seyton, the First Witch and Young Macduff. But the spaniel now sat by Georgina's feet, just staring at Neil Faulkner, as if to say that he was on guard and watching every move the man might make.

She scratched the top of Bert's head. 'Good boy,' she said softly.

Once all the headshots were done, the dress rehearsal began. Georgina sat on the front row, unobtrusively taking photographs; Liza Sheridan, the wardrobe mistress, was bustling about in the wings, making alterations to costumes with pins as the actors came off the stage, and occasionally make-up as well. Georgina noticed Liza squeezing a couple of hands and patting a couple of shoulders in reassurance; clearly the actors were having a last-minute wobble. Rich Neville, the stage manager, stopped rehearsals a couple of times to make small changes to lighting and sound.

Georgina had forgotten what a buzz the dress rehearsal was. Everyone had rehearsed their lines and movements in plain clothes, and this started the excitement that would lift them through to opening night. Despite the fact she was working, she thoroughly enjoyed watching the play and seeing her daughter shining as Lady Macbeth. Stephen would've been so proud of her. The depth Bea brought to the performance moved Georgina to tears: particularly the scene where Lady Macbeth was folding away baby clothes just before she received Macbeth's letter and it was so obvious that the queen's invocation to the spirits and hard-bitten persona was a façade to hide a deep personal sorrow, and it would crumble as her husband's character changed.

This would also be the first time Georgina had photographed a Pepper's Ghost: a nineteenth-century stage effect, made from a thin sheet of clear glass set at an angle to the stage. She knew how it worked in principle, but had never actually seen one in performance. An actor would work in a room that was hidden from the audience; the brightly lit image of the actor was projected onto the screen, and the screen would cast the translucent image onto the stage. During the feast scene,

Neil Faulkner would act Banquo's part in a room below the stage, carefully marked out, and the projection angled so his image would appear on the stage exactly where Macbeth 'saw' it.

Even to a modern audience used to special effects, Banquo's ghost really *would* look like a ghost.

But first the three hooded and masked Murderers needed to do away with Banquo.

'Ow!' Neil stepped out of role, glaring at the Murderers. 'You're not supposed to hit me so bloody hard when you stab me. Didn't you learn anything at RADA?' He turned to the First Murderer. 'Oh, wait – you didn't get *in* to RADA, did you, Rebekah?'

The snobbery was grating – and it was clearly meant to wound Neil's fellow actor.

'Sorry,' Rebekah mumbled; though it sounded more like a sorry-not-sorry to Georgina's ears.

'There's no need for that, Neil,' the Second Murderer said, and Georgina recognised her daughter's voice.

'Huh. *You're* no better, trading on Daddy's name,' Neil sneered, and Georgina had to clench her fists and press her bottom into the seat to stop herself leaping up onto the stage and delivering a strong right hook to his jaw. Bea had won that part by hard work and talent, not nepotism. Who the hell did Neil Faulkner think he was?

'Thank you for your uninformed and uninvited opinion, Neil,' Bea said crisply. 'Perhaps you need to remember that we're meant to be a *team*. It doesn't matter where you studied. Undermining other actors isn't helpful and it certainly doesn't make you look better.'

'You—'

But whatever venom Neil had intended to spew at Bea was cut off by Peter calling from the middle of the auditorium.

'Everyone, go back to the beginning of the scene, please. I know it's only a dress rehearsal, but I'd like everyone to treat it as the real thing. Remember, we open on Friday night.'

Neil rolled his eyes, as if to say he was far more professional than the rest of the cast and didn't need to be told – and he didn't need any input from the director, either.

Just how had Bea been able to stand working with someone so pompous and self-absorbed? Georgina wondered. And why hadn't she mentioned before how difficult and horrible Neil Faulkner was? Or maybe Bea was trying to make the best of it because it was a dream role for her, and she didn't want to get a reputation as a moaner-and-groaner.

The actors went back to their places at the beginning of the scene and began again. To Georgina's eyes, the three Murderers appeared to hit Banquo just as hard this time round – and rather less hard than Georgina would've wanted to hit him, in their shoes – but thankfully Neil didn't break role and complain again. Banquo bellowed, 'Fly, Fleance, fly!' and crumpled to the floor, dead; the lights went out for long enough for Neil to use the trapdoor to the room under the stage and prepare for the 'ghost' part of the performance in the next scene, while the Second and Third Murderers went backstage for a lightning-fast costume change back to their main roles as Lady Macbeth and Macbeth respectively.

The feast scene began with Macbeth welcoming his guests before slipping off to speak with one of the Murderers, worrying that Fleance had escaped. Lady Macbeth chided her husband for ignoring their guests, and Lennox asked him to sit at the table.

Now it was time for the bit Georgina had been really looking forward to: seeing her first Pepper's Ghost in action. She held her camera ready to take the shot.

Except, when the projection came onto the stage, Banquo

wasn't sitting in Macbeth's place at the table, the way he should've been.

Instead, just as Georgina clicked the first shot, everyone saw the prone, unmoving body of Neil Faulkner – at the same time as someone yelled from the room beneath the stage, 'Help!'

# THREE

'Neil? Neil?' Peter called from the middle of the auditorium. 'Leo, what's happened?'

Had the actor had a heart attack or something? Georgina wondered. And who was Leo?

'Someone needs to call an ambulance,' Aliou, the actor playing Duncan, the Porter and Old Siward yelled.

'I hate to tell you this,' Doris murmured in Georgina's ear, 'but they're not going to be able to help him.'

Inwardly groaning – this would be the third time this year that she'd been involved in a situation where an ambulance was called to a dead body – Georgina headed down to the room underneath the stage, Bert trotting beside her, with Peter and Bea a couple of paces behind.

The technician in charge of the projector, who was clearly the one who'd called for help, was kneeling over Neil's body.

'Leo, what happened?' Peter asked.

'He just – he just *collapsed*,' the technician said, looking up at Peter. 'I thought maybe he'd had a heart attack or a stroke. I couldn't find a pulse, so I moved him onto his back and tried to revive him. I did the breath all right, but then I started pushing down on his chest and I felt something wet. And... oh, God.' He shuddered. 'It was horrible!' He spread his shaking hands so Peter and Georgina could see. They were covered in blood.

'I think,' Leo continued, his face bleached with horror, 'Neil's been stabbed.'

'But who would've done that? How?' Peter asked. He looked dazed, as if the shock of a dead body under the stage had made him crumple, unable to gather his thoughts enough to know what to do next.

Whereas Georgina was getting to be a bit of an old hand at this dead body stuff and it felt natural for her to step in. 'We need to call the police as well as the ambulance,' she said. 'One of my guests died unexpectedly in my holiday cottage, earlier this year, so I know that in these sorts of cases the police will want to check a few things. We need to make sure nobody else enters this room in case it destroys any evidence. Everyone already in this room will have to talk to the scene of crimes team. And we'll all have left footprints; we'll need to give them our shoes so they can check them against any prints in the room and eliminate ours. It's probably a good idea for everyone to take their shoes off as they leave the room.'

The police would want to know what everyone saw and heard, and what had happened just before Neil died. The row Neil had with Bea a couple of minutes ago, on stage... If this was a murder case, Bea would definitely be a suspect. So would Elias Petrus, who'd been in the role of the Third Murderer, and Rebekah Khan, the First Murderer. Neil had complained that one of them had hit him too hard. Supposing one of the daggers hadn't been retractable and a blade had been involved?

She shivered. Dating a detective had clearly addled her brain; even a year ago, this kind of thought would never have crossed her mind. And of course there couldn't have been a blade. How could any of the actors have hidden a blade? Neil

Faulkner's death must've been natural causes. Maybe the blood was stage blood.

But anyone who worked in the theatre knew the difference between stage blood and real blood. Georgina had seen for herself that it was real blood on Leo's hands.

Bert whined, then pawed at the floor in a dark corner of the room.

Bert! She needed to get the dog out of here, too.

'When the police come, ask them to look where Bert's pawing,' Doris whispered.

Georgina went cold, remembering the last time Bert had uncovered a dead body: skeletal remains under the oak tree at Hartington Hall. Given that Doris obviously knew there was something beneath the floorboards, she had a sinking feeling that meant yet another dead body. Another story that Georgina would need to help uncover. Another ghost who needed closure.

'I'll take Bert upstairs,' she said. 'And then I'll come back, because it'd be useful to take photographs for the police.'

'I'll take Bert, Mum,' Bea offered quickly. 'I need to pop upstairs anyway.' She indicated the camera slung round Georgina's neck. 'You concentrate on the photographs.'

Georgina gave her a worried smile. 'Thanks, love.'

'I'll get the whole team together and we'll wait in the auditorium,' Peter said. 'And I'll call the police.'

Once everyone had left the room, Georgina took photographs of Neil's body in situ. 'Whose body is under the floorboards?' she asked in a low voice.

'His name's Fred. Fred Smith,' Doris said.

At Hartington Hall, Bert had found the skeleton of a Victorian domestic servant among the roots of an oak tree, and Doris had talked to the ghost to help Georgina piece together her story. Would the same sort of thing happen here? 'What has he told you so far?'

'He was an actor here. He died during the Blitz – though not from the bomb that fell here. He was killed the night before that,' Doris said. 'He remembers being stabbed, but not who did it. Whoever checks the remains needs to look at the skeleton's back. There'll be a mark on the bones.'

Two murders, both possibly by stabbing, several decades apart. Was there any kind of connection? Georgina wondered. Or was it just coincidence?

Colin always said he didn't believe in coincidence.

*Colin.*

Back at Hartington Hall, he'd teased her that she'd better not find another body in her next photography job because this was getting to be a habit. Even though Georgina was doing the publicity shots for nothing, to help out the theatre company where her daughter worked because she knew their budget was already stretched, it still counted as a job. And here she was with one body bleeding on top of the floorboards, and another body that Bert had found underneath the floorboards, albeit with a bit of direction from Doris.

Strictly speaking, the second body hadn't been uncovered yet, but Georgina knew from Doris that it was there. Curious, she tried to lift one of the floorboards where Bert had been scratching, but it was screwed down tightly. She'd have to ask Pete to get one of the stage crew to lift the floorboards.

By the time Georgina had finished taking the photographs and left the room to join the others in the auditorium – she saw immediately that Peter had gathered the admin team and backstage crew to join the actors – the police, the ambulance and the pathologist had arrived.

Peter introduced Georgina to Inspector Mei Zhang, the senior police officer. 'Georgina's a professional photographer, and her partner is a detective in Norfolk,' he said. 'She's taken some photographs of Neil in the room – and she was the one who told everyone there to take their shoes off outside the room so any evidence on their shoes wasn't lost, and you can rule out their footprints.'

'I've also got a photograph of the moment we saw Neil in the Pepper's Ghost, so you can see what we all saw when the room beneath the stage was lit up,' Georgina said. 'Leo thought Neil might have had a heart attack, so he moved Neil onto his back to start giving him CPR.'

'Thank you, Mrs Drake,' the inspector said. 'I'll need to interview you formally, along with the rest of the cast.'

'Of course.' Georgina paused. 'Um, this is going to sound a bit weird, but my dog was pawing the floorboards in one corner of the room. I think there might be something underneath them.'

'This is London, Georgie, and the theatre's an old building. It's probably a rat,' Peter said, looking completely unfazed.

'No. I think it might be something else.' Georgina gave the detective an awkward smile. 'Bert – my dog – found a skeleton among the roots of an oak tree, a couple of months back. I've got a feeling that this is the same sort of thing.'

Inspector Zhang swiftly wiped the incredulous expression from her face, but not before Georgina had noticed it. 'Unless it's pertinent to our enquiries about the man who died, I wouldn't expect my team to take up the floorboards,' she said.

'But we'd be able to do that ourselves, once you've dealt with the crime scene?' Georgina asked.

'It's probably a rat, Mrs Drake, as Mr Newton suggested,' the inspector said. 'But, once we've finished our work in the room, we have no problem with the floorboards being lifted.'

It looked as if they'd have to wait before they could start helping Fred Smith, Georgina thought with an inward sigh. Unless she could find a reason to convince Inspector Zhang's team to take a look at that corner.

'Mr Newton, if you could let my team know where they can

hold some private interviews, I'd appreciate it, please,' the inspector continued.

'Of course,' Peter said. 'You're welcome to use my office and the box office, and I'll make sure a couple of the dressing rooms are available.'

'Thank you.' She moved to stand in the centre of the front row, just in front of the stage. 'Everyone, if I could have your attention for a moment, please?' she called.

The low murmuring from the seats stopped, and everyone turned to face her.

'As you're all aware by now, Mr Faulkner is dead, and my team needs to investigate what happened,' the inspector said. 'We'll interview each of you individually and ask you to sign the written statements, but until we've done that, I'd ask you not to discuss what you saw or what you think happened with anyone else, here or outside the theatre. I appreciate it's unsettling when a colleague dies unexpectedly, but the best way you can help the situation now is to keep your own memories fresh and clear, not mix them up with what someone else heard or saw. I'd also ask you to keep everything confidential until we've concluded our investigation. Thank you in advance for your patience, and we'll be as quick as we can.'

'I'll make some hot drinks,' Georgina said, wanting the distraction of having something to do.

'I'll help,' Bea said immediately. 'I know how all the cast take their tea and coffee. Mum, I've left Bert with Mandy in the box office.'

'And I'll stay here,' Doris murmured in Georgina's ear, 'in case I hear anything useful.'

Georgina thought that the brisk, no-nonsense Inspector Zhang would appreciate help even less than Colin had when she'd first met him, but kept her counsel, just giving a brief nod that she knew Doris would see and nobody else would notice. She made a note on her phone of what the police officers and the pathologist drank, then headed with Bea to the little kitchen behind the box office.

'God, Mum. This is a mess,' Bea said quietly as she helped Georgina set up trays of mugs. 'And it must be particularly horrible for you.'

'Reminding me of Dad, you mean?' Georgina asked gently. She'd returned home from a photography shoot, two and a half years ago, to discover her husband dead from a heart attack.

Bea nodded. 'Plus your guest who died at Rookery Barn. And the woman in the ice house.'

'As Colin says, finding dead bodies is getting to become a bit of a habit for me,' Georgina said lightly. 'And I'm starting to understand why people in the emergency services have such dark humour.' She gave Bea a hug. 'It's horrible for the whole cast, to lose someone.'

'Neil won't be mis—' Bea cut off the words. 'Sorry. I shouldn't speak ill of the dead.'

'I didn't have much contact with him,' Georgina said, 'but it was enough for me to know your father wouldn't have cast him, even if he'd been a good enough actor. Too much negativity.'

'Working with him hasn't been great,' Bea admitted. 'But I guess this counts as discussing him.'

'So we'll just make the tea and say nothing more right now,' Georgina said. 'But we'll talk about it later.' She glanced at Bea's arm. 'I don't think you should be carrying a tray with that wrist.'

'I'm fine. It's healing,' Bea said.

Georgina peered at a stain on Bea's cast and frowned. 'Is that *blood*?'

Bea rolled her eyes. 'Stage blood. Left over from the scene where I "gild the faces of the grooms withal".' She narrowed her eyes. 'Mum, surely you don't think *I* did it?'

'No, of course not,' Georgina said. 'But you were playing one of the Murderers, and during the fight scene Neil complained that one of you hit him too hard. Maybe that was when he was stabbed.'

'We were all using blunt stage knives with retractable blades,' Bea asked, looking indignant. 'And if you mean that whoever hit him actually stabbed him with a real knife on stage, surely he would've died there and then, instead of being able to go through the trap to the room where he was setting up for the ghost scene?'

'That's not for me to deduce,' Georgina said. 'And, as you said, we shouldn't be talking about it. Though, come to think of it, you were a bit quick to offer to take Bert upstairs.'

'Because it's the first dead body I've ever seen and I wanted some fresh air – I thought I was going to throw up, but I didn't want everyone else thinking I was a wimp. Neil Faulkner wasn't the only one in the cast who thought I only got my part because of Dad.' Bea shook her head, her eyes wide and hurt. 'And I can't believe you think I could be a murderer, Mum.'

'I don't,' Georgina said. 'But, until you're excluded, you're a suspect. Just as I am.'

'How could you be a suspect? You were taking photographs. Even though you're dressed in black, anyone who wasn't on the stage would've been able to see you. There's no way you could have killed him,' Bea said. 'And I didn't have time to kill him. As soon as the lights went out at the end of the scene, he went off to the trap to get to the lower room – and I was backstage with the dressers, taking off the top of the Second Murderer's outfit and getting into Lady M's gown ready for the feast scene with Elias. We're down to the wire on time for that change as it is. I wouldn't have been able to run down the stairs, stab him to death without him making a sound, run back up the stairs again *and* get changed in the sixty seconds we have for the costume change.'

'Explain the logistics to the police,' Georgina said. 'That'll exclude you.'

Though she noticed her daughter was tugging at her right earlobe; it was a sign Georgina recognised from Bea's childhood. As a small child, Bea had always tugged at her right earlobe if she was hiding something. It was always something innocent, such as a surprise that Stephen had planned for Georgina, or while playing the card game Cheat and claiming to have put down two sevens when she'd actually laid a three and a seven.

But did that earlobe-tug mean something more sinister, today?

Did Bea know something about Neil Faulkner's murder?

And, if so, who was she protecting and why?

# FOUR

Back in the auditorium, Georgina and Bea handed round the mugs of tea. Everyone was clearly itching to talk about what had happened, but at the same time they were mindful of the inspector's warning not to discuss the situation.

Finally, it was Georgina's turn to be interviewed.

'Mr Newton mentioned that your partner is a detective – and that you'd been involved with a couple of cases recently,' Inspector Zhang said.

'Which doesn't mean I see myself as a detective who can do your job better than you can, or that I'll start interfering,' Georgina reassured her. 'I'm a professional photographer. I notice details that other people perhaps don't. Sometimes that's useful.'

Inspector Zhang inclined her head in acknowledgement. 'Can you tell me in your own words what happened today?'

'I came to the theatre to take photographs of the cast and the dress rehearsal, as a favour to Pete because he's an old friend and also because my daughter Bea's in the cast. It's her first major role, so of course I want to support her,' Georgina said. 'I can give you access to all the photographs I took. The files are quite large, so I think it would be easiest to email you thumbnails of them all and then give you private access to the full files via a password on my website. Then you can look at the ones that interest you in more detail without me jamming up your inbox.'

'Thank you. That would be helpful,' Inspector Zhang said. 'Did you speak to Mr Faulkner at all?'

'Not very much. My dog didn't like him.'

Inspector Zhang looked at her. 'And your dog's a good judge of character?'

'He normally wants to be everyone's new best friend. But he wouldn't go near Neil Faulkner.'

'Interesting,' Inspector Zhang said.

'That's what I thought. And Mr Faulkner was a little upset that I photographed the actors in alphabetical order rather than by their seniority,' Georgina said.

'He expected to be photographed first? Even though he wasn't playing the title role?'

'That was the impression he gave me,' Georgina said carefully. 'Then he stopped the rehearsal in the middle of the scene where Banquo's murdered, saying that one of the Murderers had hit him too hard.' She winced. 'I feel as if I'm throwing my daughter under a bus here, because Bea was one of the four people on stage with him at the time – along with the other two Murderers and Fleance. But, even though she's my daughter so of course I'm biased, I really don't believe she killed him. If anyone had stabbed him on stage, surely he would've died there straight away, rather than redoing the scene and then dying a few minutes later in the room below the stage?'

'I can't really comment,' Inspector Zhang said.

'There's proof that she's innocent. Like several of the cast, Bea's playing two roles; she needed to change out of the Second Murderer's costume and into Lady Macbeth's ballgown, ready for the next scene, while the lights were out,' Georgina continued, remembering how Bea had explained it earlier. 'She wasn't off the stage for more than a minute. That simply doesn't give enough time for her to go downstairs, murder Neil Faulkner in complete silence – and without Leo the technician seeing her or hearing any noise from Neil as she stabbed him – then come upstairs again and get changed for the next scene. Plus the dressers would've noticed blood on her costume as she changed – and there would've been blood on her hands, which would be hard to explain away at that point of the play.' Though there had been the stage blood on her cast...

No. It couldn't have been real blood. Bea had disliked Neil Faulkner, but Georgina was sure her daughter wasn't a murderer. Of course Bea wouldn't have done it.

'You've made a strong case, Mrs Drake,' Inspector Zhang said quietly but pointedly.

Georgina winced. 'Sorry. It's your job to ask the questions, not mine. I didn't mean to interfere.'

'You're her mother and you're worried. I respect that,' Inspector Zhang said. And Georgina warmed to the inspector when she added, 'I'd do the same, in your shoes.'

'If it helps, Bea told me the Murderers' daggers are all retractable. And blunt.'

'That's useful to know. Though I'll need to examine the daggers because they're evidence,' Inspector Zhang said, making a note. 'Has your daughter talked to you about any of the cast or mentioned any problems?'

'No. She's only just turned twenty-three, and she's thrilled to have the chance of playing Lady Macbeth at such a young age – kind of following in her dad's footsteps,' Georgina said. 'As far as I know, she was enjoying every moment.'

'She hasn't mentioned anyone she gets on particularly well with, or anyone she avoids?'

Georgina winced. 'I don't think she got on very well with Neil Faulkner. But, to be fair, I don't think anyone did.'

Including her dog, though that probably wouldn't count as evidence. 'He was quite rude about Rebekah Khan's training today, and Bea called him out on his comments not being necessary. Then he made a crack about Bea only getting the part because of her dad. I wanted to leap onto the stage and punch him on her behalf.'

'Beatrice Drake,' Inspector Zhang said thoughtfully, looking at her notes. 'Following in her dad's footsteps. Was your husband Stephen Drake?'

'Yes,' Georgina said. 'Before you ask, that's not why she got the part. Faulkner was just being nasty and trying to make her feel small. Pete's looking at bringing on young actors who he thinks have a bright future, the way Stephen used to do, and *that's* why Pete cast her as Lady Macbeth.'

'I'm sorry for your loss. I saw your husband in *Much Ado*,' Inspector Zhang said. 'He was the best Benedick ever.'

'He certainly was.' Georgina smiled. 'I met Stephen when he was playing Macbeth. I was meant to be interviewing him for the student paper, but the photographer was off sick so they gave me the camera and told me to take the headshots. He would've loved seeing Bea in this run.'

'Did he know Mr Faulkner?'

'Professionally, yes, but Faulkner wasn't one of our friends or someone Stephen had worked with much,' Georgina said. 'Stephen was a great believer in a rising tide floating all boats. He tended to give parts to people who encouraged the younger actors, and he wanted a cast who'd work together to get the best out of the play and make the audience come back for more. Which means there wasn't room for egos.'

'You said that Mr Newton had a similar attitude to your husband, when it came to casting,' Inspector Zhang said.

'Yes.'

'Would your husband have hired Neil Faulkner?'

'I very much doubt it. But maybe Pete saw something positive in him,' Georgina said. 'Or at least had a good reason for choosing him as Banquo.'

'Thank you for being honest with me,' Inspector Zhang said. 'We might have further questions, so could I ask that you make yourself available for the next few days?'

'Of course,' Georgina said. She gave Inspector Zhang her business card. 'These are my details. If you could let me have the best email address for you, I'll make sure you get those files.'

The forensics team tied up the room under the stage for the rest of the day. Peter was frantically ringing round the theatrical agents he knew well, trying to find a replacement Banquo. The dress rehearsal was cancelled and, even though they all knew that the show had to go on, nobody was keen to finish off doing the photographs.

'I know I'm being greedy, especially as you're doing this out of the goodness of your heart, but would you have time to finish the photography tomorrow instead, Georgie?' Peter asked.

'Of course,' she said.

She downloaded the photographs to her laptop and checked her email; then she sent the thumbnails to Inspector Zhang with the promise that the password to the files on her website would be with her later that afternoon. Finally, she headed for the kitchen.

Liza, the wardrobe mistress, was making a pile of sandwiches; she smiled as Georgina walked in.

'I was just about to make some tea,' Georgina said. 'Though I can see you've already got the kettle on and washed up the mugs.'

'It's like having teenagers. Not one of them can wash up a mug,' Liza said, rolling her eyes, though Georgina could hear affection in her tone. Liza glanced at the pile of sandwiches she was making. 'I worry about some of the younger ones in the cast.

I've been thinking about bringing in a big pot of veggie chilli or pasta a couple of times a week, so at least I know they've had a proper meal.'

'I used to do that for Stephen's troupe,' Georgina said with a smile. 'I'll get cracking with the tea. Milk and sugar?'

'Just a splash of milk, please,' Liza said.

'I was going to take some tea down to the forensics team, if there's a tray?'

'Here.' Liza deftly found it for her. 'On your way down, can you just let everyone know there are sandwiches in here as well as tea?'

'Of course,' Georgina said.

She duly passed on the message as she went downstairs to the forensics team. Standing in the doorway, she said, 'I'm not coming in any further because I don't want to get in your way. But I thought you could probably do with some more tea.'

'That's wonderful. Thank you – Mrs Drake, isn't it?' the lead forensic investigator said.

'Georgina,' she said with a smile.

'I'm Bryn,' he said. His name confirmed what Georgina had guessed from his accent, that he was Welsh. 'And this is Dougie.'

'Hiya,' the second investigator said, nodding his head.

Bert, who'd pattered down the stairs behind Georgina, slid into the room and started pawing at the corner again.

'Sorry,' Georgina said. 'Bert was scratching there earlier. He seems to think there's something under the floorboards.'

'Probably rats,' Bryn said. 'You know what London's like. You're never more than six feet away from a rat. Just think how many you see on the underground.'

'That's a myth, Bryn. It's more like ten or fifteen feet away,' Dougie said. 'And that's an average. Some areas you get fewer, others you get more.'

'Basements of nice warm buildings,' Bryn said. 'Like this one. No wonder your dog can hear them scratching.'

Georgina shivered. 'That reminds me of some *very* horrible student digs,' she said.

'And me. I hope things are less grim for the kids now,' Bryn said, rolling his eyes. 'Your lad here's a beauty. I've got one of these at home,' he added, making a fuss of the dog.

'Yeah, but yours is a *Welsh* springer, Bryn, not an English one,' Dougie teased.

Bryn laughed. 'True, but there's not much difference. My Cariad's just a bit smaller than this one, that's all. Spaniels are always so curious about everything. And so happy. They're a joy to have around. Let's have a look at what's got your attention in that corner, my lovely, shall we?' He shone a torch along the boards, removed the screws from a short piece, then used a crowbar to lift it.

Bert gave a soft wuff, and Bryn shone his torch into the gap. Then he frowned. 'Actually, there *is* something there. Wrapped in what looks like some sort of cloth.' He took up the next board, then knelt down and reached into the larger aperture he'd made. 'An old curtain, I'd say, by the feel of it.' Then he unwrapped the first section and gave a low whistle. 'It's not a rat – it's a body. A skeleton,' he corrected. 'And it's definitely a real skeleton, not a stage one.'

It had been there for eighty years or so, by Georgina's reckoning, though it would be too complicated to explain how she knew. 'The theatre was badly hit by bombing during the Blitz,' she said. 'Could it date from then?'

'Maybe,' Bryn said.

Dougie went over to have a look. 'Although I'm pretty sure that the dead were all pulled out of the rubble as soon as possible after the bombing, so they could have a proper burial. Why would someone wrap a body in a curtain and hide it under the floorboards instead?'

'If they didn't want it to be found?' Georgina suggested. 'Maybe it wasn't a natural death, and the bombing happened after the body had been hidden.'

'We'll need to bring up the remains so we can take a closer look,' Bryn said. 'Firstly to see how old they are, and we'll bring in the Finds Liaison Officer to help us with that.'

'And if they're more than a hundred years old, that makes them bones of antiquity and the police will have no further interest – the coroner will let us give the remains a proper burial,' Georgina said. At Bryn's look of surprise, she explained, 'Bert dug up a skeleton beneath a tree at a friend's home, earlier this summer. It turned out she was Victorian.'

'So he has form in finding bodies,' Bryn said thoughtfully. 'Maybe you should give him a secondment at your local police station.'

'Funny you should say that. My partner said something similar,' Georgina said. 'My daughter – she's the one playing Lady Macbeth – helped me identify the remains back in Norfolk. When she's not acting, she works for a probate genealogy company. She's good at tracing people. Maybe she'll be able to help me work out who this man was.'

'Well, I might have a chat with her when she's got a free moment and see if I can pick her brains, too,' Bryn said. 'My wife's doing her family tree, and she's a bit stuck at the moment.'

'I'm sure Bea would be happy to give some advice,' Georgina said. 'I'll ask her to come and see you.'

'Thanks.' He smiled. 'Right. I'd better call this in.'

'If you need photographs of the remains in situ,' Georgina said, 'I'm a professional photographer and I've got my camera upstairs.'

'That's kind, but we've got our own camera with us,' Dougie said. 'But if you could ask Mei to come down for a quick chat about what we just found, that would be great.'

Georgina went to find Mei, who'd released the ambulance

crew back to their normal duties and arranged for a funeral director to take Neil's body to the pathology lab. Meanwhile, Bryn and Dougie took up the rest of the floorboards, and, after talking to Mei, gently brought the wrapped skeleton up to floor level and unwrapped the curtain.

Thankfully, Mei didn't say that Georgina couldn't stay with the forensics team, so Georgina was able to see the extent of the hiding-place where the skeleton was found, as well as the skeleton itself.

'It's male, from the shape of the skull,' Dougie said. 'Though I'd want to check the pelvis as well to be absolutely sure, because he's not that tall – maybe five feet eight?'

'I'd say he was in his early thirties,' Bryn said. 'The sagittal suture's almost fused.' He pointed to the squiggly line running down the middle of the skull. 'But the coronal suture here at the front isn't fused, so he hadn't reached forty.'

'How did he die?' Georgina asked.

'Get them to look at the spine,' Doris said quietly.

'I can't tell,' Bryn said. 'And I'm not sure about the clothing. To me it looks like the sort of thing I've seen my great-granddad wearing in photographs – just before the Second World War.'

'That would fit in with someone who'd been killed in the Blitz,' Dougie agreed.

'But the body was wrapped in a curtain, and this is a theatre,' Bryn said. 'If he was playing a character in 1930s dress, then the body could be from just about any time from then until – well, maybe three or four years ago, for the body to have become skeletonised.'

'Is it my imagination,' Georgina asked, 'or is that a rip in the back of his shirt? And that stain on the fabric: could it be blood?'

Bryn grimaced. 'The liquid seeping into the shirt would've happened as part of the process of decomposition. And the rip could've been made by rats.'

'But the curtain doesn't seem to be damaged,' she said. 'And is there blood on the curtain?'

'It's a black curtain, so it's hard to tell what's there, under this light,' Dougie said. 'I assume you're thinking he might have been stabbed in the back?'

'It might be why the body was wrapped in a curtain,' Georgina suggested. 'If he was murdered, and someone tried to cover up what they'd done.'

'Let's have a look.' Gently, Bryn rolled the skeleton onto its front, then untucked the shirt from the trousers and checked the spine at the point where the shirt had looked torn. 'Well, I never! That looks like sharp force trauma to me,' he said, pointing at a mark on the spine. 'Unhealed, so it's probably the cause of death. Though it isn't necessarily a stabbing. He might have caught himself accidentally on something sharp and bled out.'

'But he's been wrapped in a curtain. Surely if you see someone who's been hurt in an accident, you'd call for help rather than hide them under the floorboards?' Georgina asked.

'Unless they panicked,' Bryn pointed out.

'Maybe he was put here before the theatre was bombed,' Georgina said. 'And that's why nobody found the body. Supposing the floorboards at this level were undamaged because there were several floors and ceilings above it. Maybe someone tested the floorboards at the other end of the room, and decided they were solid and there was no electrical wiring that needed replacing so they didn't need to take up the whole floor to check for problems.'

'And if the body had been here for long enough, there wouldn't be any smell of putrefaction left to alert the building team to look for something under the floorboards,' Dougie said. 'That theory definitely works.'

'Bottom line: it looks as if we have two stabbings – one today, and one decades ago,' Bryn said. 'We need to know how long this body's been here. It takes several years for a corpse to skeletonise, so we'll need radiocarbon dating to give us a scientific range for the date of death. And then we'll need to see if the two stabbings are linked or not.'

'Will you be able to identify the body?' Georgina asked.

'If we're lucky, there might be some kind of ID in his pocket,' Dougie said. 'But unless it's relatively recent and there's a missing persons report, we might not. If it happened during the Second World War, it's highly unlikely we'll be able to find out what actually happened.'

'We might not be able to identify the body at all,' Bryn said. 'We'll investigate, but it might be that all we can do is make sure that this body is properly reburied.' He looked at Georgina. 'It's lucky for him that your dog seems to be good at finding bodies...'

# FIVE

'I can't believe there were two dead bodies under the footlights.' Bea shivered. 'And one of them had been there for *years*. It's so sad to think the police might not be able to find out who he is and what happened to him.'

Georgina noticed that her daughter didn't say anything about Neil Faulkner's death being sad. 'Maybe that's something we can look into,' she said, knowing full well that she planned to look up Fred Smith. 'Did Bryn talk to you about his wife being stuck on something in the family tree?'

'Yes. I've given him my email. He's going to get his wife to give me access to her tree, and I'll see if I can find a way past some of those brick walls for her,' Bea said.

'That's kind of you.'

Bea shrugged. 'You and Dad always taught me that kindness makes the world go round.'

'It does,' Georgina said. 'But there's a difference between kindness and telling lies for someone when they've done something wrong.'

'Well, yes. You don't need to tell me that,' Bea said, and tugged at her right earlobe.

Georgina sighed. 'Sweetheart, I can only help you if you talk to me.'

'I don't know what you mean, Mum.'

Georgina tugged her own right earlobe and raised an eyebrow.

'Oh.' Bea grimaced.

'I don't think for one minute that you killed Neil Faulkner,' Georgina said. 'But I think you might know who did.'

'I don't know for sure, only suspect it,' Bea said. This time, she wasn't tugging her earlobe. 'But Neil wasn't very nice, Mum.'

'He was snobby about people's CVs, definitely,' Georgina said. 'And I'm proud of you for standing up for Rebekah, the way you did. Your dad would've been proud of you, too.' She paused, gentling her tone. 'But what else did he do, sweetheart? Did he look or touch where he shouldn't?'

Bea shook her head, disgust on her face. 'Not that. If he'd tried it, I would've kicked him where it hurt.'

Which in some ways was a relief, but in other ways was more worrying. 'What did he do to you, darling?' Georgina asked softly.

Bea's eyes filmed with tears and a single one slid down her cheek. 'Oh, Mum. I did something so stupid. When I was twenty. I...' She dragged in a breath. 'I was seeing someone. I thought I loved him. I thought he loved me. And I let him... take photos.' She swallowed hard. 'Intimate photos.'

Neil was nearly forty years older than Bea – more than old enough to be her father, and old enough for it not to have been an equal relationship. Georgina made the effort to keep her voice calm. 'Did Neil coerce you into letting him take those photos?' Even though, at twenty, Bea had been over the age of consent, it still wasn't acceptable.

'Neil didn't take them,' Bea said with a grimace. 'I'd never have let him touch me.'

'Who?'

'You don't need to know who,' Bea said, shaking her head. 'He's not in my life now. But he kept the photographs. And Neil found out. I don't know *how* he found out, but he did. And he said he'd make sure people saw them if I... if I didn't give him money.'

'He was *blackmailing* you?' If someone hadn't already killed Neil Faulkner that morning, Georgina would've battered the man's dressing-room door down and strangled him with her bare hands.

Bea hung her head. 'I didn't know what to do, Mum.'

'I love you. Nothing's going to change that.' Georgina wrapped her arms round her daughter. Why didn't you tell me?'

'I was too ashamed. Not of the photos, but of being such an idiot and not making sure I got them all back when we split up,' Bea said. 'I couldn't tell you how stupid I'd been.'

'If you didn't want to talk to me, you could've talked to Colin. He wouldn't have told me anything without your permission, and he would've helped to stop Neil Faulkner blackmailing you,' Georgina said, her voice gentle. 'And he would've helped you nail him in court.'

'I couldn't take him to court. Pete couldn't afford any scandal and Neil said Pete would drop me from the production if the truth came out. And I know Neil had mates in the press. It would've been everywhere before I could stop him.'

Was it an open secret that Peter was struggling financially? Georgina wondered. Or did Neil know something about Peter, too? Because blackmailers rarely stopped at demanding money from just one person; from what she'd seen of Neil Faulkner, he was very far from the kind of person who would've helped build a team and she couldn't understand why Peter had cast him.

'You were young, you made the mistake of trusting someone with intimate photos, and Pete would *never* have held that against you,' Georgina said. 'You could have talked to him. I would've supported you.'

Bea's breath hitched. 'I thought Pete would probably be OK about it – I mean, people in the theatre or films have survived all sorts of scandal in the past, haven't they? But Neil threatened to tell my boss at the probate genealogy place. And that's where I have to be super-respectable. Any hint of wrongdoing and I'd be out for good.'

The job that kept Bea going between acting roles. The job her daughter loved and was good at.

Neil Faulkner had threatened to lose it for Bea, if she didn't pay up.

And Bea had clearly caved.

'When did you start paying him?' Georgina asked.

'About a week after I started here. When he said he wanted a chat, I thought he wanted to talk to me about my performance and maybe give me a few tips on how to improve it – the way actors who worked for Dad used to do with rookie actors,' she said.

'How much money did you give him?'

Bea looked miserable. 'I've used almost all my savings. I was looking into taking out a loan.'

'Oh, love.'

'And my wrist – that wasn't an accident. Neil made sure I tripped. It was a warning, the day before I gave him the money: pay up, or he'd do a lot more damage and release the photos on the internet. I couldn't take the risk.'

'I'm so sorry you've been through this,' Georgina said. 'If I'd had any idea, I think I would've murdered him myself. I thought he was rude and unkind, but this goes way behind that. And I hope you know that *he's* the one in the wrong, not you.'

'Oh, Mum.' And this time Bea really did cry, sobbing into Georgina's shoulder. Georgina stroked her daughter's hair, holding her close until she'd stopped crying.

'You know you're going to have to be really brave, love, and tell Inspector Zhang about this.'

'But she'll think I killed him!'

'She knows you didn't,' Georgina said. 'Though if I'd known about this, I would've been her prime suspect because I would cheerfully have broken every bone in his body – twice – before wringing his scrawny neck.'

'He's dead. He can't blackmail me anymore. What's the point of telling anyone else now?' Bea said, her voice cracking.

'Because,' Georgina said gently, 'he was probably doing the same to someone else in the company. Maybe even more than one person.' And maybe that was why Pete had hired him in the first place; maybe Neil had blackmailed him into it.

'It's such a mess.' Bea dragged in a breath. 'Dad would be so disappointed in me.'

'Your dad,' Georgina said firmly, 'would've been hugely proud of you. Just as I am. And your brother. You're doing a great job and I can't wait for the opening night. But your dad would've agreed with me that you need to tell the police. I'll go with you, to support you.'

Bea's shoulders drooped in defeat. 'All right.'

'Go and wash your face,' Georgina said gently. 'Then we'll go and see Inspector Zhang. After that, I'll take you out for something to eat, and then we're going to watch *Mamma Mia!* and dance and sing our way through it. You'll feel better after that. And the important thing here is that Neil Faulkner can't threaten you ever, ever again.'

Bea hugged her. 'I love you, Mum.'

'I love you, too,' Georgina said.

'Will Bea be OK?' Doris asked anxiously, when Bea headed for the bathroom.

'She will be,' Georgina said. 'But if that man wasn't dead already, I'd kill him myself. And break those expensive white teeth of his.'

'He'd better not come to me, asking for help,' Doris said. 'If ghosts could punch, he'd have a broken nose as well as whatever else.' She paused. 'Are you OK, Georgie?'

'I will be, when this mess is cleared up and Bea gets to shine on stage,' Georgina said. 'Has Fred said anything else to you?'

'No. I'll need to be at the theatre to ask him. What do you need to know?'

'What he was performing. It'll help me look things up in the archives,' Georgina said. 'And where he lived. The names of anyone he lived with or his landlady.'

'Who are you talking to, Mum?' Bea asked.

Georgina started. 'Myself,' she fibbed. 'I was thinking out loud about a list of things I want to find out about the body under the floorboards.'

'Count me in for helping you look at the documents,' Bea said.


Inspector Zhang listened to Bea's account of Neil's blackmail, making notes.

'I'm sorry. I should've told you this morning,' Bea said. 'But I *didn't* kill him.'

'You should've told us when he first started to blackmail you,' Inspector Zhang corrected. 'Blackmail and extortion both carry a prison sentence. So does sharing intimate photographs of someone without their permission. And we can certainly have a chat with the young man who took the photographs in the first place, if you'll give me his details. We'll find out if he gave the photographs to anyone else and follow up with them.' She raised her eyebrows. 'I'm sure that as soon as they realise we can seize their phone and laptop, and they're looking at a possible custodial sentence and a large fine for their part in things, they'll do the right thing. Don't worry – we'll get any photos deleted.'

'Thank you.' Bea's voice cracked.

'I'm sorry you've had to go through something like that,' Inspector Zhang said. 'But I do need to ask, do you have any idea if Neil Faulkner was blackmailing anyone else in the company?'

'I didn't talk about what he was doing to me, so if he was blackmailing anyone else in the company I'm guessing they've kept it quiet, too,' Bea said, though Georgina noticed that her daughter was tugging at her earlobe. Bea definitely knew something. 'For the same reasons – none of us wanted to lose the chance of being in this production. Peter Newton's a good director. This is going to look so good on our resumés.'

Inspector Zhang sighed. 'We won't bring your name into it, but we'll need to interview everyone again and make it clear that we know he's done it before, so they feel safe telling us what they know. Thank you for coming in, Miss Drake. And if you do hear anything, I'd appreciate hearing it, too.'

'Of course,' Bea said.

'But,' Inspector Zhang added, 'I should remind you that I'm investigating the murder of Neil Faulkner. The blackmail gives you a motive to get him out of the way, and you were close enough to stab him, a minute or two before he died.'

Bea's eyes widened. 'But I didn't kill him!'

'At the moment, I can't rule *anybody* out,' Inspector Zhang said. 'Please make sure you keep yourself available, in case we need to ask you further questions.'

'I...' Bea's eyes welled with tears, and her head drooped.

'We came here to ask you for help,' Georgina said quietly, a note of steel in her voice.

The inspector met her gaze unflinchingly, then nodded. 'Please don't worry about the blackmail, Miss Drake. I'll make sure it's dealt with.'

'Thank you,' Bea whispered.

When they left the police station, they found a nice café for afternoon tea, and Georgina was relieved to see that Bea looked a bit less strained than she had since Neil was first killed.

The scones had just been served when Georgina's phone rang.

'Do you mind if I get this?' she asked Bea.

'Sure.' Her daughter smiled at her.

Not Colin – of course it wasn't, when he was busy at work – but the number wasn't one Georgina recognised. Word had probably started to spread that she was working again, so it was probably a magazine with a commission, she thought. 'Hello?'

'Is that Mrs Drake?'

'Yes. Who's calling?'

'Harrison Taylor.'

Even though she'd hoped that Harrison would act on the messages she'd sent and ring her, Georgina nearly dropped the phone in surprise. 'Thank you for calling me, Mr Taylor,' she said.

'I'm not quite sure what you wanted to talk to me about,' he said, 'but I had a message that it's to do with local history.'

'Yes. I live in Little Wenborough,' she said, 'and I'm researching the history of my house.'

'I'm not sure I can be much use to you. I haven't lived there for half a century,' he said. 'I'm sure there are plenty of people still living there who'd be able to tell you a lot more than I can.'

'There aren't that many with a connection to my house.' She paused. 'I live at Rookery Farm.'

There was silence.

For a panicked moment, Georgina thought he'd hung up. 'Mr Taylor?'

'Yes. Sorry. I haven't heard that name in a while.'

'I know this must be difficult for you, but I wanted to talk to you about Doris. If you have the time,' she said.

'Doris.' His voice cracked. 'I'll always have time to talk about Doris.' He paused. 'I assume you know what happened?'

'Yes. I'm sorry for your loss,' she said. 'I read the newspaper reports and I've talked to her brother.'

'Jack's still in Little Wenborough?' He sounded surprised.

'No. The Beauchamps moved away. In 1972,' she added.

'Ah.' He paused. 'Do you ever come to London?'

'Yes. Actually, I'm here at the moment, doing a job,' she said.

'I'm in London, too,' he said. 'Perhaps we could meet.'

She'd promised Colin that she'd only see Harrison Taylor if he was with her. But Colin was up to his eyes in a case; he'd sounded so tired when they'd spoken on the phone last night. It wouldn't be fair to ask him to squeeze another five or six hours out of his day after work to drive to London, talk to Harrison, then drive back to Norwich. At the same time, she didn't want to risk losing her chance of speaking to the love of Doris's life. It had already taken her months to find him. 'I'd like that,' she said. And maybe if she suggested a neutral place to meet, in public, it would stop Colin fussing about her taking risks. With Doris being a huge Beatles fan, there was an obvious place to meet. 'Shall we meet at Abbey Road zebra crossing?'

'Perfect,' she heard Doris say, at the same time as Harrison said, 'Yes. Would three o'clock tomorrow afternoon suit you?'

'That'd be lovely. I'll see you then.'

'Who was that?' Bea asked.

For a moment, Georgina almost confided in her. Bea was sensitive and kind.

On the other hand, her daughter had enough on her plate, without worrying that Georgina had suddenly gone crazy, talking to a ghost.

'Remember the poor girl who died in my house?' she asked. At Bea's nod, Georgina said, 'That was her boyfriend.'

'And I'm going to see him again. At last. After all these long, lonely years,' Doris whispered, sounding as if she was crying. Georgina's heart squeezed.

'But I thought you found out what happened, Mum,' Bea said, looking surprised. 'That it was a tragic accident.'

'I'm just putting in the last pieces of the puzzle,' Georgina said. 'You know yourself what it's like when you follow a trail.'

'I do.' Bea tipped her head on one side. 'Why are you meeting him at Abbey Road zebra crossing?'

'They were both big fans of George Harrison,' Georgina said, only just remembering to add, 'apparently.'

'You're still sharing your location with me on your phone, right?' Bea asked.

'Yes. Why?'

Bea rolled her eyes. '*Mum*. You're meeting someone for the very first time. If it were the other way round, you'd be reminding me to take precautions.'

Georgina knew that was true; but how could she explain that Harrison Taylor wasn't a complete stranger to her, even though she was a stranger to him? 'We're meeting in a public place,' she said, 'and we'll probably go for a coffee somewhere. I promise I won't go anywhere that's not in the public eye. Plus I've got the emergency SOS call set up on my phone.'

'All right. And make sure your phone's charged and you haven't accidentally switched off your location,' Bea said. And then she grinned. 'I sound like you.'

'Indeed,' Georgina said dryly. 'Your dad would be pleased.'

'I miss him,' Bea said. Her eyes filmed with tears. 'I'd give anything to see his face in the front row on opening night.'

'Oh, he'll be there in spirit. Dead centre,' Georgina said.

'Do you believe in ghosts?' Bea asked.

This was the opening Georgina had longed to hear from someone close. To share what she knew about Doris. But before she could start to explain, Bea added, 'Because I don't.'

Georgina damped down her disappointment. 'Love never

dies, though,' she said. 'Your dad will be there, because he's part of you.' She raised her eyebrows. 'And, even though we both hated Larkin, that last line from "An Arundel Tomb" is a good one. Taken out of context, that is – Larkin's a miserable sod.'

# SIX

Georgina had been away for three days. And Colin *missed* her.

He missed her sound common sense. Her smile. The way she saw things.

He missed her dog plonking himself on his feet.

He missed the warmth of Georgina in his arms.

They said that absence made the heart grow fonder; but she was in London. His old stomping ground. *Her* old stomping ground, too. Back in the city, among theatres and museums and art galleries... would it make her realise how much she missed London?

What if she decided she wanted to stay?

He shook himself. Too far, too fast.

And it had only been three days. He wasn't going to become clingy and ridiculous, like a teenager. For pity's sake, he was fifty-three years old. Nearly three and a half decades away from being a teenager.

But he called her anyway and did his best to sound casual. 'Hi. How's it going?'

'Um, *interesting*,' Georgina said.

He felt his antennae twitch. 'Meaning?'

'One of the actors in Bea's company was murdered on stage as part of the play – except he really *was* murdered. And then Bert, um, found a skeleton under the floorboards.'

'Two dead bodies? So much for you not finding a corpse in the middle of your next job,' he said, keeping his voice much lighter than he felt. 'When did this all happen?'

'This morning,' she said.

'If I didn't have this case,' he said, 'I would've been with you. I could've helped.'

'I know,' she said. 'I'm not expecting you to drop everything and rush up here.'

'I couldn't be of that much help anyway,' he admitted, 'because it's out of my jurisdiction. Though I still have friends in the area, so I could put you in touch with them, if you need it.'

'Thank you,' she said. 'I appreciate the support. Though the inspector in charge is lovely, if a bit stern. She interviewed the cast and crew today, and Neil Faulkner – the victim – has been taken to the pathologist.'

Something in her voice alerted him. A hardness he wasn't used to. 'I'm not far away, Georgie. I can get in the car now and be with you in a couple of hours, if you need me.'

She blew out a breath. 'No, it's fine. Just that, um, Bea was one of the four people on stage with him just before he died.'

'So she's a suspect?'

'She didn't do it,' Georgina said.

'No, of course not,' Colin said.

'The inspector seems to think she has motive and opportunity.'

'It's still the early stages of the case,' Colin said. 'You can't rule someone out until you've ruled them in. Remember what I said about taking the emotion out of it when you examine a case, and looking at the facts. I've met Bea, and she's a sweetheart. But, given specific circumstances, I think anyone has it in them to kill someone.'

'You've said that to me before and I never really believed you until now. You have a point. If I'd known what Neil Faulkner had done,' Georgina said softly, 'I would've strangled him with my bare hands.'

The suppressed anger in her voice shocked him. 'What did he do?'

'The slimy bastard blackmailed Bea.'

'He *what*?'

'I can't tell you the details, but it was a mistake she'd made when she was younger and it might've affected her job. The job she does when she's resting, I mean,' Georgina said.

'Didn't she tell you about it?'

'No,' Georgina said. 'She was...' She sighed. 'She paid up.'

But Colin had already made the connection. It sounded as if Bea had given her trust to someone who'd betrayed it. And somehow this Neil Faulkner had become involved. 'Blackmail's illegal. We're looking at a fine or even a custodial sentence. I hope Bea knows she could've come to me with a problem and I would've helped her without judging. And without telling you anything, if that was an issue.'

'She knows,' Georgina said. 'I already told her.'

The fact that Georgina trusted him so much warmed him all the way through. 'Is she officially a suspect?'

'I think so. I don't know, because obviously DI Zhang can't discuss anything with me.'

'I can give you names of good legal counsel, if you need it,' he said. 'I assume DI Zhang's the senior officer? Would that be Mei Zhang?'

'Yes.'

'I know her. Actually, I've worked with her a few times,' Colin said. 'She was one of the juniors on my team. She's good. Thorough and fair.'

'Can I tell her I know you? Pass on your best wishes, or something?'

Thankfully Mei Zhang hadn't worked on the case that had broken him. But she'd know about the fallout. 'I think I told you that I left London under a bit of a cloud,' he said. 'So maybe not. Or maybe. I don't know.'

'You sound out of sorts. Tough case?' she asked sympathetically.

'Mmm.' No. He just missed her. But he wasn't going to whine; right now it sounded as if she and Bea could both do with his support. 'Tell me about the skeleton.'

'The body was wrapped in an old stage curtain,' she said.

'Under the floorboards?'

'Under the floorboards of the room underneath the stage,' she said. She explained to him about the Pepper's Ghost and them seeing the image of Neil Faulkner's dead body on stage. 'When I went down to take photographs, Bert kept scratching in one corner. He did it again when I took some tea down to the forensics team. Everyone said it was probably a rat.'

'You're always within six feet of a rat in London,' he said.

She chuckled. 'I'm reliably informed that's a myth. But the forensics team were nice and they had a look under the floorboard. They realised something was down there and took up another floorboard to get access – and that's when they realised it was a skeleton wrapped in a curtain. The clothing looked to be 1930s or 1940s.'

'So it had been there for years? I'm surprised nobody noticed the smell, when the body started to decompose,' he said.

'The theatre was bombed during the Blitz,' she said, 'so if the body was put there before the bombing, the theatre would've been closed. It wasn't restored until the early 1960s.'

'By which time the body would've been a skeleton and the smell of putrefaction would've dissipated. You're sure the body's that old? It wasn't someone who was wearing a costume of something set in the 1930s?' he checked.

'The forensics team is going to let me know.'

'And you're going to find out the identity of the body?' Just as she had at Hartington Hall, when Bert had discovered a body underneath the Great Oak.

'I hope so.'

'Unless you have an idea of the identity, you can't use dental records to trace them, though,' he said. 'And DNA won't be much help without a living relative. What did the forensics team say?'

'Probably male, about five feet eight, and there was a rip in the back of the shirt that corresponded to some damage to the bones – sharp force trauma, I think Bryn said.'

'Bryn? Would that be Bryn Morgan?'

'I'm not sure of his surname,' Georgina admitted.

'About five feet nine, very Welsh, in his forties, fluffy hair,' Colin said.

'That's him.'

'I know him, too,' Colin said. 'He's very good.'

'And his colleague, Dougie. With me not being a detective – as I've reassured Inspector Zhang – I didn't think to ask their surnames.'

Colin couldn't help grinning. Georgina was good at deduction, and he'd discovered that thinking aloud with her made his brain work better. 'Bryn Morgan and Dougie Ball. Give them my best when you talk to them,' he said. 'So we're looking at murder. An actor?'

'Maybe,' she said. 'I was wondering if there was some kind of connection between the death of the unknown man and Neil.'

'Other than their profession?'

'Neil was older than me – older than Stephen, too. Nearly sixty. He wouldn't have been born when my poor victim was killed and hidden under the stage. But what if Neil's father was the original killer? Neil's death might have been revenge – by the victim's child.'

'That,' Colin said, 'is extrapolating so far that you've over-reached yourself.'

'Like Macbeth,' she said.

'I doubt there's a connection,' he said. 'Who are the other suspects for murdering the blackmailer?'

'At the moment, the other three who were on the stage with him, as well as Bea. Though, to be fair, the boy who plays Fleance is only twelve, a slight lad, and I very much doubt it's him. Faulkner complained that someone hit him too hard, made a fuss and held up the rehearsal.'

'So someone could have stabbed him on the stage. Depending on where the wound was, he might not've realised he'd been stabbed rather than punched. And a stabbing victim can bleed out in less than five minutes,' Colin said.

'They redid the scene he interrupted. And he was fine on stage. All the staggering was acting... At least, I think it was.'

'Was he a good actor?' Colin asked.

'I'm probably not the best judge,' Georgina said drily, 'given my feelings towards him.'

'Take the feelings out of it,' he said. 'You're good enough at analysis to be able to do that.'

She was silent for a few moments. 'No. He was definitely one of the weaker actors, despite having the most experience. Stephen wouldn't have cast him – not just because he wasn't good, but because he was nasty with the younger actors. I heard him on stage, being snooty about where one of the actors had trained and claiming that Bea only got the part because of Stephen.'

'Which is utter bollocks,' Colin said. 'Bea got that part because she's *good*.'

'I know. But thank you for taking her side.'

'I happen to like your daughter very much,' he said. And he was pretty sure he had even stronger feelings for Georgina herself, but now wasn't the time to bring that up. 'If he was blackmailing Bea, he was probably blackmailing other people, too,' Colin mused.

'That's what I thought.'

'Does Bea know who else he might have targeted?'

'She claims not.'

'But you think she does?' Colin asked, noting the way she'd phrased it.

'I don't think she wants to cause problems for anyone.'

'Even if it would clear her name?' Colin asked.

'They're quite a tight-knit company, apart from Faulkner. I think they want to protect each other.'

'She needs to think about it and realise it'd be more helpful to tell the police than to hide it,' he said. 'Or tell you. You could—' He stopped abruptly. What the hell was he thinking? He could never, ever put the job before Georgina. 'No, ignore me.'

'I could what?' she asked.

He backtracked swiftly. 'No. I'm not involving you.'

'Bea's my daughter and I'm a witness. I'm already involved,' she reminded him.

She had a good point. And she was bright enough to work it out for herself. He'd rather know what she was doing so he could give her some kind of protection than let her do this alone and be vulnerable. 'I was thinking. You're observant and you're good at getting people to talk to you. Have you done all the photographs yet?'

'No.'

'Then maybe,' he said, 'if there's anyone who looks as if they're...'

'Hiding something?' Georgina suggested.

'Not so much hiding something as looking as if they need

someone to talk to. Someone who could give them good advice. Someone who could tell them to trust Mei and talk to her,' he said. 'You could do that. *Provided* you're not putting yourself at risk.'

'I could take a leaf out of Cesca's book and make cake,' she said thoughtfully.

He gave a wry smile. 'Cesca's lemon cake would make anyone talk. But, as I said, you're observant and you've got good instincts.'

'Goes with the job – like you and paranoia,' she said dryly.

'Just please don't take any risks,' he said. 'You're too imp...' Well, hell. He'd said enough for her to work it out for herself. He might as well blurt out the whole lot. 'You're too important to me,' he finished, squirming slightly as he said it.

'You're important to me, too,' she said, and his heart squeezed sharply. 'I was feeling a bit out of sorts,' she added, 'and you've just made it better.'

'Any time,' he said. 'If you want me to drive up to Camden, give you a hug, and drive back again, just say.'

'A four-hour round trip, just for a hug? No. You've got enough on your plate,' she said.

Was it his imagination, or did she sound wistful? Maybe he just wanted to think she missed him, too. Or maybe she really did miss him. He'd forgotten how messy and confusing emotional stuff could be.

'Oh, and there was one teensy other thing,' she added.

'What?'

'Harrison Taylor rang me,' she said.

His breath caught. 'Please tell me you haven't agreed to meet him on your own.'

'I've been looking for him for months,' she said. 'I can't turn down the chance to meet him now, and you wouldn't either in my shoes.'

'I suppose not,' he said grudgingly.

'Colin, I'm meeting him in a very public place tomorrow afternoon – the zebra crossing on Abbey Road. There will be tourists everywhere. Here, there and everywhere, in fact.'

He groaned. 'I get what you just did. Though that song was on *Revolver*, not *Abbey Road*.'

'Still works.' She laughed. 'And Bea has my location on an app on her phone.'

Colin would've rather liked to have Georgina's location on an app on his phone, too, for peace of mind, but he knew that suggestion needed to come from her. If he asked, it'd feel a bit like coercion. Which it wasn't. Just that Georgina had a very sunny view of life, and he knew from years of experience in his job that people could change from nice to extremely nasty in a very short space of time. 'Can Bea go with you? Safety in numbers, and all that?' he asked.

'Bea has a job to do, Colin. And I don't need babysitting by my own child. I'm probably going to a café with Harrison after our rendezvous, just for a chat,' she said. 'I understand why you're concerned, but your job makes you overprotective. Not everyone you meet is a secret baddie waiting to abduct people for nefarious purposes.'

He winced. 'I know. But not everyone who seems stable actually *is* stable. The wrong question could land you in' – he stopped, knowing that saying what he really thought would make her defensive – 'a difficult situation.'

'I promise that wherever we go will be in public, and I won't give him any personal information that would let him' – she paused briefly – 'trace me.'

That pause told him exactly what she'd done. 'You've already told him you live at Rookery Farm, haven't you?'

She sighed. 'Yes. But you've been over my security measures at the house with a fine-tooth comb, and remember I have Bert.'

'Is Bert going with you tomorrow?'

'Yes.'

He was only aware of how tense he'd been when he felt his shoulders drop. 'Good. Humour me and check in with me afterwards, to let me know you're safe?' he asked.

'You're being overprotective,' she said, 'and Bea's as bad. But yes, I will.'

'Bea's sensible,' he said. 'Though I admit I might be a *tiny* bit overprotective, as you said. It kind of goes with the job.' He paused. 'Do you want me to brainstorm questions with you?'

'No, but I appreciate the offer,' she said gently. 'I might pick your brains when Bryn and Dougie come back to me, though.'

'Do that,' he said, determining that somehow he'd get a day off soon so he could go to London and see her. 'Good night. Give Bea my best. And good luck for tomorrow.'

# SEVEN

The next morning, Peter called Georgina. 'I know I'm being the most enormous pain,' he said, 'but can we do the photography tomorrow rather than today, please? The police still have the trapdoor taped off and they're analysing the costumes and props, so we can't do a proper dress rehearsal. I'm still trying to find a replacement Banquo. I could kick myself for doubling up the cast so much instead of letting people be understudies. I thought I could save on the wages bill, for once, but I've been an idiot.' He groaned in apparent frustration. 'And, to be honest, the whole thing's making me tear my hair out.'

'It's not a problem, Pete,' Georgina reassured him. 'I'm enjoying spending some time with Bea. And being in London for longer than originally planned means I get time to do a few things I haven't done in ages. I'm going to see the mummies at the British Museum, later today.'

'You're a good egg, Georgie,' Peter said. 'No wonder Stephen could focus the way he did at work. He knew you had everything else under control, and there was never any of that needless *drama* outside the theatre.'

She laughed, knowing what he meant. 'You just never found the right one for you, Pete.'

'Say the word and I'd marry you tomorrow,' Peter said.

'You're a dear friend, Pete, but that's all it can be between us. You just need to find someone who isn't totally dependent on you for her happiness,' she said gently.

'And Bea says you're seeing someone anyway,' Peter said. 'I hope he doesn't take you for granted.'

'He doesn't,' Georgina said with a smile. 'It's still early days. And we're not looking for someone to replace someone else.'

'I envy you,' Peter said with a sigh.


'Who was that?' Bea asked, walking into the kitchen.

'Pete. He's asked me to do the photographs tomorrow rather than today. The police are still working with the stage, so you'll probably need to check in to see if they need you at the Regency today or not.'

Bea did so and came back to report that she was free for the day. 'I might see if I can do some office stuff today to top up my bank account a bit,' she said. 'Unless you want me to come with you to meet this Man of Mystery?'

'I'll be fine,' Georgina said. 'Colin nagged me last night about personal safety, too.'

'Good.'

'He sends his best wishes,' Georgina said.

Bea's eyes narrowed. 'Did you tell him about me?'

'Not the details,' Georgina said. 'Just that Faulkner was murdered, you're one of the four people under suspicion – five, really, because there's Leo the technician as well – and that Faulkner had blackmailed you. He says to ring him if you need help, and it won't go further than him – even to me,' she added.

'I like Colin. So does Will,' Bea said. 'He's one of the good guys.' She raised an eyebrow. 'Dad would have approved of him.'

'I agree,' Georgina said. 'Colin says that blackmailers normally target more than one person, and to think about anyone who might be acting... not as they usually would.'

'So I should throw someone else under a bus to clear my name, you mean?' Bea asked, folding her arms.

'No. There are already others in the frame with you,' Georgina said. 'I was thinking more of someone who might've been struggling, like you, and could do with a bit of support. And he's worked with Inspector Zhang. I know she's a bit stern, but he says she's fair. You could talk to her.'

'I'll think about it,' Bea promised.

Again, Georgina noticed her daughter tugging at her earlobe. She was convinced that Bea was protecting someone – but who? And why?

She texted Harrison.

> My schedule has changed so am free all day. If you'd like to meet at Abbey Road crossing a bit earlier, maybe I can buy you lunch?

Five minutes later, he responded.

> Lovely. See you at eleven?

> Perfect!

she typed back.

'Are you sure you're ready for this?' she asked Doris as she left the house, Bert trotting along beside them.

'Seeing Trev again, for the first time in half a century? Oh, I'm ready,' Doris said softly. 'I've waited for this moment for years and years and years.'

'One thing – he doesn't call himself Trevor anymore. He's Harrison.'

'After George? Like a stage name,' Doris said. 'Harrison Taylor. It sounds good.'

Georgina took the tube to St John's Wood, only needing to change lines once. It was a five-minute walk from the tube station to Abbey Road Studios. In front of the studios was the iconic zebra crossing, and on the other side of the road stood a tall, slender man with pure white long hair, worn just the way George Harrison had worn his for the Abbey Road album cover.

'Trev! Harrison, I mean. He still has that beautiful hair,' Doris said. 'When I last saw him it was almost black. He wore it like that back then, and his mother *hated* it and kept on at him to have it cut. But I always thought it made him look like what I imagined Aragorn to look like, all dark hair and grey eyes.'

Of course Doris and Trev would've read Tolkien back in 1971, Georgina thought. 'Did you approve of Viggo in the films?' she asked.

'Oh, yes. He's very easy on the eye. And the people who put it on DVD when they were staying at the farm *really* liked him.' Doris gave an earthy chuckle. 'But Trev – he was *my* Aragorn. And even though he's... well, I suppose we're both old now. But he's still beautiful. *To me, fair friend, you never can be old. /For as you were when first your eye I eyed, /Such seems your beauty still,*' she quoted.

Sonnet 104, Georgina thought. And Doris was right. Even though Harrison must be seventy, the age Doris would've been now, he still had a youthful air about him.

She crossed the road. 'Mr Taylor. Good to meet you,' she said.

'Harrison,' he said, shaking her hand. 'Good to meet you, too, Mrs Drake – or may I call you Georgina?'

Even though she knew she was supposed to be on her guard, and Irene had hinted that Trev was the one who'd pushed Doris down the stairs, she couldn't help warming to him. Especially with Doris sighing beside her, 'He always had such a lovely way with him.'

'My friends call me Georgie,' she said.

'If you're interested in my Doris, that makes you my friend,' he said. 'And who's this handsome lad?'

Bert sat nicely and offered a paw. Harrison chuckled and bent to make a fuss of him.

'This is Bert,' Georgina said.

'He's a beauty. Doris loved dogs. She had a black Labrador called Moppett – named because you always had to mop—'

'—the floor after she'd had a drink of water,' Doris said in tandem.

'I have the same thing with Bert. He never swallows that last mouthful,' Georgina said with a smile. Bert seemed to like Harrison, which was reassuring; dogs were usually good judges of characters. Irene had insinuated that her son had a dark side to his character, but Georgina couldn't see it, and it seemed that Bert couldn't, either.

'I never got over Doris,' Harrison said. 'I've missed her every day for more than half a century.'

'Oh, Trev. How much I missed you, too,' Doris said. 'How I wish I could hold you now. Kiss you. Tell you how much I love you still.'

Georgina had to blink back the tears. It was how she'd feel if she could see Stephen again but he couldn't see, hear or touch her. 'That's a long time.'

'I've had pink carnations put on her grave on the fourteenth day of every month ever since I left Norfolk,' he said. 'They were her favourite flower.'

Now Georgina understood the mystery that Jack hadn't been able to clear up. The date was obvious, because Doris had died on Valentine's Day. If only she'd thought to ask the local florist if anyone had a regular order for the churchyard, maybe she would've been able to find Harrison sooner. 'I saw them in the churchyard,' she said. 'And Jack keeps her grave nice with pink silk roses, too.'

'Jack, as in Doris's little brother?' Harrison asked.

'Yes. I met him when I started researching the history of the house, and he told me all about you both,' Georgina said. It was true – just not the whole truth. And, mindful of when she'd told Jack about being able to hear Doris, and his reaction, she wasn't yet ready to tell Harrison the truth. 'You were very hard to track down. I've spent months looking for Trevor Taylor.'

'I changed my name years ago,' he said.

'I assume Harrison is after George rather than Ford?' Georgina asked.

'George was Doris's and my favourite Beatle,' Harrison confirmed. 'Though I admit I loved *Star Wars*.'

'The name suits him,' Doris said. 'My Trev. My *Harrison*.'

Georgina smiled at him. 'I'm named after George Harrison, too. "My Sweet Lord" was number one, the day I was born.' She took a deep breath. 'I'm sorry to hurt you, but it was Valentine's Day.'

'1971. The day my world fell apart,' Harrison said. 'And not just mine. Doris's family were devastated. I could hardly face them afterwards.'

Because he'd been the one to push her down the stairs, the way his mother had suggested?

Georgina liked to think she was a reasonable judge of character. Her work as a photographer had taught her to sum people up quickly, and it was clear to her that Harrison Taylor had loved Doris every bit as much as Doris had loved him. He wasn't a murderer, or even an accidental killer. And he'd spent half a century mourning her.

'I always imagined walking here with her,' he said. 'The way half the tourists do, recreating the album cover.'

'Oh, *yes*,' Doris sighed.

'Let's do it,' Georgina said impulsively. 'I know there are the only two of us and Bert' – three of them, though Harrison wouldn't know that – 'but you can be George and Paul, and Bert and I will be John and Ringo.'

'Bert really ought to be Paul, with the bare feet,' he said. He smiled properly for the first time, and Georgina had a very good idea of just how lovely a couple he and Doris would have made.

'Walk as slowly as you like. I'll match your pace,' he said. 'The cars are quite used to having to stop for people walking slowly over this particular crossing.'

Was Doris walking next to Harrison right now, or had she slipped her hand into the crook of his elbow? Georgina wondered. Could Harrison even feel her presence?

Not that she could ask.

'Thank you,' Doris said as they reached the far side. 'I've always wanted to do that.'

'Thank you, my dear,' Harrison said. 'I could almost feel her beside me, just now.'

Maybe because that was exactly where Doris had been. 'I'm glad,' Georgina said. 'Did you end up studying in London, then playing in a band and teaching, the way you planned?'

His grey eyes widened. 'How did you know that?'

She couldn't tell him how. 'Something Jack said.' It was a slight fib, but it was forgivable, in the circumstances, she thought. The truth was too complicated.

'No. I didn't finish my A levels or even go to university,' Harrison said. 'I came to London in the end, but it wasn't the same without Doris. I didn't want to teach and I didn't even want to play guitar. But eventually I got a job as a barman in a Soho club. They had a back room where bands would play on Friday and Saturday nights, and one evening there was a problem with the sound. I sorted it out for them, and they talked me into learning to become a proper sound engineer – not going to college, but learning on the job.'

'That sounds great. I'm glad you still kept music in your life,' Georgina said.

'So how is Jack?' Harrison asked.

'He's doing fine. He's retired now, happily married with grandchildren,' Georgina said. 'And you might be amused to know that, despite the fact that he always hated weeding, he's become a keen gardener as he got older.'

'I always liked him. He was a good kid,' Harrison said. 'What about her parents, Lizzy and Albert?'

'Albert died ten years ago,' Georgina said. 'Lizzy's still around. I haven't met her, but Jack sees a lot of her.'

'That's good.' Harrison smiled wryly. 'In another life, I would've retired to Norfolk. And Doris and I would definitely have taken our children to Rookery Farm for the summer, even though we lived in London.'

'Have you been back to Little Wenborough since you left?'

He shook his head. 'There was no point. Without Doris, there was nothing left for me in the village,' he said. Which told Georgina everything about his relationship with Irene. 'But I'm not the only one who lost her. Neither's her family. There are all the kids she would've taught who missed out on her, too. She would've been brilliant. She loved Shakespeare.'

'My late husband was an actor and director. He loved Shakespeare, too,' Georgina said.

'Did you lose him very long ago?' Harrison asked.

'Two and a half years. He had a heart attack,' she said. 'But he's always with me in my heart.'

'I know exactly what you mean. Doris is always with me,' he said. 'I keep her picture close to my heart.'

'Let me buy you lunch, and you can tell me all about her,' Georgina said.

'My dear, I was brought up that a gentleman always buys a lady lunch. I *insist*,' he said. 'And I know just the place, because they're dog-friendly. Do you like Turkish food?'

'Very much,' Georgina said with a smile.

# EIGHT

Harrison offered Georgina his arm, and they walked with Bert to a small restaurant with maroon velvet seating, jewelled light fittings and white damask tablecloths. When Georgina confirmed that Bert had perfect manners and wouldn't annoy other customers, just sit under their table, they were shown to a table in a bright conservatory filled with olive trees. They ended up sharing several *mezze* – the best spinach and feta *borek* Georgina had ever eaten, along with excellent hummus and stuffed vine leaves, followed by a wonderfully spicy chicken tagine and rice, finishing up with the most gorgeous tiny pastries and fresh mint tea. And best of all the waiter sneaked them bits of grilled chicken for Bert, who lived up to Georgina's promises.

Then Harrison took the photograph from his wallet and handed it to her. 'This is my favourite photo of Doris and me.'

The photograph was slightly creased and the colours had changed with age. The picture showed Harrison with dark hair – in the same style as he wore it now – wearing jeans and a Beatles T-shirt. Doris was wearing her favourite shirt, lilac cheesecloth with purple flowers; his arm was round her shoulders, hers was round his waist, and they were smiling broadly.

'It's a lovely shot,' Georgina said. 'May I take a snap of it so I can send it to Jack?'

'Of course. And give him my best,' Harrison said.

'I will.' She took a snap on her phone. 'You both look really happy, with the world at your feet. You were what, eighteen at the time?'

'Seventeen,' he said. 'Though I was a couple of months younger than Doris. It was the middle of our A level years. We'd gone to Stratford to see *Hamlet*.'

Georgina remembered Doris's description. 'Miss Shields drove you, and you were all convinced the minivan would fall to bits on the way.'

Harrison looked surprised. 'Who told you that?'

When Georgina had told Doris's brother that she could communicate with Doris, it had rapidly turned into a sticky situation. She needed to feel her way a bit more carefully, this time. 'Something Jack said,' she improvised, glad of the excuse she'd kind of set up earlier. 'It stuck in my memory because I had a similar experience with my own first trip to Stratford-upon-Avon. My mum was our English teacher, and she was the one driving the minibus. Much as I love my mum, she was a *terrible* driver. We were all glad when school stuck to booking shows at the Barbican.'

'You grew up in London?'

'I did,' Georgina confirmed. 'And I stayed here for uni because I loved the city.' She explained about her work on the university newspaper leading to meeting Stephen and her career as a photographer with the occasional bit of journalism on the side.

'But you've moved from London to Little Wenborough.'

'I couldn't bear walking into the house and remembering all over again that Stephen wasn't there – and knowing that he wasn't going to be coming in late that evening after a performance,' she said. 'I needed space. Somewhere with no memories.'

'That's why I came to London,' Harrison said. 'I couldn't handle Little Wenborough. Not without Doris.' He dragged in a breath. 'I had a nervous breakdown after her funeral, and I spent a few months in a mental hospital in Norwich.'

'Oh, my poor Harrison,' Doris whispered, sounding anguished.

'I'm so sorry.' Georgina reached across the table and squeezed his hand. 'That must've been hard.'

'People talk a bit about mental health now, but back then it was something people hid. Something to be ashamed of,' he said. 'Women could almost get away with "having nerves", because they were seen as being weaker than men – even though nowadays we know better than that. But for a man to take an overdose...' He shook his head. 'My mother never got over the shame of having a son who ended up in the nuthouse. She told everyone I'd gone to stay with an aunt, but the truth leaked out and she hated it.'

'Your mother didn't deserve you,' Doris said fiercely.

And now it clicked. *It's not my fault that Trevor did what he did...*

Georgina had got completely the wrong end of the stick. Irene hadn't been insinuating that Trevor had been the one to push Doris down the stairs; she'd been trying to disassociate herself from his overdose and mental health issues. Even though she must've known that she was responsible for Doris's death, which in turn had triggered Trevor's – Harrison's – breakdown.

'It sounds as if your mother was a bit difficult,' Georgina said. 'Maybe if you'd confided in Lizzy Beauchamp, she would've helped you, so you and Doris could still go to London together. She would've helped you find —' She stopped. 'I'm sorry. I know about the baby. A family member told me,' she said. He didn't need to know it was Doris herself.

'I did the wrong thing,' Harrison said. 'I should've told Doris I'd make my parents give their consent and we'd get married. Or we could've waited until we were twenty-one and didn't need their permission anymore. The baby would've had my name and Doris could've called herself Doris Taylor and worn a wedding ring – we could've just gone to a register office quietly, the day after my twenty-first birthday, and nobody would've been any the wiser afterwards because she'd have worn the same ring and had the same name she'd used before the baby was born. The main thing is we would've been together.'

'It never occurred to me.' Doris gasped. 'We could've been students together *with* the baby.'

'Childcare was harder to come by, back in those days, and it wouldn't have been easy being parents and studying at the same time – it's not like it is now, where universities offer nursery facilities,' Georgina said gently. 'Don't blame yourself.'

'I should've been braver and stood up to them,' Harrison said. 'Doris and I could still have studied together. We could've worked part-time to pay for a childminder. It would've been hard, but we could've managed.'

'Why didn't you tell Doris's mum instead of yours?' Georgina asked.

'I *didn't* tell my mother,' Harrison said. 'Doris went to the doctor for advice. He prescribed hot baths, gin and a few falls down the stairs.' His jaw tightened. 'At the time, we were both panicking and it seemed the only thing we could do. I borrowed my best friend's motorbike to get to Norwich – I knew I could buy the gin there and nobody would see me and tell my parents or hers. We thought we could sort it out without anyone knowing.' He closed his eyes for a moment. 'But my mother found the gin in my room. She went on and on and on until I admitted that Doris was pregnant. I said we were going to take the doctor's advice.' He shook his head. 'I should've resisted her. But she said she was going to help.'

'So you weren't at Rookery Farm at all, that night?'

'No. She said it was women's work and made me stay home. She took the gin over to Doris. When she came back, she told me everything was done. It was only the next day, when Doris didn't turn up for school, that I realised something was wrong. The rumour went round that she'd slipped on the stairs, hit her head in the wrong place and died. Only I knew it wasn't that.' He rubbed his hand across his face. 'If only I'd gone with my mother instead of being a lousy, rotten coward. I could've stopped it happening.'

'You think she... pushed Doris down the stairs?' Georgina asked, her skin prickling.

'That's *exactly* what she did,' Doris said. 'I remember now. I was getting ready to roll down the stairs for the third time, and she pushed me. Hard. I fell awkwardly and hit my head. And then it felt as if the lights had all gone out.'

'I asked her once. If she pushed Doris down the stairs,' Harrison said. 'She said she did what had to be done and got snappy with me when I asked her exactly what she meant. Her reaction made it obvious: she'd killed the love of my life and she was trying to justify it. I tried to tell the police, but they didn't take me seriously. Of course an upstanding citizen like my mother would never push someone down the stairs – besides, I didn't have any evidence. I couldn't prove it. The coroner said it was an accident, and of course the coroner knew more than a stupid teenager like me ever would.'

'Oh, Harrison. That's...' Georgina shook her head. 'I'm so sorry nobody would listen to you.'

'Everything seemed hopeless. Doris was dead, and there was nothing worth staying for. That's when I took the overdose,' he said. 'Unfortunately, my father found me in time to get my stomach pumped. My mother made sure I was locked up under supervision and couldn't do it again. When they finally let me out of the mental hospital, I refused to go back to

Little Wenborough. Instead, I got the bus to London with nothing except the clothes I was wearing. The only time I went back to Norfolk was for my dad's funeral, but I stayed at the back of the church and I didn't go to the wake or speak to my mother.'

And Georgina didn't blame him.

'When her social worker rang me to say she needed more care, I came back to make the arrangements to sell her house and fund her care at the nursing home, but I won't visit her. Ever.' His face tightened. 'Because I can't forgive her for what she did to Doris.'

'Unfortunately, she'll never stand trial for it,' Georgina said. 'She doesn't have capacity.'

Harrison's eyes narrowed. 'You've met her?'

'When I was trying to find you.' She paused. 'She's lonely and bitter.'

'Good,' Harrison said. 'Don't try and persuade me to lighten her last days with forgiveness. Because I won't.'

'I wouldn't dream of it,' Georgina said. 'I know she's your mother, but I didn't like her – or the way she spoke about Doris.' She paused. 'She didn't admit to what she'd done, in so many words, but she told me she "did what she had to do". It's pretty clear now what she meant.'

'Then let her loneliness be her punishment,' Harrison said.

'I can't forgive her, either,' Doris said, 'but it breaks my heart to know what happened to Trev. It's such a waste. Such a stupid, *stupid* waste. I wish he'd found someone who'd make him happy – someone who'd love him as much as I did. Someone who'd given him children. He would've been an amazing dad.'

'I'm so sorry,' Georgina said again. 'I took her flowers, actually. Orange lilies.'

Harrison's mouth quirked. 'She would've thought them vulgar. Good choice.'

'In the language of flowers, they also mean contempt,' Georgina added.

Harrison grinned. 'Perfect. And Doris would've quoted *that* Shakespeare sonnet.'

'*Lilies that fester smell far worse than weeds.* Exactly. That woman's a festering lily,' Doris said.

'I'm just sorry that you had to go through what you did,' Georgina said.

Harrison shrugged. 'I muddled through. As I said, I found a job and I ended up doing sound engineering. I loved that even more than playing – if I'm honest, I was never good enough to make it to the big time, either as a singer or a guitarist. But I knew sound and I could make a difference there. I still had my challenges with the black dog – once you've had depression, it never goes that far away. But I've learned to recognise when things are bad, and I've checked in to a clinic every once in a while, to keep me going. Once I was qualified in London, I went to work in America, and I even had the chance to see George Harrison play – but it didn't feel right, going to see him without Doris.'

'You should've gone and enjoyed the show,' Doris said. 'For pity's sake, we did that Christina Rossetti poem in class together!'

Georgina knew the poem Doris meant. *Better by far you should forget and smile /Than that you should remember and be sad.*

But she could understand how Harrison felt, because she never wanted to forget Stephen, either. They'd shared so much. Forgetting would make her sadder than remembering, and she was pretty sure it was the same for Harrison.

His next words confirmed it. 'People told me I had to move on. But it made me sadder to think of forgetting her than it did to just keep missing her.'

'I know what you mean,' Georgina said. She thought about telling him what she knew about Doris; but how did you tell someone that you'd become friends with the ghost of the woman he'd lost fifty-odd years ago? 'People mean well,' she said.

'But until you lose someone you really can't understand how it feels.'

'It was a Thomas Hardy poem that tipped me over the edge,' she said. 'The last line: *The look of a room on returning thence*. When you go back to a familiar place and the person you expect to see just isn't there and you realise you've lost them all over again. That poem made me sob buckets.'

Harrison reached over and squeezed her hand. 'Oh, my dear. I think we need to make a toast.' He lifted his glass of mint tea. 'To those we love and will never forget.'

'To those we love and will never forget,' Georgina echoed, lifting her own glass. 'Though people have told me that Stephen would've wanted me to be happy. To find someone who made me see the joy in life again. And I've come to realise they have a point. If it had been the other way round, I would've wanted Stephen to find someone who loved him – not in the same way that I did, because you can't replace someone, but as *much* as I did. Because living without love is a lonely place to be.'

'That's it exactly,' Doris said. 'I want my Harrison to be *loved*.'

'And have you?' Harrison asked. 'Found someone, I mean?'

'I've met someone. It's early days, but I think we're good for each other. My children – well, they're grown up, but you know what I mean – they like him. And I think Stephen would've liked him, too, if they'd met. He would've said I'd found someone who'd be good *for* me as well as good *to* me.' She looked at Harrison. 'How about you?'

'I'm seventy,' he said.

'That's not old. Not in this day and age. Tell him I want him to find love again. Don't compare me with whoever he meets, because we won't be the same, but find someone who'll fill his days with joy,' Doris said. 'And tell him what happened to me wasn't his fault.'

'I never met Doris,' Georgina said carefully – and she hadn't, at least not when Doris had been alive. 'But I'm pretty sure she was one of those people who made the world feel a better place.'

'She was,' Harrison agreed.

'I think she was all about love,' Georgina said. 'That's what Rookery Farm feels like. A place where people loved and lived and laughed. And I think she'd want that for you, Harrison. Not to see someone as trying to be a replacement for her and failing, because you can't replace one person with another, but someone who'll make you feel joy and understand that you want to keep Doris in your heart, too. Someone who'll put brightness in your days. Share music and good food and poetry. Who'll love you for who you are – and someone you can love for herself.'

'Maybe you're right,' Harrison said.

Seventy and alone in the world, except for the mother who'd ruined his life by killing the girl he loved. Georgina's heart squeezed. He'd left his friends behind in America, too. She'd been in a similar place, after Stephen's death, but thankfully she'd had the children, her mum and a host of good friends. She'd made some new good friends, too, since moving to Norfolk.

Right at that moment she wanted to adopt Harrison as the uncle she didn't have, with both her parents being only children; so he wouldn't have to be alone anymore. But she didn't want to patronise him or appear as if she were playing Lady Bountiful.

Maybe, in time, he could become a family friend. Perhaps he'd agree to come back to Little Wenborough and heal some of the pain of the past, sitting in Doris's old garden, eating Cesca's lemon cake and enjoying the birdsong and the butterflies. She made a mental note to find out if there were carnations or roses called Doris, and ask Young Tom to plant them in the garden in her memory.

'You know, what happened to Doris really wasn't your fault,' Georgina said.

Should she tell him what she'd told Jack?

The glimmer of tears he blinked back decided her. 'Tell me, Harrison, do you believe in ghosts?' she asked.

'*There are more things in heaven and earth, Horatio, /Than are dreamt of in your philosophy,*' he quoted. 'I don't know. A lot of the musicians I've worked with have their superstitions and their rituals to calm them down before a show, and some think it's lucky to sleep with the score under their pillow.' He smiled. 'And you never whistle backstage, because sailors used to do the rigging and they used whistles to communicate. A whistle in the wrong place could mess up the cues and cause havoc with the show. And then,' he added, 'there's the opera equivalent of the "Scottish Play".'

Georgina smiled, knowing that he meant *Tosca.* 'My husband was an actor-director and my daughter's an actor, so I know where you're coming from about superstition around a stage. Actually, I'm taking some headshots of a cast that's performing *that* play, including my daughter.' And there was definitely a ghost in that particular theatre, along with a bit of superstition, a lot of bad luck and a real-life murderer. It would take time to sort out those particular tangles. 'But what I meant was, do you, personally, believe in ghosts?'

'I've had things happen where I couldn't find a rational explanation,' Harrison said thoughtfully. 'But, no. I don't really.'

'Don't tell him about me,' Doris said, surprising her. 'He's fragile. It'll be too much for him. Let him remember me as I was.'

Georgina gave a subtle nod of agreement. 'You're probably right. It's superstition.'

'Why?' he asked.

'No matter. Just that sometimes I feel Stephen's close by, that's all. I wondered if it was the same for you, with Doris.'

'It felt as if she was with me when we walked across Abbey Road,' he said. 'But that was wishful thinking, remembering the might-have-beens. But I'm not going to be a tiresome old man, banging on about the past. Tell me about you. You said your daughter was an actor?'

'Yes. And my son's a scientist.'

By the time they'd finished their second pot of mint tea, they'd become firm friends. And Georgina ended up telling him about the Regency Theatre and Bert's habit of finding skeletons.

'Quite a character, your dog,' he said, making a fuss of Bert.

Bert thumped his tail in agreement.

'Are you retired now?' Georgina asked.

'Yes, but I miss work,' he said. 'I've been tempted to see if I could keep my hand in, though it'd be selfish to take jobs away from the youngsters who've been struggling since Covid.'

'He'd be a great teacher,' Doris said.

Georgina nodded again to show Doris she'd understood. 'Unless,' she said, 'you mentored people. As a volunteer. Maybe you could work with kids who are struggling at school and don't know what they want to do – and you could bring them the joy of music.'

Harrison looked at her. 'Like the way the guys in the club brought music back to me? I'd never thought of that. It's the sort of thing Doris would've suggested.'

'Maybe that should be your mantra when you're feeling

stuck. What would Doris suggest you should do?' she asked lightly.

'I'll think about it,' Harrison said. 'Though I do know she would've really liked you.'

'I do like you,' Doris said. 'Very much. You're like the daughter I never had and the sister I never had, mixed up with an aunt or two. My mum would love you, too.'

And then it was Georgina's turn to blink back the tears.

'I think it would've been mutual,' she said.

When they left the restaurant, she gave him a hug. 'I'd really like to stay in touch, Harrison. And, if you can bear it at some point, I think Jack would love to see you again.'

'I'd like that,' he said.


When he'd left, Georgina headed for one of the small parks in the area to let Bert stretch his legs. 'Are you all right, Doris?' she asked. 'You must feel you've been through the wringer – seeing Trev again after all these years, plus remembering what happened to you.' She blew out a breath. 'Yet again, I'd really love to be able to give you a hug and I'm so sorry that I can't.'

'But you're *there* for me,' Doris said. 'And that means a lot.' She paused. 'It's weird, finally knowing the truth. When you went to see her, Irene tried to blame him for my death, didn't she?'

'How do you know?' Georgina asked, surprised.

'Because you kept changing the subject or refusing to answer when I asked you. It felt as if you were protecting me, like the way you protect Bea and Will.'

'You might be technically eighteen years older than me,' Georgina said, 'but at the same time you're younger than Bea.'

'Which makes me a cross between being like an aunt and a daughter for you, like you are for me,' Doris said. 'Did she say he pushed me?'

'She said she did what had to be done. And she said it wasn't her fault that he did what he did. She implied he was involved, and I hated the thought you might've spent half a century loving someone who didn't feel the same way about you,' Georgina said. 'I wanted to see Harrison face-to-face, so I could judge for myself, before I told you what Irene said.'

'And?' Doris asked.

'Even before he told us about the overdose, I knew he hadn't pushed you. It's so obvious that you're the love of his life. But I don't think Irene was deliberately trying to make me think the wrong thing; I think she was talking about his overdose not being her fault and trying to convince herself that it was true. Even though her killing you is exactly what pushed him into taking that overdose.' She sighed. 'I liked him very much, and I think you would've been happy together. And I wish I could do something to help.'

'If you tell him about me, I think that'll push him over the edge again,' Doris said. 'I don't think people necessarily need a partner to validate their life, but I do think Harrison needs someone in his. Someone to help him keep the dark thoughts away. That was a good idea you had about mentoring. Hopefully he'll think about it.'

'I wish there was a way of bringing that woman to justice,' Georgina said.

'Harrison has a point. Loneliness is a fitting punishment,' Doris said. 'If she hadn't killed me, she would've had at least one grandchild. And maybe she would've come round to our way of thinking, in the end. But, instead, she lost her son. He walked away and refused to see her again. She's had a whole lifetime of being lonely.'

'I think you're a nicer person than I am,' Georgina said.

'No, I'm not. I don't forgive her for what she did. But she's not going to stand trial, and she's never going to apologise, so it's pointless getting upset about something I can't change,' Doris said. 'Let her be lonely. It's what she deserves.' She paused. 'But I could do with some space to sort out how I feel about Harrison, in the back of my head. Could we go to the British Museum?'

'Let's drop Bert back at Bea's and do that,' Georgina said.

# NINE

Back on the Tube, Georgina texted Colin.

> Confirm am perfectly safe, post meeting. Bert liked Harrison and so did I. He didn't kill Doris, but he knows Irene did. Is there a way of bringing her to justice? Speak later xx

Then she texted Bea.

> Harrison was lovely. Bert liked him, too. On my way back. Love you xx

Colin was clearly busy because he didn't respond, and when Georgina got back to Camden, Bea was clearly up to her eyes in admin.

'If I make you a cup of tea, can I leave Bert with you and swan off to the British Museum?' Georgina asked.

'Course you can. So Harrison Taylor was nice, then?'

'*Really* nice,' Georgina said. 'He's promised to stay in touch. And he told me a lot about Doris. I think it makes it even sadder for me, because they would've been so happy together.'

'I hope,' Bea said, 'he found someone lovely to share his life with.'

Georgina shook her head and hugged her. 'He wasn't that lucky.' Not like her. 'I love you.'

'Love you, too, Mum. Will and I have been talking about it,' Bea added, as if Georgina's thoughts had been written all over her face. 'We want you to be happy rather than lonely.'

They'd accepted Colin as a potential fixture in her life, clearly seeing that love expanded rather than replaced, and it brought tears to her eyes. 'Thank you.' Georgina blinked the tears back. 'Harrison's lonely. He's spent more than half a century mourning Doris.'

'Poor man. I mean, of course you don't just stop loving someone when they die. But life goes on, and you have to adapt the best way you can.' Bea gave her a speaking look. 'I know Dad would've been furious if you'd walled yourself off from everyone.'

'I pretty much did that for a while,' Georgina reminded her.

'I know. But you made friends in Norfolk. Sybbie, Cesca and Jodie are fabulous. You've got Bert. Plus you're back to working again now, and that suits you.' Bea raised an eyebrow. 'Even though you seem to spend as much time investigating murders as you do taking photos, or in your darkroom.'

'Speaking of work – well, and investigating – I'm going to pop into the theatre on the way home. Just in case there's any information about the body Bert found,' Georgina said.

'You're planning to find out who it is, if they can't?' Bea asked. At Georgina's nod, she added, 'As I said, count me in for helping you with that.'

'Thank you.' Georgina hugged her again. 'I'm going to ask Pete if there's an archive at the theatre.'

'If there isn't, he might know where the records are deposited. If it's at the National Archives in Kew, you can ask them to get the records for you before you go.'

'Thank you. I'll do that.' Georgina smiled at her. 'See you later, sweetheart.'

At the British Museum, Doris thoroughly enjoyed the Egyptian rooms, from the mummified crocodile to the Rosetta Stone and all the cases. 'This is amazing. And to think I might've been able to see the Tutankhamun exhibition here in 1972 – when they actually had the blue-and-gold mask on display.'

'My mum went to that,' Georgina said. 'It's a shame I'm still the only one who can hear you, because I think you and my mum would get on incredibly well. You have a lot in common.'

'Same favourite subject, same favourite Beatle, same love of Shakespeare, same love of Egypt...' Doris mused. 'Did she like Ancient Rome, too?'

'Yes,' Georgina said. 'She watches every documentary going.'

'We would definitely have been friends,' Doris said.

'We'll come back and see the Roman Britain area next time,' Georgina promised. 'But I really want to check in with Pete. Do you mind if we go to the Regency now?'

'Of course not. And I can speak to Fred, hopefully,' Doris said.

Peter Newton was in his office at the theatre when Georgina got there.

'I'm checking in on you and whether you've actually eaten today,' Georgina said.

He gave her a weary smile. 'Bless you, Georgie. Yes. Liza' – the wardrobe mistress, Georgina remembered – 'made me a sandwich earlier.'

Georgina had a feeling that Liza worried as much about

Peter as she did about the younger cast members. 'Which is good of her, but you can't live on sandwiches, Pete. Come over to Bea's tonight. I'll cook.'

He shook his head. 'Too much to do. But thank you for the offer. Don't worry. I'll order something in.'

'Just make sure you do,' she said. 'Have you heard anything back from the police?'

'They're going to interview everyone again tomorrow. Which was supposed to be opening night – but, given that I'm still short of a Banquo, that's not going to happen,' he said with a sigh. 'And neither's the dress rehearsal; the police are still looking at the stage.'

'You've already got most of the cast playing more than one role,' she said, 'so you can't even switch to the understudy because then you'll be short elsewhere.'

'I need someone who's played Banquo and the Doctor before, to take Neil Faulkner's roles – and someone who's going to fit in with what I'm trying to do here, rather than battering people with their ego,' Peter said. 'I've got a couple of auditions this evening. But, with the problems we've had already, I can't risk anything going wrong on opening night. I've cancelled the performances on Friday and Saturday, and Monday isn't looking hopeful either. I've said it's due to cast indisposition.' He groaned. 'As soon as the press find out that Neil's dead, they'll besiege us to find out what happened. Plus there's the fact that someone in the theatre is a murderer – who's going to be their next victim?'

Should she tell him about the blackmail? Whoever had killed Neil had probably been blackmailed by him, the way Bea had; with that out of the equation, there would be no more reason to kill anyone.

Then again, had Peter himself been blackmailed by Neil? Was that why Peter had cast him as Banquo?

'I gather Neil wasn't very popular among the cast,' she said carefully. 'He was fairly snide with Rebekah and Bea, in front of me. It might be that his behaviour pushed someone over the edge.'

'Or it's the start of something that will end up completely out of control.' Peter grimaced. 'Maybe I should just cancel the whole thing.'

'And then what? Pete, give the police time to find out who did it. Then – even though it's horrible to think that someone you work with could be a killer – you might need to replace someone else in the show. But everyone else in the cast and crew will still be safe. And I know Bea was so excited about this opportunity. I'm sure everyone else is, too. They'll stand by you and give you their best for the show.'

'Or maybe I'm kidding myself and the production really is cursed.'

'You know what?' Georgina asked. 'That sounds like lack of sleep and lack of food talking. You know you've got a good team here.'

'With a murderer in the middle,' he said, looking bleak. 'But you're right. If I cancel, that means refunding the tickets we've already sold. I've been talking to Sheena about it – the finance and admin manager – and the Regency will definitely have to close if we cancel the whole run. I'm not sure which of us is having more sleepless nights over it. As it is, I'll have to extend the run on the other side, and hope that not too many people ask for a refund instead of a reschedule.'

'Money's that tight?' she asked.

'Money's that tight,' he confirmed. 'We're still not really back on our feet after Covid. The limited opening helped, but the tickets we did sell didn't cover our costs. You need to sell at least half your seats to break even. And even though we put some virtual performances online, so our theatregoers knew we understood how much they missed live performances and we were trying to fill that gap as best we could, quite a few of our patrons weren't working either. When they didn't have their usual money coming in, they couldn't afford to donate money to help us. And then, once that was starting to stabilise and we were all starting to hope things would get better, the cost of living crisis hit...' He blew out a breath. 'Sorry. You don't need to know all this.'

'I get it, Pete,' she said. 'And I'm sorry – it didn't help when Bert found that body underneath the floorboards. Do you want me to leave him at Bea's tomorrow when I finish the headshots?'

'No – he's a lovely dog, and maybe it'll help the more jittery members of the cast feel a bit safer, having a dog around.'

'Making a fuss of a dog does make you feel better when you're antsy,' she said.

'I agree.' He raked a hand through his hair.

'Is there anything I can do to help?' she asked.

'Short of finding a magic wand, probably not,' he said. 'And you're already doing the publicity shots as a favour. I appreciate that.'

'OK. Then I'll see you tomorrow,' she said. Tonight, she'd make a big batch of Cesca's lemon cake to cheer everyone up; and it would have the useful side effect of persuading them to talk to her.

She headed down to the stage, in case Bryn and Dougie were there; to her pleasure, they hailed her.

'No dog today?' Bryn asked.

'He's back at Bea's,' she said with a smile. 'How's it going?'

'Not to be rude, love,' Dougie said, 'but it's a forensic investigation.'

'You can't tell me anything about it because I'm not part of your investigation,' she said. 'I understand that. But, as it happens, I have a message for you. Colin Bradshaw sends his best.'

'Would that be Colin "oh, for God's sake, I am *nothing like*

Colin Firth" Bradshaw?' Bryn asked, doing a fair impersonation of Colin at his most exasperated.

Georgina burst out laughing. 'It would. Some of our friends were teasing him about it recently, and he admitted that his team used to do things to his desk whenever a new Colin Firth film came out.'

'They did. The best though was the frilly shirt they gave him when he left uniform,' Dougie said with a grin. 'Mr Darcy. How do you know our Colin, then?'

'We're, um, friends.'

Bryn gave her an arch look. 'Would that be as in "just good"?'

'It's early days,' she said, feeling the colour flood her face. 'He was originally planning to come to London with me while I did the photography here, but then he was caught up in a case. I was talking to him last night and told him about what happened here, and I mentioned you. That's when he asked me to give you his best.'

'He's a good man, Colin Bradshaw,' Dougie said. 'Settled in all right in Norfolk, has he?'

She nodded.

'Terrible case he had at the end here, though I expect you know all about it,' Bryn said.

'I do,' she fibbed. Colin still hadn't opened up to her, and she wasn't going to pry or gossip. When he was ready, he'd tell her.

'Actually, although we can't discuss Neil Faulkner with you, we do have some news on your skeleton,' Dougie said. 'I was hoping you'd be in today so we could tell you, or we would've asked Pete to pass it on. The Finds Liaison Officer's had a look, and he says the clothes are original, not modern replicas for a costume. That means we're looking at late 1930s or early 1940s and, although it's clear from the sharp trauma on the skeleton that he was murdered, the person who did it would have to be more than a hundred years old by now.'

'If by some miracle they're still alive, the chances are they won't have capacity and they couldn't go to trial,' Bryn said.

Just like Irene's murder of Doris, Georgina thought sadly.

'Which means we have zero chance of getting a conviction,' Bryn finished. 'Sadly, we can't investigate.'

'What's going to happen to the remains?' she asked.

'They'll be buried with respect in an unmarked grave,' Dougie said.

'What if,' she said, 'I could find out who the victim is? Could you hold off burying him until then?'

'That's a tall order,' Bryn said. 'He could be anyone.'

'But if there's a paper trail? If he was one of the actors here, maybe I could follow it up,' Georgina said. 'As I told you before, my daughter works for a probate genealogy firm when she's resting.'

'Yes. I had a chat with her, like you suggested, and she's given my wife some tips for her family tree,' Bryn said. 'I appreciate that.'

'She also helped me find the identity of the skeleton Bert dug up a few months ago,' Georgina said. 'I'm pretty sure she could do that again.'

Bryn and Dougie looked at each other. 'In that case, I'm sure it could take us a while to file the paperwork,' Dougie said.

She smiled. 'Thank you. Are you likely to be here tomorrow?'

'Possibly,' Bryn said.

'Then there will be lemon drizzle cake with your name on it,' she said.

'My favourite,' Dougie said. 'Thank you. And let us know how you get on with your records.'

'I will,' she promised.

She headed back to see Pete. 'You might have one story for the press that will bring people in, out of curiosity – and hopefully they'll enjoy the show and book for the next,' she said.

He frowned. 'What's that?'

'The body under the floorboards counts as "bones of antiquity". I'm going to try and find out the story behind it, with Bea's help. Do you happen to have an archive for the theatre?'

'Only since I leased it. The rest, I think, was deposited in the National Archives in Kew.'

'Perfect,' she said. 'I know the theatre was bombed in the Blitz, so that's somewhere between 1940 and 1941 – but do you know the exact date the bomb hit? Because my theory is that there's a connection.'

'Hold on,' he said, and checked something on his computer. '15 October, 1940.'

'Thank you. That gives me a good starting point,' she said. 'I'll see you tomorrow. And I'll bring cake.'

'You,' he said, 'are wonderful.'

'Hang on in there, Pete. It's going to get better,' she said.


Doris joined her on the way out of the theatre. 'I talked to Fred,' she said. 'Actually, he wasn't Fred. He was Friedrich Schmidt, but they billed him as Fred Smith for obvious reasons.'

'He was German?'

'Austrian,' Doris said. 'He moved to London before the war started – the autumn of 1937, because he could see where things were going in Vienna. He knew he would've singled out anyway, because of his religion, but his political views made him even more of a target. He left Vienna in an attempt to draw eyes away from his family.'

Which probably hadn't been enough, Georgina thought. 'Poor man.'

'It's scary to think that all happened when my mum and dad were young,' Doris said.

'My mum was born a few months after the war ended,' Georgina said. 'I agree. It's still within living memory.' She paused. 'Does Fred – Friedrich – remember what happened to him?'

'Yes and no,' Doris said. 'He goes by Fred, because he married an English nurse who lived two doors down the street from him, and she used to call him Fred. She kept her surname, because – well, he wasn't allowed to change his name and, with people's feelings towards anyone who sounded German, it saved a lot of ill-will. Her dad didn't approve of their relationship, because he didn't see any difference between Austria and Germany. Plus, back then, Esther would've been expected to give up her job as a nurse as soon as she got married. She didn't want to do that. So they got married quietly.'

'Did he tell you her name?' Georgina asked.

'Esther Bailey. She was pregnant when he was killed – but he doesn't know what happened to her or to the baby, and he can't rest until he finds out.' Doris sighed. 'He's terrified that she thought he'd deserted her and lied to her about which side he was on. I guess his situation is a bit like mine was, when I first met you.'

'Stuck, with no way of finding out what happened. OK. We'll do our best to find out what happened to her – and find records for him to prove who he is, so he can have a proper burial with his name,' Georgina said. 'Can he remember what happened, that night?'

'He had a fight with another actor – a guy whose dad was killed in the First World War, so of course he'd have it in for anyone with a German-sounding name. And I get the impression there was a bit of rivalry between them. Fred got the part the other actor wanted, and it didn't go down well.'

'That sounds like professional jealousy, as well as grieving for his father, and deciding to take it out on the wrong person,' Georgina said. 'Can Fred remember his name?'

'It's fuzzy,' Doris said. 'But he remembers white-hot pain in his back, then at his throat, and then everything went dark. He's had a long time to think about it and conclude that he was stabbed in the back, and then maybe his throat was cut to finish him off.'

'That's horrible. Poor guy. The marks on his skeleton bear out the stabbing, but obviously slitting a throat wouldn't have left marks on the bones, so I won't be able to prove that,' Georgina said. 'I'll start with the theatre records and see who acted with him, in case he recognises a name. My theory is that the guy who killed him hid him under the floorboards, and nobody found him because the theatre was bombed the next night. That's so sad – and his family would never have known what happened to him.' She bit her lip. 'Right. I have a cake to bake, and some documents to search through.' She glanced at her watch. 'Actually, I'll check with Kew now and book what I want for tomorrow.' It was the work of a couple of minutes on her phone to sort that out.

Back in Bea's house in Camden, she called Colin to update him.

'So you'll be staying in London for longer?' he asked.

'Looks like it,' she said. 'I'll have to ring Jodie and ask her if she can handle the Rookery Barn holiday cottage changeover for me, and be the contact point if the guests need anything.'

He paused. 'I miss you,' he mumbled.

The fact he'd admit that made her feel warm all the way through. 'I miss you, too,' she said.

'Just promise me you won't do anything dangerous.'

'Of course I won't do anything dangerous. I'm going to the National Archives. Do you think someone's going to brain me with a digital census record?'

He coughed. 'You know exactly what I mean. I haven't forgotten what happened at Hartington.'

Neither had she. Coming face-to-face with her own mortality – twice – had been a shock. Not that she was going to admit it to him. 'Bryn and Dougie send their best, by the way. And they mentioned the frilly shirt.'

'Oh, no.' Colin groaned. 'Will I ever live that down?'

She laughed. 'I think you already know the answer to that!'

# TEN

'Until we know who killed Neil Faulkner, how do any of us know that we're safe?' Anjali Chander, who played the First Witch, Donalbain and Lady Macduff, asked. 'And it's not just him, is it? Bea fell off the stage and broke her wrist. Rebekah had food poisoning for a week. There was John, the carpenter – he had a bang on the head and hurt his shoulder when the scenery fell on him. The broken lights could've hurt someone. And that weight from the flies that only just missed Elias. How do we know that wasn't the murderer just warming up? Who's going to be next?'

There were murmurs of agreement from the other actors massed in the Green Room.

'And there are weird sounds under the stage. Not rats – I know what that sounds like,' Aliou Faye, who played Duncan, said. 'I don't know what's causing them, but I don't like it.' He shivered. 'I wouldn't want to act in that room. I don't know how Leo stands it, being down there on his own waiting for Banquo to come through the trapdoor.'

'Of course you're all worried,' Peter said. 'I'm worried about the situation, too. But I've almost got someone to agree to join us as Banquo – someone I've worked with before and who'll be supportive. It's going to work out. I promise.'

Georgina noticed several of the cast glancing at each other and looking awkward at the mention of supportiveness. From what she'd seen, Neil had been far from supportive. She knew he'd blackmailed Bea, and it was likely that he'd blackmailed others. But who?

Jake Atkins, the twelve-year-old boy who played Fleance, Banquo's son, looked particularly anxious, and she resolved to have a quiet word with him. It could be his youth that made him nervous, especially if this was one of his first roles; or it might be that he knew something.

'I think it's true what they say – you know, that there's a curse on the play,' Aliou said. 'Look at all the productions in that past that went wrong. I learned about it in stage school, years ago: the riots, the real-life murders—'

'What real-life murders?' Peter asked.

Everyone was clearly thinking of Neil Faulkner and didn't make eye contact with anyone else.

'There was one in Amsterdam – where the guy playing the lead had an affair with the wife of the guy playing Duncan and stabbed him for real on stage,' Aliou said.

'Which was meant to happen in, what, the 1670s? But I bet you can't find the name of the people involved,' Peter said. 'It's all part of the myth, Aliou. Loads of productions of other plays have had accidents on set and people being ill.'

'Not as many as *this* play,' Anjali muttered.

'And there was a production where Macduff actually ran the lead actor through with his sword, by accident,' Edith Miller, who played the Second Witch and Malcolm, said. 'Maybe their ghosts are the ones we can hear in the basement. Or maybe the play's unlucky.'

'My husband directed and acted in the play a few times,' Georgina said. 'He said it was the play companies always put on when things were a bit tight and they needed something that they knew would sell out. That's probably where the "unlucky" feeling comes from. And think how many productions of this play have run *without* any problems, especially as it's one of the most often performed Shakespeare plays. It's only human to look for patterns – but sometimes we look too hard for patterns when we're scared, and see things that aren't really there.'

Aliou, Anjali and Edith didn't look convinced.

'Your husband directed and acted in it, and he d—' Rebekah, the First Murderer, clapped her hand over her mouth. 'I'm sorry.' She reached over to Bea and squeezed her shoulder. 'Sorry. That was tactless. I didn't mean it.'

'Stephen died of a heart attack, two and a half years ago,' Georgina said calmly. 'And I can assure you that he wasn't working on a production of the Scottish Play at the time. These things just happen, sadly.'

'The police want to interview everyone again today,' Peter said, clearly trying to change the subject. 'It's just routine. But nothing's going to happen to any of you while they're in the building, is it? You're all going to be fine. We'll get through this and the show's going to be a hit. *And* Georgina brought cake.'

'To sweeten you all up for the photographs,' Georgina said with a smile.

Nobody smiled back, and she sighed inwardly. It looked as if today was going to be tough.

When she checked the stage, Bryn and Dougie weren't there. But a man was lying on the stage. Very, very still. 'Hello? Are you all right?' she called.

He didn't answer, and she quickly clambered up onto the stage. If someone else had collapsed...

She'd just reached him when he jumped and banged his head against the corner of the stage. 'Ow!'

'Sorry,' she said. 'I didn't mean to make you jump.'

He sat up and took out one of his earbuds. 'What?'

'I said I'm sorry – I didn't mean to make you jump,' she repeated. 'Just, you were lying very still. With everything that's been going on, I just panicked that you were...' She couldn't bring herself to say any more.

'It's my own fault,' he said, giving her a rueful smile and rubbing his head. 'I had my music on too loud.' He grimaced. 'It's a bit spooky when you're in here on your own.'

'I think everyone in the theatre feels like that at the moment,' she said, holding out her hand. 'I'm Bea's mum, by the way. Georgina Drake.'

'John Riley,' he said, shaking her hand.

The carpenter who'd had a set fall on him. Was he another of Neil's blackmail victims, or had it been a genuine accident?

She eyed the chisel, hammer and utility knife in his open toolbox. 'Just as well I didn't make you jump when you were using any of those.'

'Just fixing the trapdoor. It squeaks, and we don't want the audience to hear it,' he said. He shivered. 'Though it's not very nice, thinking about the last time it was used. Or about that skeleton they found under the floorboards. I wouldn't do Leo's job, not if you paid me double!'

Georgina decided not to tell him her dog had been the one to find the skeleton. 'Sorry again for making you jump. I'll let you get on.'

'All right,' he said. 'Nice to meet you. Bea's very good.'

'Thank you,' she said.

John *seemed* nice. Then again, so did some of the others who were on Mei Zhang's suspect list...


Peter had given Georgina a quiet, private space to do the headshots. Her first subject was Jake Atkins.

'Hello, Jake. Grab a seat. I meant to tell you, I really enjoyed your performance the other day,' she said with a smile, taking a couple of snaps. 'And I've seen a lot of productions of this particular play.'

'Thank you.' He went very slightly pink.

'Are you enjoying working here?' she asked, taking another shot.

'Yes.' But his smile was a little too bright.

'Are you all right, love?' she asked gently.

'Ye-es.' But he didn't sound too sure. 'It's just' – he took a sharp intake of breath – 'it's a bit scary, seeing a real dead body.'

'Of course it is. Especially if you've never seen one before,' Georgina reassured him. 'Tell you what, I'll download the shots I've taken so far to my laptop. Let's have a look at them together, and you can tell me if you like them or if you'd prefer me to try a different approach.'

'Really?' He looked surprised. 'I thought I'd have to – well, do what I was told. You being a top photographer and me still being at stage school, and all that.'

'It doesn't matter that you're still at school; you're part of the cast. You have exactly the same rights as the others – and I like my clients to be happy with their headshots, not feel they're stuck with something they don't like.' She cut him a slab of cake, which he accepted gratefully, and they went through the photos on her laptop.

'I like that one,' Jake said, pointing to the third shot.

'That's good. I'll make a note,' she said with a smile.

She kept him chatting for a little longer; then, when he seemed more relaxed, she said, 'I know Neil upset some of the cast. Did he do anything to upset you?'

Jake bit his lip. 'No.'

That sounded almost like a yes, Georgina thought. 'Some-times,' she said, 'it helps to have someone who isn't on the cast on your side. You can talk to me about anything. Or to my daughter, Bea, if you'd rather talk to someone in the show.'

'Bea's nice,' he said. 'But...' He looked awkward. 'Neil didn't upset me. But I heard him having a row with Elias, a few days ago. It sounded as if – as if Neil was threatening him. And – well, Elias is a bit scary. He's *big*.'

Elias was a good six foot two and broad-shouldered, Georgina thought, whereas Jake was small and slight, more like a Puck or an Ariel. No wonder the boy was nervous of him.

'And I was thinking, what if Elias was the one who killed Neil?' Jake's eyes were wide with fear. 'I mean – he was one of the Murderers. On stage with Banquo, that is,' he added hurriedly. 'I'm not saying he's an *actual* murderer. He probably isn't.' But he sounded as if he was trying to convince himself.

'Have you spoken to the police yet, today?' Georgina asked gently.

Jake shook his head.

'Tell them what you just told me,' she said, 'and they'll look into it.'

'But what if I got it all wrong and Neil wasn't threatening him? Then Elias will get into trouble for nothing. And if he finds out it was me who grassed on him, he might...' He shivered, clearly not wanting to name his fears. 'And if he *did* kill Neil, and he finds out I know something...'

'The police won't tell him who told them,' Georgina reassured him. 'You won't get in trouble with Elias or anyone else, I promise. It just gives the police another lead to go on.'

Jake bit his lip. 'I can't.'

'What if,' she suggested, 'I mention it to the inspector? Then you're not the one who said anything. And I'll ask her to be discreet. She'll talk to you in private, and she'll talk to a few other people in private as well. Nobody will know what you say to her.'

'Would you?' He looked relieved.

'Of course. You can talk to me any time while I'm here, if you're worried. And talk to Bea when I'm not here,' she reassured him. 'Pete's really approachable, too.'

'This is my first proper part,' Jake confessed.

'And it's for a solid director, with a good cast. You did the right thing, accepting the part. It'll look great on your CV,' she said. 'I'm sorry this week's been so tricky and upsetting, but I promise you things will get better.'

There were a couple of other people she wanted to talk to, as well. Anjali and Aliou were both clearly jittery, worried that the killer would strike again. Given that she hadn't heard any rumours about Neil blackmailing anyone other than Bea, if they were worried they might be the next targets of the murderer, did that mean he hadn't tried to blackmail them?

And she definitely wanted to talk to Elias and Rebekah, the other two of the three Murderers on stage when Neil had complained about being hit too hard.

When Jake left her, she went to see Inspector Zhang, who was using Pete's office, and caught her between interviews. 'I wondered if I could have a very quick word, perhaps in exchange for lemon cake?' Georgina asked.

'Thank you.' Inspector Zhang took a polite bite of the slice Georgina gave her, then smiled. '*Really* thank you, if I can have the recipe for this,' she said. 'What can I do for you, Mrs Drake?'

'Actually, it's what I can do for you,' Georgina said. 'As a photographer, I'm good at getting people to open up to me. I was talking to Colin about it last night. I thought if I made some lemon cake and mothered the cast a bit, I might be able to persuade them to come and talk to you sooner rather than later if they knew something.'

'Colin "don't call me Darcy" Bradshaw.' Inspector Zhang chuckled. 'Bryn told me.' Her expression softened. 'I worked with him a few years ago, before – well, never mind. How's he doing?'

The concern in her eyes was yet another hint about the case that had broken him, Georgina thought. Would he ever trust her with what had happened to him? 'He's doing fine.'

'That's good.' She looked at Georgina. 'In the circumstances, I'd be happy for you to call me Mei.'

'I'm Georgie, to my friends,' Georgina said.

'Georgie.' This time, Mei Zhang's smile was broad. 'So, did you get anyone to open up to you? Do you have any idea who else Neil Faulkner blackmailed? Because I agree with you: it's not a huge leap to think he was blackmailing people other than Bea.'

'Jake – the young lad who plays Fleance – told me he overheard a row a few days ago, between Neil and Elias Petrus, who plays Macbeth; Elias also plays the Third Murderer. Jake said that Neil was threatening Elias.'

'And Elias was on stage when Neil complained about being hit too hard – when he might have been stabbed. Interesting,' Mei said. 'Does Jake think Elias killed Neil?'

'He's not sure. He didn't want to tell you about it himself, because he's worried that Elias might blame him and take it badly.'

'And Elias Petrus is a lot bigger and stronger than he is. I get it,' Mei said. 'But that's definitely worth following up. Thank you. Did Jake say if he heard what the row was about?'

'No. And he's really worried that Elias is going to find out and blame him if there's any trouble.'

'I'll reassure him about confidentiality,' Mei said. 'Anyone else?'

'Pete was briefing everyone this morning. Aliou Faye – he's playing Duncan – was very jittery, saying that he thinks there's a curse on the production. So was Anjali Chander. She's Lady

Macduff, Donalbain and the First Witch. And Edith Miller – she's the Second Witch and Malcolm.'

'None of them was on stage when Neil was stabbed, I take it?'

'No.'

'Could they be blackmail victims?' Mei asked.

'I haven't heard anything, and neither of them have done their photos with me yet so I haven't been able to talk to them properly,' Georgina admitted. 'But I wanted to let you know what Jake said. And I'm happy to take the blame and deflect Elias from Jake, if need be.'

'We'll be discreet,' Mei promised. 'Actually, do you happen to know if any of the cast is diabetic, particularly Neil Faulkner?'

'Bea hasn't mentioned it. Pete might have a better idea – or somebody might refuse cake on those grounds, in which case I can let you know. Why?'

Mei looked at her. 'I'll trust Colin's judgement that you know how to keep things confidential. I had the pathology report through this morning. Not only was Neil Faulkner stabbed, he was injected with insulin. The pathologist spotted the needle puncture – not too far from the stab wound, actually. She ran tests and that's when she picked up that his blood glucose was very low.'

Georgina frowned. 'If Neil wasn't diabetic, does that mean that the person who stabbed him also gave him insulin – so if one didn't kill him, the other would?'

Mei didn't answer the question, instead asking, 'What do you know about insulin, Georgie?'

'One of my friends at uni was diabetic,' Georgina said. 'She always carried jelly babies with her, so if her blood sugar dropped too low, she had some fast-acting carbs to fix it. I remember her saying once that if she was sweaty and staggering about, it didn't mean she'd been drinking too much, it meant her blood sugar was low and we needed to get sugar into her; and if she was drowsy and smelled like pear drops, her blood sugar was too high and we needed to get medical help.' She looked at Mei. 'So if Neil wasn't diabetic and someone gave him insulin, it'd make his blood sugar drop below normal levels.'

'To the point where he'd collapse,' Mei said. 'And if they gave him enough insulin, it could cause death.'

'So what killed him? The insulin or the stab wound?'

'We're still working that out,' Mei said.

Georgina nodded. 'I'll keep it to myself. Well – myself and Colin.'

'Give him my best when you speak to him,' Mei said. 'And if he has any thoughts on this, I'd be happy to hear them.'

When Georgie continued with the headshots, Anjali, Aliou and Edith were all still nervous but made it clear that it was the alleged 'curse' of the Scottish Play rather than Neil that had upset them. Rebekah did her best to smile, and Georgina managed to get a reasonable set of pictures, but it was clear that the actress was worried about something.

'Are you all right, love? It looks to me as if you could do with a friend,' Georgina said, cutting her a bit of cake and pouring her a mug of tea.

'I...' Rebekah closed her eyes. 'I've been so *stupid*,' she whispered. 'It was five years ago. I thought nobody would know.'

Georgina gave her an encouraging smile and waited.

'I'd only graduated the year before. It was my first real break. And I was so flattered when the star of the show started paying me attention. He said...' Her breath hitched and she opened her eyes again. 'He said his wife didn't understand him because she wasn't in the business. Obviously I know now it was just a line, but I fell for it.'

You and quite a few others, Georgina thought. 'You had an affair?' she asked gently.

'I was so in love with him, and I thought he loved me. I

thought we were going to be the new golden couple of the West End. Until I fell pregnant.' A tear slid down her face. 'He dumped me as soon as I told him. A week later, I lost the baby. And I don't know how the hell Neil Faulkner found out about it, but he said he'd dredge it all up again and make sure everyone knew unless I paid him.'

Another blackmail victim.

Someone with a motive to stop him; and an opportunity because she'd been one of the last on stage with him.

Could Rebekah have stabbed Neil Faulkner?

'Do you think he had anything to do with your food poisoning?' she asked gently.

'It was a warning. Like—' Rebekah stopped abruptly.

'You knew he was blackmailing someone else?' Georgina deliberately made her voice gentle. She had a feeling that Rebekah might be the person Bea was trying to protect.

Rebekah closed her eyes. 'Not for definite. But I've been thinking about it. He gave me a dodgy sandwich to warn me. Bea tripped and broke her wrist – what if he was the one who made her fall? And the weight that nearly hit Elias? But I could hardly ask them if he was blackmailing them, too, without admitting that he was blackmailing me, and I didn't want my past all coming out. I didn't know what to do.' She rubbed her hand across her face. 'So I paid up,' she whispered. 'I'm only just back at work after maternity leave. I didn't want to lose this part. And I really didn't want my partner finding out how stupid I was, back then. I don't want him walking out on me and the baby – or, worse, walking out on me and taking the baby with him.'

'I understand,' Georgina said. 'Just for the record, any partner who's worth their salt would stand by you.'

Rebekah winced. 'He's worth it. Just... he's a bit traditional. He didn't even want me to come back to work. He said we could manage on his salary and I didn't have to work.'

'That's still not an excuse to leave you struggling,' Georgina said. 'And I'm pretty sure Pete wouldn't let you go for something like that.'

'Neil said he would. He said people would think I got rid of the baby on purpose and they'd say I was a monster and they'd boycott the play, so Pete would have to sack me or the show would fold.' Her breath hitched. 'I'm glad he's dead. I didn't kill him – but I'm grateful that someone stopped him and I'm glad I don't have to pay him any more money. Except...' She bit her lip and whispered, 'What if Neil already told someone else what he knew and they want me to pay them to keep it quiet?'

'Talk to Inspector Zhang,' Georgina said gently. 'She'll help you sort it out. If anyone comes to you and tries blackmailing you, make sure she knows. Blackmail's illegal and it carries a jail sentence.'

'What if he's already told someone in the press?' Rebekah looked haunted.

'Then the press officer here will help you with damage limitation,' Georgina said. 'You might be able to spin it about how delighted you are to have a baby after suffering the heartbreak of a miscarriage, and you want to give hope to other women who've been through similar pain. There's always a way.'

'Really?'

'Really,' Georgina said. 'Go and have a quiet chat with Inspector Zhang. She'll help you.'

Elias was the next actor on her list.

'Is this going to take long?' he asked, not smiling. 'I have things to be getting on with.'

'I'll try and be as quick as I can,' she said. 'Did you have any particular pose in mind?'

'Whatever,' he said, rolling his eyes.

In Bea's experience, actors enjoyed having headshots done – especially when they weren't paying for it. They chatted about their favourite roles, the parts they dreamed of playing, or told her scurrilous stories to make her laugh. This man was taciturn to the point of rudeness.

She made one last attempt. 'Would you like some lemon cake?'

'I don't eat cake.'

Talk about hard work. Georgina could normally get anyone talking. Elias wasn't just a closed oyster, he was stuck together with barnacles. No way would he open up willingly.

He was also, as Jake had pointed out, *big*. From muscle, rather than fat. It was easy to see him as Macbeth the *berserkr*, a wild warrior fighting ferociously, besmeared with blood.

Georgina decided not to try pushing him, particularly in light of what Jake had said. Bea had paid up; so had Rebekah. But if Elias had argued with Neil, did that mean he'd resisted Neil's attempts to blackmail him? Had Elias been the one to kill Neil? Any real questioning, Georgina thought, needed to be done by Mei and her team. If she meddled, she could make things worse. She'd tell Mei about it, though.

Bert placed himself between Elias and Georgina during the shoot; he sat quietly, but Georgina was aware of the tension in the way he was sitting. Bert clearly didn't like Elias.

'OK. Would you like to pick your top three shots?' she asked.

'I'll go with whatever,' he said, not looking at her.

It wasn't said with the tone of wanting to make life easy rather than being a diva, more as if he couldn't care less. What was his problem? She was pretty sure she hadn't done or said anything to upset him. 'Fine,' she said.

The rest of the cast made a fuss of Bert and told Georgina how worried they were about a murderer being in their midst. None of them gave her the impression that they were involved, and none of them refused cake, let alone mentioned being diabetic.

Was Elias perhaps diabetic? Was that why he'd said no to the lemon cake?

No. It was more that he'd given her the impression he trained hard in the gym and wouldn't touch refined carbs.

She rang Colin at lunchtime, when she left the theatre, to talk to him about it.

'Be careful,' he said. 'Either you have a desperate murderer doing a belt-and-braces approach and using two different methods of murder to make absolutely sure Faulkner dies, or you have two desperate people who snapped at the same time.'

'Which is a coincidence – and you don't like coincidences,' she reminded him.

'He complained of being hit too hard. That could either be the stab or the insulin – but my money would be on the insulin,' he said, 'because you said the scene was repeated. If it'd been the stab, you would've seen blood on his costume or dripping on the stage. Which of the four people on stage with him would've had access to insulin?'

'Not Bea, and I think Jake was too scared to do anything,' Georgina said. 'Which leaves Rebekah and Elias.'

'Faulkner sniped at Rebekah on stage,' Colin said, 'which to me suggests he felt he was powerful enough to get away with it because she wouldn't protest or complain to the director.'

'Originally I thought maybe he did it because Rebekah was younger than him and female, and he thought that gave him the right to behave how he liked,' Georgina said. 'But now I know he blackmailed her, so it was power play on his part. Though I don't think she killed him.'

'Are you sure? If people are desperate enough, they can act out of character – and I'm afraid, much as neither of us would like to think she could be guilty, Bea would be included in that.' He paused. 'You mentioned Elias. How was he with you?'

'Grumpy. Sadly, cake didn't sweeten him and get him to talk to me.' She decided not to tell Colin that Elias had made

Bert tense; the last thing she wanted was Colin being overprotective.

'That's unusual,' Colin said. 'Normally people respond to your warmth – or the cake.' He paused. 'Maybe he's worried that the police would find whatever material Neil had on him.'

'I hadn't thought of that.'

'What did you think?' Colin asked.

'Jake was scared of him, and I could see why.'

'Did he intimidate you?'

She sighed, recognising the overprotective instinct coming out. 'No. Just he's big and he clearly spends a lot of time in the gym.'

'Maybe he colluded in the murder with either Rebekah or Bea: one of them using the insulin, and the second using a blade just before the lights went out so nobody would see the blood. I don't like this, Georgie.'

'Firstly, I still think Bea's innocent – even if you take out the bias because she's my daughter. Secondly, Bea wouldn't let anyone harm me. And, thirdly, nobody's going to do anything to me with Bert around,' she said firmly. Or Doris. Not that she could tell Colin that Doris had helped Bert save her at Hartington Hall.

'Hmm,' Colin said. 'I know I suggested maybe you could have a chat with people earlier, but it was the wrong decision. Of course you're worried about Bea, but please stay out of it from now on, Georgie. For your own safety.'

'I'm going to drop Bert back at Bea's then go to the National Archives, this afternoon,' Georgina told him. 'Nothing's going to happen there, either.'

'Hmm,' Colin said again, but to her relief he said no more. 'Call me later. And tell Bea to ring me if she's worried.'

'Even though you think she might be a murderer?'

'I've said to you before, to investigate properly you need to take the emotion out,' Colin reminded her gently. 'You need to rule her in as a possibility before you can rule her out effectively.'

'I know you're right. Though I'm still sure she didn't do it. I *know* her, Colin.' Though she knew he had a point. Even if you gave birth to someone, you didn't know all of them. Georgina hadn't had a clue about the photos that had landed Bea in trouble in the first place. She sighed. 'I'll call you tonight.'

# ELEVEN

At the National Archives in Kew, Georgina went to talk to one of the archivists about the documents she'd ordered.

'There are several large boxes in the Regency Theatre's archive,' the archivist said. 'Were you looking for something in particular?'

'I'm looking at the casts of plays performed in London from 1936 to 1945,' Georgina said. 'I was hoping to see playbills or programmes, especially ones with photos, and I'm fairly sure I can narrow down what I want to the Regency Theatre in Islington – definitely from 1940, anyway.'

'You might find it useful to start with the calendar of plays and players,' the archivist said. 'There's one covering each decade, listing all the performances in the West End with their opening and closing dates, usually the cast, and sometimes comments as well as notes about reviews.'

'So if I look at the calendar first, then I'll know which specific programmes and playbills I need to look at from the Regency's archives?' Georgina checked.

'It's probably the best place to start,' the archivist said. 'I'll show you where they're shelved. Come and see me when you've found which particular documents you need, and I'll do my best to help you locate them.'

Georgina took the volume for 1940–49 over to one of the tables and started to work her way through it. 'Look at this,' she whispered to Doris. 'October 1940 – the week we think Fred was killed – guess what they were performing?'

'That's a spooky coincidence,' Doris said, clearly looking over her shoulder.

Georgina chuckled, enjoying the pun. 'Isn't it? *Macbeth* by William Shakespeare, Regency Theatre, Islington, 1/10/40 to 15/10/40, all matinees. And Fred's listed as Macbeth.' She glanced through the rest of the cast. 'There aren't any names I recognise here.'

'Ooh, look – there's a name I know. Donald Wolfit. He's listed at the Strand, for *A Shakespearean Entertainment*,' Doris said. 'Excerpts from the plays and sonnets.'

'So was Fred's rival an actor from Wolfit's company or someone from the Regency?' Georgina asked.

'Maybe you should take a copy of the entries on the other Shakespeare productions as well, so we can cross-check,' Doris suggested.

Georgina worked her way through 1940, taking photographs of all the entries for the Regency and all the Shakespeare productions outside it – most of which seemed to star John Gielgud at the Old Vic or Donald Wolfit's company at Kingsway or the Strand. 'Fred's here at the Regency at the start of 1940, but between May and August he disappears, and he doesn't seem to be listed at any of the other theatres, either,' she said. 'The Regency produces *Othello* again in June, but this time it's with Eric Daubeney as Othello instead of Fred.' She checked the previous production. 'Eric played Iago, last time. He seems to have been in the second most important male role in the productions where Fred's the lead, and he seems to have taken over Fred's roles between May and August.'

'We need to find out why Fred disappeared,' Doris said. 'Fred's back in September; I'm guessing the two weeks in the middle of September with nothing listed at the Regency were because of the Blitz, because virtually nothing else is open either; and that's also why *Macbeth* is matinee-only in September and October.'

'There aren't any listings for the Regency at all after 15 October 1940, but I expected that because we know the theatre was badly bombed that night,' Georgina said. 'Fred's not listed in any other London productions after then. So we have documents which strongly suggest he's the body under the floorboards at the Regency.'

She checked online and found an article about theatre performances in London during the Second World War. 'The theatres closed in September 1939 by government order, until GB Shaw led a protest and they were allowed to open again. That ties in with what the calendars say. And the theatres closed again in the middle of September 1940, after the Blitz started; a couple stayed open for matinees only, to avoid the blackout. That explains the gap in September, but not the gap between May and August.'

Looking through the previous volume of the calendar, Georgina found Fred listed at the Regency from September 1937 until September 1939. 'It looks as if Fred acted only at the Regency,' she said. 'And the reviews seem to praise his performances as much as they do Donald Wolfit's. My gut feeling is that the rivalry's within the Regency – and most likely Eric Daubeney, because he's the one who took over Fred's roles.'

'So what happened in 1940?' Doris asked. 'Why did Fred go missing?'

'I'll ask Bea.' She texted her daughter quickly.

> Where can I find out about Austrian people
> living in London in WW2? Xx

Internment tribunal records

> ???

Hang on.

A few moments later, Bea sent her an internet link.

It's an article about enemy aliens – horrible
name, but that's what they were called. Check
1939 register as well. Replaces 1941 Census.
Can help you tonight if you want.

> Thanks. Love you xx

She clicked on the link, read the article and winced. 'This is horrible. Under the 1914 Aliens Registrations Act, any "enemy alien" wanting to live in England had to register with the local police office. Those poor people, trying to get away from Hitler and yet still being treated with suspicion. They were on the same side as us, not our enemies, and "alien" is such a vile word to describe someone.'

'I remember Dad talking about the POWs who worked at Rookery Farm in the war,' Doris said. 'The way my gran saw it, our boys captured in Germany or Italy would be in the same position, so we treated their boys the way we wanted our boys to be treated. Some of them came back in the 1960s and brought their families to meet us. They remembered my grandparents with a lot of affection.' She paused. 'Though obviously there were others who didn't see the refugees or the POWs the way my grandparents did. They saw only a German, not the real person in front of them, and they wanted revenge for what they'd lost in the bombing or for people they loved who'd died fighting Hitler. So they'd start fights, smash windows and paint slogans.'

'Even though the refugees hated Hitler as much as they did.' Georgina shook her head, feeling a mixture of pity and frustration. 'That's so sad.'

'And the article talks here about the tribunal records Bea mentioned,' Doris said. 'The Home Office set up committees to interview enemy aliens and decide how to classify them. High-risk people were put in category A and interned; people in category B weren't interned but had special restrictions on their movements; and people in category C could carry on life as usual.'

'Until May 1940,' Georgina said, reading further forward, 'when the authorities thought the risk of invasion was so high that they rounded up all the "enemy aliens" and sent people in category A and B to camps. Some people from category C were sent to the camps as well. That could explain Fred's disappearance. Was he sent to one of the camps? And what made them change their mind and let him go back to London?'

'We need to find Fred's tribunal record,' Doris said.

The records had been digitised, and Georgina was able to find Fred's card easily. As soon as she looked at it, the words "male enemy alien" leaped out at her, typed in capitals and underlined. Then the card explicitly stated that he was a refugee.

It gave his date of birth in Vienna, and to her surprise showed his nationality as German rather than Austrian. His address in Florence Street, Islington, was listed, along with his police registration certificate number, and his occupation was 'actor'. His employer was shown as the Regency Theatre in Islington, and the tribunal declared him exempt from internment or restrictions.

'He must've been category C,' Doris said.

The next page was titled:

*Reasons for Decision*

*SCHMIDT came to this country on 15 September 1937, and is of Jewish race.*

*His father was deprived of his business as a pharmacist in Vienna, and his parents are living in America. He also has a younger sister in America.*

*The alien is at present working at the Regency Theatre in Islington. He is listed on all playbills as Fred Smith, his 'stage name'.*

*He was vouched for by Mr Alan Havers, the director of the Regency Theatre, and Mr Michael Rowan, the owner-manager of the Regency Theatre, who both state that Schmidt bears an excellent character and there is no doubt as to his loyalty to this country.*

*The Committee regarded the alien as a genuine racial refugee whose being at liberty in no way constituted a danger to the State.*

The report was signed by the chair of the Regional Advisory Committee, dated 1 November 1939.

'So he was category C, and it's likely that he was interned between May and August 1940,' Georgina said.

'What about Eric? Is he still acting in the West End after the Regency was bombed?' Doris asked.

Georgina checked the listings. Eric Daubeney was listed in the cast at the Kingsway Theatre, but he didn't seem to have been given any of the major roles. When she checked listings from before September 1937 at the Regency, he hadn't been cast in major roles before Fred's arrival, either.

'I'm really not sure what's happening here. Is it professional jealousy, like actors who loathe each other and only just manage to put it aside on stage? I mean, Wolfit and Gielgud apparently hated each other,' Georgina said. 'Did Eric have a grudge against Fred because he thought he should've had Fred's roles? Or could there be another reason why he killed Fred?'

'Maybe he was like those people my grandparents talked about – the ones who hated anyone with a German name because they'd lost someone in the war?' Doris suggested.

'Good point,' Georgina said. She glanced at her watch. 'We're running out of time. I know Bea can access some of the records online at home, but she can't access the playbills and theatre programmes. I want to see if we can put a face to Fred.'

'There might be something on the internet,' Doris said, 'but I agree. Start with the theatre records.'

The archivist Georgina had spoken to earlier helped her to dig out the information she wanted. There were several programmes from 1940, including for *Macbeth*, but none of them had photographs.

She tried 1938, when she knew Fred had starred as Elyot in *Private Lives*, and was thrilled to see a black-and-white head-shot in the programme. She took a snap of it on her phone.

'Look at this. The way he wears his hair, slicked back but he's obviously got slightly curly hair.'

'He reminds me a bit of Paul Henreid,' Doris said, 'who played Victor Laszlo in *Casablanca*.'

Georgina looked up the actor on her phone. 'You're right,' she said. 'He does.'

'Poor Fred,' Doris said. 'To be separated from his parents and his sister, know that others in his family were at risk of being dragged into the camps if they didn't get out in time, have to make a whole new life in another country while being treated like an enemy – and then, when he'd just found love and a chance of happiness, to be murdered.'

'It's a shame,' Georgina said. 'But at least we'll get him buried properly, under his name. And maybe we'll be able to find out what happened to Esther and the baby.'

'I hope so,' Doris said. 'Can you find an excuse to go to the theatre tomorrow? Then I can have another chat with Fred. Maybe what we've found out will jog some of his memories, the way it did with Anne at Hartington – and like talking to you jogged mine.'

# TWELVE

When Georgina got back to Bea's house in Camden, Bea was in the middle of making curry and Bert was thrilled to see Georgina, wagging his tail and circling her for a good five minutes.

'That's what she gets for deserting you for a whole *century*,' Bea teased. 'You tell her, Bert.'

Bert wagged his tail even more.

'You fraud. It was a few hours,' Georgina protested, making a fuss of the dog. 'How has your day been, love?'

'Good,' Bea said. 'And the really good news is that Pete's found us a Banquo. A nice guy, this time. Inspector Zhang says we can have the stage back, so we're going to have a run-through tomorrow, a dress rehearsal on Monday, a school workshop on Tuesday and then hopefully open on Wednesday night.'

'That's wonderful,' Georgina said.

'Just as long as Neil didn't leave all his secrets with someone who decides to take advantage of it,' Bea said dryly.

'I doubt it – and if that does happen, we'll get Colin involved.'

'Agreed,' Bea said. 'Pete wondered if you wouldn't mind

coming in with me tomorrow morning to grab a headshot of our new Banquo, then finish the dress rehearsal on Monday?'

'Of course,' Georgina said.

'Great. Dinner will be about another twenty minutes.'

'Bea – how well do you really know the other people in the cast?' Georgina asked.

Bea shrugged, her expression completely open. 'Pretty well.'

'Jake?'

'He's a sweetie. A bit nervous, but this is his first professional role, so you'd expect that,' Bea said.

'Elias?'

'I don't think anyone really knows Elias,' Bea said thoughtfully. 'I'm not entirely sure that cool, menacing Macbeth of his is entirely acting, and I wouldn't want to get on the wrong side of him.'

Exactly what Georgina had thought, but she didn't want to make Bea uncomfortable by agreeing too loudly.

'But I don't think he's a murderer,' Bea continued.

'What about Rebekah?'

'She's lovely. She came with me to the hospital when I broke my wrist and kept me in coffee during the wait.'

'Do you think she was another of Neil's victims?' Georgina asked.

Bea rubbed her earlobe. 'No.'

'No?' Georgina coughed and rubbed her own earlobe.

Bea grimaced. 'That bloody tell! I don't *think* she was being blackmailed, but I think Neil knew something about her that made her unhappy.' She looked awkward, and then gave a brief nod, as if she'd decided something. 'I trust you not to break a confidence, Mum.'

'Of course,' Georgina said.

'Even to Colin,' Bea checked.

'It stays with me,' Georgina promised.

'You know that bit in the play when I'm folding baby

clothes? The first time I did it on stage, Rebekah had tears in her eyes, and she was quiet for the rest of the day. I walked to the Tube with her after rehearsal, and I said I'd noticed her looking upset and asked if everything was all right. That's when she told me she'd lost a baby, and she'd folded clothes just like that afterwards. She put them in a box she gave to a charity shop, because she couldn't face giving them to a friend and seeing them being worn by a baby who wasn't hers.' Bea sighed. 'I think Neil found that out and was using it just to be nasty and bully her. I can't think how he could've blackmailed her over that.' She frowned. 'She did mention her partner was a bit difficult about her coming back to work. Maybe Neil was putting extra pressure on her because he liked feeling powerful, and Rebekah's a bit vulnerable.'

'I don't think anyone in the cast is going to miss him,' Georgina said.

'And you promise you're not going to talk to Colin about her? She doesn't need the hassle.'

'You're a good friend, Bea. Actually, she did tell me a little bit about it when I was taking her photograph,' Georgina admitted. 'I advised her to have a quiet chat with Mei Zhang.'

Bea's eyes narrowed. 'So if you knew already, why are you questioning me? Do you actually think I did it?'

'No. But I think you might suspect someone.'

'Rebekah wouldn't have stabbed him. I certainly didn't. Jake wasn't near enough to him on the stage to stab him.'

'So that leaves Elias – and maybe Leo, when Neil went through the trapdoor. What do you know about Leo?'

'We haven't worked together for very long. He's very good with lighting,' Bea said.

'Pete told me there's been some trouble with the lights. Expensive breakages.'

'And you think that was a warning to Leo, like the way Neil tripped me?' Bea looked shocked. 'Oh, God. It sounds as if Neil was working his way through the cast and crew, picking them off one by one.'

'That's what I was wondering,' Georgina said. 'He knew that nobody would talk to anyone else, because they wouldn't want whatever he had on them getting out.'

'So that makes everyone in the cast and crew a potential suspect,' Bea said with a shiver. 'Everyone in the theatre, even. And if whoever killed Neil was desperate enough to kill him, they'd also be desperate enough to kill anyone who guesses who they are.'

'Hopefully the forensics team will come up with evidence of who killed him,' Georgina said. 'In the meantime, I think everyone just needs to be very, very careful.'

'I don't want to let Pete down, and I really want to do this play. But a tiny bit of me wishes I'd never been cast,' Bea admitted. 'And I don't want to think about it anymore tonight. How did you get on at the National Archives?'

'I'm pretty sure I've found the identity of our actor under the stage,' Georgina said, and explained the theory she and Doris had worked out. 'Fred came to England in 1937. I've got his tribunal notes and a record of everything he acted in at the Regency. But there's a gap I can't account for, between May and August 1940. I think he might have been at one of the camps.'

'Do you know what category he was placed in?' Bea asked.

'C – the least dangerous. I took a photo of his card. The committee called him "a genuine racial refugee" – he was Jewish,' Georgina said.

'Sadly, that doesn't make a difference,' Bea said. 'There was a "collar the lot" campaign in 1940, partly whipped up by the press. A lot of people were interned in May 1940, regardless of their category. Because there were so many, some were sent to Canada and Australia; one of the ships, the *Arandora Star*, was torpedoed in July 1940 on the way to Canada. It was awful – more than half the people on board lost their lives. That swayed public opinion back again, and from August the category C internees started to be released. So that fits with the dates.'

'Interned in May and released in August,' Doris agreed. 'That definitely fits.'

'Fred, you said?' Bea checked.

'Friedrich Schmidt, but his stage name was Fred Smith in the programmes and playbills.'

'Legally, from the end of World War One until, would you believe, as late as 1971, anyone from a foreign country who came here wasn't allowed to change their name, unless they were women who got married. It would've made sense for him to use a stage name, to stop anyone linking the theatre with Germany – even though a lot of German actors from Jewish backgrounds had come to England and America, after the Nazis purged the film and theatre industry of anyone who disagreed with them.' Bea grabbed her laptop, logged in and checked a few things. 'How old was Fred in 1940?'

'Thirty-five,' Georgina said.

'Yup, he's here. He was taken to one of the Liverpool camps.' Bea glanced up from her screen. 'He was very lucky not to end up on one of the ships.'

'He got to stay, only to be murdered and buried under the stage of the theatre where he worked,' Doris murmured.

Georgina gave a tiny nod of acknowledgement. 'What happened about conscription?'

'Just before the war, it was for men aged twenty to twenty-two,' Bea said. 'When war was declared, it was for all men between eighteen and forty-one, unless they were in a reserved occupation or medically unfit.'

'Was acting a reserved occupation?' Georgina asked.

'No. The main ones were medics, police, farmers, teachers and skilled labourers,' Bea said. 'In practice, the government realised actors would be more useful in helping with morale than they would be as infantry, so they weren't called up as quickly.'

'That fits, too,' Georgina said thoughtfully.

After dinner, Georgina cleared the table and Bea got her laptop out again. 'Did you check the 1939 register, Mum?'

'No. I've got three people I want to check,' Georgina said. 'I'm not sure whether Fred will be listed under his original name or his stage name.'

'Probably his original name, but we'll try both. Do you have any idea where he lived?'

'Somewhere in Islington. I'm guessing maybe a boarding house?' Georgina suggested.

Bea quickly typed in some information. 'He's listed under his real name. Friedrich Schmidt, aged thirty-five, actor at the Regency Theatre. He lived in Florence Street.'

'The same place as on his tribunal card. Just round the corner from the theatre,' Georgina said.

'The landlady was a Mrs Martha Stephenson – and there are a few other actors listed,' Bea said.

'Would one of them be an Eric Daubeney?' Georgina asked.

Bea shook her head. 'There's nobody with that first or last name at the boarding house.' She turned her screen round so Georgina could see it. 'Do you recognise any of the other names?'

'Three or four – they seem to have been regulars at the Regency,' Georgina said, and showed Bea the snaps she'd taken of the cast lists.

'Hang on. The Scottish Play was the last production before the Regency was bombed?' Bea's eyes widened in surprise. 'That's a bit of a coincidence.'

'Don't read anything into it,' Georgina warned, 'and especially don't mention it at work.'

'I won't. People are spooked enough as it is,' Bea said. 'Please tell me Fred wasn't playing Banquo.'

'No. He played the title role. Eric was Banquo,' Georgina said. 'And I have a feeling that there wasn't much love lost between the two of them.'

Bea shivered. 'Just like there wasn't much love lost between Neil and Elias.'

'I'm not sure if it was professional jealousy, because Eric took over Fred's roles while he was interned, or whether it was something else,' Georgina said. 'And I might be completely wrong about everything. But can you see if you can find Eric anywhere in Islington?'

Bea typed swiftly, after checking the spelling of Eric's surname. 'Aged forty-six, actor at the Regency Theatre. His address is in Liverpool Road, just round the corner from the old workhouse – and actually not that far from Fred. It looks as if he lived with his mum.'

'That sounds like Eric was too old to be conscripted for war,' Georgina said. 'Maybe he'd lost a younger brother who'd been called up. Or a son, perhaps.'

'Or even his dad, in the First World War, and Eric saw Fred as representing the Germans who killed his father,' Bea said.

'I'll look at tracing that in the birth, marriage and death records tomorrow. Could you check the houses next to Fred's in the register?'

'Sure.' Bea went to work. 'Two doors down, it looks as if there's another boarding house. This one's full of nurses, and they all worked at the Liverpool Road hospital. Which makes sense, because they're nearby. Were you looking for someone in particular, Mum?'

'I'm sure I saw something somewhere about Fred getting married to a neighbour – she's the last one I wanted to check. Esther Bailey.'

'She's here,' Bea confirmed. 'A nurse, aged twenty-five.'

'Thank you. Things are slotting into place,' Georgina said. 'Does her name change at all?'

'No, so she might not have married him. Or maybe she kept her name.' Bea paused. 'Do you think you've got enough to identify him officially?'

'I hope so,' Georgina said. 'And then we need to find his family.' Had Esther carried the baby to term? Had she survived the war? Had she remarried? 'If Esther's still alive, she'd be a hundred and eight now.'

'If she was still alive, we wouldn't be able to see her entry in the 1939 register,' Bea pointed out.

'The baby – assuming Esther was eight weeks pregnant in the middle of October 1940 – would have been born in May 1941, making him or her eighty-two now,' Georgina said.

'And if they had a baby, Fred and Esther's grandchild might be around your age,' Bea added.

'And a great-grandchild might be around *your* age,' Georgina said. 'I wonder if there's a connection between Fred and someone in your company?'

'Nobody's talked about having a granddad or great-granddad who trod the boards, let alone acted here,' Bea said doubtfully.

'It's still something to consider,' Georgina said.

'Nurses were supposed to give up work when they married, or if they had a baby,' Bea said.

'But if Fred was dead and Esther couldn't claim a widow's pension, she'd have had to work. Does the register show if someone moved?' Georgina asked.

Bea shook her head. 'That'd be at a local level.'

'The closer I think we're getting, the further away we really are,' Georgina said with a sigh.

# THIRTEEN

Colin glanced at his watch for the tenth time in five minutes, knowing that he was being utterly ridiculous. Georgina was probably chatting to Bea and had lost track of the time. Besides, she hadn't said exactly when she'd call him, that evening. She'd left it vague.

Though that in itself wasn't like Georgina. She was usually organised and meticulous.

He shook himself. If anything had happened, Georgina would've got a message to him, or Bea would've called him, or Mei would've messaged him. Perhaps Georgina was right, and his job had made him paranoid.

He forced himself to watch TV, but found himself flicking aimlessly through the channels.

If Georgina was in Norfolk, they might've gone out for a meal this evening, taking Bert with them to the Feathers in Great Wenborough and sitting by the huge open fire as they ate; or they might've spent the evening curled up together on her sofa listening to music, with Bert snoring happily in the armchair opposite them.

He just *missed* her. Even more than he had earlier in the week.

But he could hardly demand to know when she was planning to come back. And he didn't want her thinking that he was needy – even though, right now, he rather suspected that he was.

When his phone shrilled, he grabbed it and sagged in relief as he saw her name on the screen. 'Hello, you,' he said, striving very hard to sound casual. 'How did you get on at the National Archives?'

'Really well. I'm pretty sure we've found evidence of who the actor was; I've looked at the cast from two years before the war until the Regency was bombed, and one actor in particular fits,' Georgina said. 'Bea's helped me find him in the 1939 register, too. He lived just round the corner from the theatre.' She filled him in on Fred Smith.

'It sounds a reasonable theory,' he said. 'I'll have a word with the forensics team, if you like, and find out if there was anything personal with the body – a wallet with a driving licence or an ID card, or even a watch or a signet ring that could be traced back.'

'Thanks. That would be helpful,' Georgina said. 'Did Mei say anything to you about the theatre?'

'It's not in my jurisdiction,' Colin pointed out.

She coughed. 'Since when would that stop you asking her?'

He chuckled. 'I'll give you that one, but it doesn't mean that Mei told me anything.'

She waited.

Normally, he had the edge on her when it came to this sort of thing. But today he caved. 'She has a few suspects. Obviously I can't tell you anything.'

'Not officially.'

He sighed. 'All right. You already know some of it, because

you persuaded Jake to talk to her about Elias and Rebekah to talk to her about her own situation.'

'Did Elias tell her anything?'

'No. He stonewalled her. She's waiting for full details from the bank, but she knows there were regular cash deposits into Neil Faulkner's account. How much was Bea paying him?'

She told him.

'Assuming that Rebekah paid a similar amount, I'd say that leaves at least one other person being blackmailed, possibly two. And Mei's team haven't narrowed it down to who they are, yet, so be careful,' he said.

'Elias is the only one of the cast who makes me feel a bit intimidated,' she said. 'Jake felt the same. Bea, too. She says she wouldn't want to get on the wrong side of him. I'm not stupid enough to accuse him of anything without any proof, or to try to bluff him into admitting that he's been blackmailed. If it's something he was prepared to pay to keep quiet, it might well be something that'd make him react physically to what he perceives as another threat.'

'That's what worries me,' Colin admitted. 'Look, I'll try and get some time off, and come down to join you.'

'Colin, I know you're really busy,' she said gently. 'I don't expect you to drop everything for me.'

The thing was, he *wanted* to. Though he wasn't quite prepared to tell her that. 'All right. Just watch your back. And I've been thinking: you said there have been some accidents at the theatre over the last few weeks?'

'Bea's broken wrist,' she said, 'and one of the carpenters had a set crash onto him, plus a weight came down from the flies and nearly hit Elias. Bea said Neil tripped her as a warning to pay up.'

'The set and the weights might have been warnings, too,' he said. 'I'll mention it to Mei. If you can find out who the carpenter was, that could be helpful.'

'One of the cast mentioned it, when they were saying they thought the production was cursed,' Georgina said. 'Actually, one of the carpenters was fixing the trapdoor on stage and I chatted to him. His name's John Riley.' She paused. 'A couple of expensive bulbs were broken, as well. And Leo – the technician who was in the room where Neil died – is a lighting specialist. Bea and I both think that Neil was picking off his victims one by one, sure that they wouldn't tell anyone else because they didn't want their secrets exposed. You know, the divide-and-rule thing.'

'I know,' he said grimly. 'All right. I'll tell Mei. Just be careful, OK?'

'Of course. You, too,' she said.

On Saturday morning, the story of Neil's death broke in the press, and the headlines were full of sensationalism, focusing on the curse of *Macbeth* and a real-life murder on stage, and bringing up the alleged murders on stage from the past. Thankfully nobody had picked up that 'Shakespearean star Neil Faulkner, 59' was also a blackmailer; but someone had definitely leaked the news that the police weren't sure whether the cause of Neil Faulkner's death was stabbing or an overdose of insulin.

When Georgina walked to the theatre with Bea, from a fair distance away they could see that the entrance was packed with journalists and photographers wanting more details on the story.

'Hang on,' Bea said, grabbing her mobile phone from her bag and ducking back. 'It's Bea. Can you let me, Mum and Bert in round the back, please? The front's full of press and we'll never get through. Cheers. Yeah, I will.' She ended the call and turned to Georgina. 'This way, Mum.'

Bea led her through a narrow street to what Georgina

assumed was the back of the Regency, then rapped four times on an unobtrusive grey door. It opened a crack, and then there was a rattling that told Georgina the door had been on a security chain. They slipped in, and Liza, the wardrobe mistress, locked the door behind them and put the chain on again.

Everyone was waiting in the auditorium, in ordinary clothes rather than costume, and Peter introduced Geoff Kerr as their new Banquo.

Georgina liked him immediately; he had an easy way about him, and he didn't try to shove himself into the centre of an already established troupe. She took his headshots, then sat and watched the cast mark through the play. Geoff fitted in very well; and to her relief the tension on stage seemed to be only the dramatic tension caused by the play itself rather than any background worries of the actors.

At the end of the play, they all agreed to run through it a second time after lunch. 'I'll see you later,' Georgina said, and slipped out of the back with Bert.

Once she was sure that nobody from the press was following her, she pretended to be talking into her mobile phone. 'Did you manage to speak to Fred, Doris?'

'Yes. He remembers his landlady Martha; she was in her sixties and very much a Victorian lady, stern but very fair. She was an amazing cook; she took over the ration books of her guests so she could keep them fed. Obviously, as a Jew, Fred had a slightly different ration book where his ham and bacon allowance was swapped for cheese. He remembers the smell of yeast when Martha had been baking bread – little brown squares she used to melt in water.'

Georgina's own mother had made bread that way, too, and Georgina could still remember the distinctive scent of the fresh yeast from her childhood. 'Could he tell you anything about Eric?'

'Apparently Eric fought in the First World War and had a

bit of a bad time. He was invalided out a couple of times, but was sent back again. He made it home, but his dad and his older brother both didn't, and his mum was very bitter. She lived on her nerves after that, all gin and ciggies.'

And if she'd resented Eric for being spared, that would've made him bitter, too, Georgina thought.

'His first marriage broke up because his wife couldn't stand his mum – Bessie – living with them and complaining all the time. Eric never forgave the Germans for his dad's and his brother's death, and for making his mum unhappy. He couldn't see that Fred was Austrian rather than German or that Fred was against Hitler; instead, he read all the ugly stuff in the newspapers and spouted it to anyone who'd listen.'

'That figures,' Georgina said. 'So Eric would've had it in for Fred because of who he was.'

'Fred remembers marrying Esther, by the way. He got a special licence because they didn't want to wait. Her dad disapproved and refused to come to the wedding. And Bea was right about nurses who married; they were expected to leave the hospital and concentrate on being a wife. That's why she kept her name rather than taking his – it meant she could look as if she was unmarried, at work, plus with him having a German surname, it stopped any potential trouble outside the hospital.'

It all stacked up with the evidence that Georgina and Bea had uncovered, so far.

'He says they got married in St Mary's Church in Upper Street, a couple of days after he was released from being interned – being kept apart made them realise how much they loved each other,' Doris added.

'They were both over the age of twenty-one, so they didn't need permission from anyone. I'll look up the licence records,' Georgina said. 'I'll check with Bea if anything changed during the war, but at least that narrows down what we're looking for and when. A special licence, August 1940.'

'Because it was a summer wedding, they had the wedding breakfast as a picnic in the church gardens at lunchtime. Everyone chipped in with their rations to help with the wedding breakfast, and Martha Stephenson, his landlady, made them a cake while Esther's landlady cut flowers from her garden for the bouquet. The wardrobe mistress altered a wedding dress from the theatre's costumes for Esther, and all the boarders in both their houses came, as well as everyone from the theatre and some of the nurses Esther worked with who weren't on duty – even the matron from Esther's hospital came. Esther was terrified that meant she'd have to leave her job, but the matron gave them both a hug and said in wartime you had to take your happiness where you could find it, and that she wished them both all the very best.'

Georgina had a lump in her throat. 'So she kept it quiet. That's lovely.'

'Esther's dad refused to come to the wedding, but her mum said he'd come round in the end because everyone knew that Fred hated Hitler as much as the rest of them did. Her little sister, Muriel, and her best friend, Amy, were the bridesmaids – again with dresses altered from the theatre's costumes,' Doris said.

'Was Eric at the wedding?' Georgina asked.

'Fred didn't say. Just that he remembered how beautiful Esther looked, walking down the aisle to him on her mum's arm. She had to go straight from the wedding breakfast to work at the hospital, and he was on the stage, but the actors clubbed together to give them money towards a night in a hotel as their honeymoon – Mr Rowan, the theatre manager, made up the difference so they had a room and a bottle of champagne at a hotel round the corner from the hospital. Fred walked there after the show ended, that night.'

The whole community had rallied round the newlyweds, Georgina thought. The nurses and the actors, all seeing that love was more important than fighting and brushing aside the fact that Fred spoke the enemy's tongue. They'd even gone against regulations so Esther could keep her job.

'They were looking to find a place of their own,' Doris said. 'But then the Blitz started. And then, on the third day of the Blitz, the church was blown up. Only the spire and the tower were left intact. It was the first church in London to be destroyed in the war, and Esther worried about it being a bad omen.'

More superstition, like those surrounding the production of *Macbeth*. Maybe that was the link, Georgina thought. 'You said the other day that she was pregnant. How far gone was she when Fred was killed?'

'Two months. They thought she'd got pregnant on their wedding night. She hadn't started showing; they'd said if they had a boy he'd be Robert Frederick, after her dad and Fred, and if it was a girl she'd be Mary-Ann Rosa, after her mum and his.'

So the baby had been due in May 1941, Georgina thought. 'That's helpful. I can at least look them up,' she said. And hopefully in the meantime Esther hadn't married anyone else, or at least had left a paper trail for them to follow.

'Fred couldn't remember anything else. He tried to keep out of Eric's way, to defuse the tension, but he can't remember if anything specific had set Eric off, that night, or why Eric had killed him,' Doris added.

'We need to work out what happened to Esther and the baby,' Georgina said, 'and what happened to Eric.'

'Agreed,' Doris said. 'Do you have plans for this afternoon?'

'I'm going to visit my mum,' Georgina said. 'The weather's nice, so thought I'd take her out for afternoon tea. Would you like to come with us?'

'Yes, I'll do that,' Doris said.

'You sound a bit flat,' Georgina said, worried about her friend.

Doris sighed. 'I'm just worrying about Harrison. I hope he thought about what you suggested.'

'We could see if he's free to join us,' Georgina said.

'Could we?'

'Of course.' Georgina rang Harrison, but the call went through to voicemail. She left a message. 'Harrison, it's Georgina. I'm taking my mum out for afternoon tea.' She gave him the address of the café. 'You're very welcome to join us, if you're free. Give me a call and let me know.'

Her mum was on form that afternoon, and Georgina loved having the chance to spend some time with her. That was the only downside of living in Norfolk: she couldn't just pop round and see her mum for half an hour. And she missed her mum. Seeing Irene had brought it home to her how lonely an older person's life could be. She was lucky that her mum still had good friends living near, and that she had made friends in the sheltered accommodation. But afternoon tea with her mum was a really precious treat, now.

Even though they spent the afternoon talking about London in the 1960s, and Doris was clearly fascinated by everything Georgina's mum said, Georgina could tell how disappointed Doris was that Harrison hadn't called them back. She'd try him again tomorrow.

When she arrived back at Camden, Bea was struggling to sort out some mending at the kitchen table.

'Do you want me to do that for you?' Georgina offered. 'It's pretty hard to sew when you've got one hand in a cast.'

'Thanks, Mum.' Bea gave her a wry smile. 'It's my own fault. I went out to get some fresh air at lunchtime, and I was trying to get away from the press pack without banging my wrist. I caught my shirt in the door.' She smiled ruefully. 'And I'm not exactly the best at sewing anyway. Luckily Liza Sheridan, the wardrobe mistress, pinned it up for me, so I wasn't trailing half my sleeve around. I've never been so grateful to see a string of safety pins on someone's sleeve!'

Georgina frowned. 'I know it's not your costume, but wouldn't a running repair be as quick as safety pins, and hold better?'

'Liza did offer,' Bea said. 'But then she couldn't find her scissors.'

A wardrobe mistress always had the basics of scissors, needles and black and white thread with her, as well as safety pins, Georgina thought. She carried a similar repair kit in her own handbag, just in case anything happened when she was on a shoot and she needed to make running repairs to a subject's clothes. 'That's a bit odd.'

'I guess,' Bea said. 'But she pinned up my shirt and then I was too busy with the rehearsal to think any more about it.'

Missing scissors?

Had they been used to stab Neil? Maybe someone had taken the scissors from the case Liza usually kept them in, and that could have happened at almost any time.

Unless Liza was yet another of Neil's blackmail victims... Or maybe she was overthinking this.

'Hand it all over, and I'll fix it for you,' Georgina said, sitting at the kitchen table next to Bea and taking the needle, thread and damaged shirt from her. 'So is everything still on track?'

'Yes. One more rehearsal tomorrow,' Bea said, 'dress rehearsal on Monday, the school visit on Tuesday, and hopefully we'll have the first night on Wednesday.' She rolled her eyes. 'Sheena's stomping round, muttering.'

'The finance and admin manager?' Peter had mentioned her earlier, though Georgina hadn't met her yet.

'Yes,' Bea confirmed. 'She's got to contact everyone about their tickets for Monday and Tuesday and offer a refund or a reschedule.'

'I sympathise; it's always awkward, especially when it's late notice,' Georgina said. 'Though at least most of the customers on a Monday or Tuesday night will be mainly local. Friday and Saturday nights, and matinees during school holidays and weekends, are trickier, because people often travel and they're more likely to have hotels to cancel too.'

'I guess.'

'How's Geoff settling in?' Georgina asked.

'Really good. He's a lot better than Neil – and not only because he's not a blackmailer,' Bea added with a wry smile. 'He's a better actor, and he's doing his best to fit in to the direction rather than thinking he knows best and insisting that everyone should listen to his opinions.'

'That's good,' Georgina said. 'It'll work out.'

'Having an opening night planned is helping to settle everyone's nerves,' Bea said.

'And then everything will settle down again,' Georgina said. 'Neil Faulkner isn't going to ruin the Regency. We're absolutely *not* letting that happen.'

# FOURTEEN

'Are you planning to stay in London for ever?' Sybbie asked when she phoned Georgina on Sunday morning. 'We missed you at Pilates on Thursday. And Max and Jet' – her two black Labradors, who often played with Georgina's spaniel – 'miss Bert. When are you coming home?'

'Soon,' Georgina promised, realising with a shock that Norfolk really did feel like home, rather than the city where she'd grown up, worked, married and raised her children. When had that happened? 'Anything exciting happening in Little Wenborough?'

'Actually, now you come to mention it, there is some talk in the village. About that woman you went to visit in the nursing home.'

'Irene Taylor?' Why were people talking about Irene? Had Harrison perhaps visited her and denounced her as a murderer?

'She died yesterday.'

'*Died*?' Georgina hadn't expected to hear that. She blinked, shocked.

'Don't worry – I don't think Colin will be arresting you any time soon. You've been in London all week; I'd say your alibi's pretty solid,' Sybbie said.

Georgina ignored the comment. 'How did she die?'

'Old age, I presume. At least, you didn't say anything about her being frail.'

'She wasn't. She'd just got over that horrible cold that had gone round – she had pneumonia,' Georgina said, 'but she definitely wasn't anything like frail when I saw her.' She paused. 'What are people saying?'

'Some of the older residents remember her as being a frightful snob,' Sybbie said. 'She was the mother of the boyfriend of that poor young girl who fell down the stairs and died, wasn't she?'

'Yes,' Georgina said. Though Doris hadn't fallen. *Irene had pushed her.* 'Actually, I finally tracked down her boyfriend earlier this week and we met up. He was a nice guy. Bert liked him, too.'

'I'm glad you had the sense not to meet a complete stranger *completely* on your own,' Sybbie said crisply.

'Don't worry – I've already had that lecture from Colin and Bea,' Georgina said.

'How are things at the theatre?' Sybbie asked.

'Peter's managed to find a replacement Banquo, who seems to be getting on well with the rest of the cast,' Georgina said.

'That's good. Do we have the rescheduled date for the opening night, yet?'

'Hopefully Wednesday this week,' Georgina said. 'We just have to hope that nothing else goes wrong.'

'I can certainly see now why actors are superstitious about *that* play,' Sybbie said. 'Let me know when you're on the way back to Norfolk – and when we can all come and cheer on our Bea when she steals the show.'

'I will,' Georgina promised.

When Sybbie ended the call, Georgina was thoughtful.

Irene was dead; and yet she'd seemed physically strong a week ago.

Something about this didn't sit right.

She rang Colin. 'How do I find out a cause of death?'

'You'd have to get a copy of the death certificate,' he said. 'Why? Who died and why do you want to know the cause?'

Of course a detective would ask that. 'Irene Taylor. When I visited her a week ago, she seemed perfectly healthy – and yet apparently she died yesterday.'

'The elderly woman whose son was the boyfriend of the girl who died in your house half a century ago?' Colin checked.

'Yes.'

'The mother of the man you met a couple of days ago,' he said.

She sighed. 'Before you suggest it, I'm sure he didn't kill her.'

'But you think her death is suspicious.'

'Surprising,' she corrected. 'Irene seemed fine when I saw her.'

'I trust your instincts,' Colin said. 'I'll have a quiet word with Sammy Granger, the pathologist we usually use, if she's on duty today. Leave it with me.'

He texted her a few minutes later.

> Doctor who signed death cert thought Mrs
> Taylor probably died in her sleep. She was
> reportedly confused and irritable that afternoon,
> but that goes with dementia diagnosis. Sammy
> says will take a look. C x

A second text, a couple of hours later, after Georgina had taken her mum out for lunch, said,

This is your *third* suspicious dead body in a week. Sammy reports needle puncture at hairline. Blood sample shows glucose levels way too low. Am checking meds and alibis at nursing home. Can you give me contact details for her son, pls? C x

Am sure Harrison had nothing to do with it

Georgina texted back.

He hadn't seen her since his father's funeral, and that was at a distance. They were estranged. G x

Her phone rang seconds later. 'I know you liked him,' Colin said, 'and you're a good judge of character. Think of this as a chance to rule him off the list of suspects.'

'It feels more as if I'm throwing him under a bus,' Georgina said. 'His mother pushed his girlfriend down the stairs and Doris hit her head and died. He's blamed himself for that for decades. I know you're not supposed to speak ill of the dead, but Irene Taylor was utterly poisonous. When I saw her, she was sniffy about Jodie's family and Sybbie's. In his shoes, I would've avoided her, too.'

'Objections noted,' Colin said. 'And I can find out his details from other sources, if I have to. But, if you want him cleared quickly, it would help to have his contact details sooner rather than later.'

'I don't have his address, only his phone number,' Georgina warned.

'That will do,' Colin said.

'I'll text it to you.'

'Thank you,' he said quietly. 'I realise this isn't very nice for you, Georgie. And there's another thing I need to ask. You didn't happen to take a photo of him, did you?'

'No.' Though she rather wished she had. She should've taken a shot of him on the zebra crossing.

'OK.' He paused. 'I'm not going to give you a lecture about assisting an offender or the fact that it carries a custodial sentence.'

'How to tell me I'm in trouble without telling me I'm in trouble?' Georgina asked softly.

Colin sighed. 'We want to rule him out, remember? Can I ask you to describe him for me?'

'Just under six feet tall, quite slender. Grey eyes.' Knowing that Colin would do his job without prejudice, but feeling as if she was shoving Harrison into a prison cell, she added, 'Look at the *Abbey Road* album cover. Imagine George Harrison but with white hair and clean-shaven.'

'Thank you, Georgie. I know this is hard. And with someone with the kind of personality you've described, I'm sure there will be other suspects. I'll call you later, OK? And if he gets in touch with you, ask him to call me.'

'All right,' she said.

'Was that about Harrison?' Doris asked as Georgina was texting Colin with Harrison's phone number and a note that he'd changed his name from Trevor to Harrison when he left Norfolk.

'Hopefully clearing him of any involvement in Irene's death,' Georgina said.

'Oh,' Doris said.

Georgina waited. And waited a bit more. 'Don't go quiet on me, Doris,' she said softly.

'Just thinking. Irene's dead. After all this time.' She paused. 'And not from natural causes.'

'There's a needle puncture at her hairline, and a blood sample says her glucose levels are too low,' Georgina said.

'So did someone give her insulin, the same way someone gave insulin to Neil Faulkner?' Doris asked.

'They're still not sure whether Neil died from being stabbed or being dosed with insulin,' Georgina said. 'But, yes. Essentially it looks as if it's the same.'

'Colin doesn't really think Harrison killed Irene, does he?' Doris asked.

'He's checking alibis at the nursing home and trying to find evidence to rule Harrison out,' Georgina said. 'Which I don't think is going to be that easy. Harrison has a motive: he suspected his mother pushed you down the stairs, and I told him what she'd told me – which pretty much confirmed his suspicions. You said yourself he was fragile. Supposing what I told him pushed him over the edge and he decided to take matters into his own hands?'

'He hated his mother for what she did to me, but he's not a killer,' Doris said. 'OK, I admit he has a motive. But it sounds as if Irene was killed by insulin. Harrison isn't diabetic. Why would he even think of killing someone with insulin?'

Georgina winced. 'I told him where I was working – and Neil Faulkner's murder was reported in the press on Saturday. Maybe what he read about the possible method of murder gave him the idea.'

'Even if it did, how would he get hold of insulin? Isn't it only available on prescription?' Doris asked.

'Yes. Maybe he knows someone who's diabetic and talked them into letting him have some insulin? Or he might have bought some from a dealer,' Georgina said.

'Not all people in the music industry take drugs, you know,' Doris said, sounding cross.

'I wouldn't insult Harrison by stereotyping him,' Georgina said. 'I'm trying to rule him out. To do that, I need to see what the arguments are to rule him in, so I can find the evidence to counter them. That's how Colin does it, anyway.'

'Hmm.' Doris sounded faintly mollified. 'All right. Supposing he does manage to get hold of some insulin. What next? Irene lived in a nursing home. How would he get in to see her?'

'Sign in as a visitor?' Georgina suggested.

'If he used his real name, he'd incriminate himself. Even if he used a false name, someone in the home would have seen him and would remember what he looked like. Plus there's bound to be CCTV in the nursing home, and he'd show up on that. I know I'm biased, but you look at him and you remember him,' Doris said.

'Particularly his hair,' Georgina said. Long, flowing white hair wasn't exactly easy to hide. Even if he'd tied it back, it was still distinctive enough to have made people notice him.

'If he'd gone to the nursing home, he might just as well have walked into the police station and held out his wrists, asking someone to arrest him, cuff him and throw him in the cells,' Doris said. 'Besides, how do we know it isn't someone in the home who gave her the insulin? If she was as vile to them as she was to me, they'd have motive, method *and* opportunity.'

'Colin's checking them, and he wants to talk to Harrison as part of the alibi-checking process.' Georgina sighed. 'I'm clutching at straws, here. If he didn't sign in as a visitor, maybe he signed in as agency staff, filling in for someone who was off sick or on holiday.'

'Surely it's obvious he's over retirement age? That'd look suspicious, to start with. And he'd need an ID card to work for an agency,' Doris said. 'It'd take a while to forge a card. Plus, how would he know which agency the nursing home used?'

'True. If he went to Lake View, it's more likely he went as a visitor than a carer.' She grabbed her phone again. 'I need to tell Harrison that I gave his number to Colin. I hope he doesn't think I'm betraying him.'

Harrison's phone went straight through to voicemail, and Georgina ended the call without leaving a message. 'What do I say? I can hardly ignore Irene's death. But it doesn't feel right to offer him my condolences, not after what she did to him.'

'Acknowledge it, and move on,' Doris said.

'Good idea.' Georgina rang his mobile again, this time leaving a message. 'Harrison, it's Georgie Drake. It's about Irene's death. I'm sorry that this might be difficult for you. Detective Inspector Colin Bradshaw is trying to get in touch with you. He's my...' She stumbled over what to call him. 'My friend,' she said. 'I gave him your phone number, but with the best of intentions. I trust him, and he'll help you. He's checking a lot of alibis, right now. He wants to rule you out. Can you call me back when you get a chance, please?'

She ended the message. 'Now what?'

'We can't do anything to help Bea at the theatre. So my vote is we look at Fred's family,' Doris said.

# FIFTEEN

Georgina scribbled down some notes. 'We know the baby was due in May 1941. So if I look at the registers a couple of weeks either side, to allow for the baby being early or late, I should be able to find something. We also know they were going to call a boy Robert and a girl Mary-Ann. Even if Esther ended up using different first names, we can still check under both her surname and Fred's for any births in that period. I guess at least because Fred was still officially Schmidt, it'll be a bit easier to trace than Smith.' She bit her lips. 'Fingers crossed that Esther didn't miscarry when she discovered Fred was missing.'

'We need to check Eric, too, and see what he did after the theatre was hit. Did he join another company of actors, or did he join up to fight?' Doris asked.

'He definitely acted at the Kingsway in the year after the Regency closed, so I suppose it was the former.'

She spent the rest of the morning on her laptop, researching. There were several Robert Baileys; none of them were born in London, and only two had a mother called Esther. Of those, one had a father listed and Esther had a different maiden name; the other had no father listed.

'I think this is the most likely Robert,' Georgina said, rereading the final record.

'Agreed. Better check the death records, next,' Doris said. 'If he's still alive, we can get Bea to help us trace him; if he's not, then we'll need to see if he had any children.'

Georgina drew a blank. 'That's promising,' she said. 'Unless Esther remarried and changed Robert's surname.'

'Keep going on the death records, to find Eric,' Doris said.

But Georgina couldn't find anything. 'We know he was at the Kingsway in 1941, but if he'd been killed in a bombing raid in London, as a civilian, he would've had his National Registration identity card with him. You were supposed to carry it with you, partly so they could identify you if you were killed in a raid, and partly because you had to use it with your ration book.'

'Did Bryn and Dougie find Fred's identity card?' Doris asked.

'They would've told me if they had, because they know I'm trying to identify him,' Georgina said. 'What are you thinking?'

'Either it's still under the floorboards, or maybe Eric panicked when he realised he'd killed Fred and took his card, so he could get away from London and change his identity,' Doris suggested. 'They didn't have photographs in the identity cards, did they?'

Georgina checked online. 'Not unless they were government officials,' she said. 'But, Doris, why would Eric change his identity to that of someone he considered to be the enemy, when he hated anything German-sounding?'

'Because back then they still hanged murderers,' Doris said. 'Maybe he thought changing his identity to that of the enemy and staying alive was a better deal than being hanged for what he did to Fred.'

'But remember,' Georgina said, 'he's listed as an actor in the cast at the Kingsway Theatre after the Regency was bombed. So he stayed in London.'

'Sorry. I tuned out for that bit. Scratch my theory, then,' Doris said.

'Maybe he went abroad *after* the war,' Georgina said. 'If he died abroad, we wouldn't have the record here.'

'The only definite information we have is the date the theatre was bombed,' Doris said.

'Maybe someone local has recorded memories,' Georgina said. 'There might be a clue there.'

The internet wasn't as helpful as she'd hoped. 'There are snippets about people who were rescued, and sadly one about a school where a lot of people were killed in a shelter. But the only other thing I can see about Tuesday, 15 October 1940 is that it was a full moon,' she said.

'Didn't they call a full moon a "bomber's moon"?' Doris asked. 'Because it made things easier for a bombing crew to see their targets.'

'Horribly, yes. And that night was a heavy raid, by the looks of things.'

'So Esther would probably have been working flat out at the hospital,' Doris said. 'She might not have heard about the Regency Theatre being bombed until long after it happened – and even then she might not have worried too much, because she knew the performances were all matinees and Fred wouldn't have been there.'

'But then she discovered Fred was missing. And it wasn't that he was part of a rescue team who lost his life, because enemy aliens weren't allowed to be ARP wardens or part of the Home Guard. People might even have refused to let him help lift rubble to rescue someone.' Georgina shook her head. 'This is all so sad.'

She continued her research until it was time to make dinner – a traybake of piri-piri chicken, sweet potatoes, peppers, onions and long-stemmed broccoli, following Bea's request to make enough for them to heat through for dinner the next evening.

She tried ringing Harrison's phone a couple more times, but her calls went straight through to a recorded message: 'The person you are trying to call is unavailable. Please try again later.'

In Norfolk, she'd assume someone was in a dead signal area; there were a couple of those in Little Wenborough itself. In London, it was more likely that Harrison had switched off his phone. She messaged him, letting him know that Colin was trying to get hold of him and including Colin's number.

She'd just about had enough of the dead ends in her research and switched out of the website when Bea came in. 'Hi, Mum. Something smells good! I'm *starving*.' She gave Georgina a hug.

'Perfect timing. It's about ready to dish up,' Georgina said.

'And you've made loads. That's good, because I found a couple of people loitering outside.'

'Loitering?' Georgina asked, having no idea what her daughter was on about.

'You can come in now, guys,' Bea called.

To Georgina's surprise and huge pleasure, in walked Will and Colin.

'I brought pudding,' Colin said. Georgina recognised the tub as ice cream from the Italian deli round the corner which opened late even on a Sunday.

'And *I* brought wine,' Will said, handing her two bottles of red.

'Fabulous! Thank you – both of you. It's so good to see you both.' She hugged Will first. 'My boy. This is the best surprise. Bea kept this quiet.'

'Because I asked her to. I've got a training course in the city tomorrow,' he said, 'and Bea said you were still staying, so she told me to meet her at the theatre and come for dinner tonight.'

'So that was what all the "make enough for tomorrow night as well" was about,' Georgina said.

Bea grinned. 'It was.'

'She's filled me in on all the drama,' Will added. He looked at Colin. 'Mum isn't actually a suspect for any of these dead bodies, is she?'

'No, but she's managed to get herself involved with all of them,' Colin said dryly. 'I'm only investigating one of them – the one in Norfolk.'

'Norfolk? Who else has died?' Bea asked.

'Irene. Harrison's mother,' Georgina explained. 'Sybbie rang me this morning to tell me the news.'

'I know you're not supposed to speak ill of the dead, but from what you said she sounded as bad as Neil Faulkner,' Bea muttered.

'Agreed,' Georgina said, and held Colin close, realising just how much she'd missed him. 'I know I'm not supposed to ask you, but did Harrison show up on the CCTV at the nursing home?'

'No.'

But, before Georgina could sag in relief, Colin added, 'Apparently, their CCTV hadn't worked for weeks. The nursing home will be in trouble for that – and for giving the front door's key code to regular visitors and not maintaining a full register of visitors.'

'And Harrison still isn't ruled out,' Doris said.

'Harrison's still a suspect?' Georgina asked.

'Sorry. I've left my team working through the alibis of the staff and visitors that day. Plus checking with the staff in case they can remember other visitors.' Colin grimaced. 'I ought to be with them, really. But I've taken a couple of days off. I wanted to see for myself that you and Bea were OK, with all the stuff that's gone on at the theatre. I'm staying with a friend, and I was planning to see my daughter tomorrow night as well.'

'That's good,' Georgina said. She knew it was too soon for him to introduce her to Cathy, who was still at school and needed stability, rather than being worried about someone new in her dad's life; but she was glad that Colin and his ex seemed to be finding a way forward that worked for them all.

'I didn't leave you out either, gorgeous boy.' Colin made a fuss of Bert, then gave him a plaited rope toy. Bert threw it into the air, then did a little dance of joy around it before happily carrying it over to his bed and cuddling up to it.

Will found the crockery and cutlery; between them, he and Bea laid the table, and Colin sorted out a jug of water while Will opened the wine and Georgina dished up.

'Mmm. It's so nice to eat dinner that I haven't had to cook,' Will said.

'You mean, that you haven't just taken out of the fridge and plonked into the microwave,' his sister said acerbically.

'Takes one to know one,' Will retorted. 'I bet you've had Mum slaving over a hot oven ever since she got here.'

'Children,' Georgina admonished, rolling her eyes.

'I'm with both of them, I'm afraid. That's three of us for a quick microwaved dinner after work,' Colin said with a grin. 'And three of us who much prefer your food.'

'But it isn't your food they're after – it's *you*. You're the one who makes a place feel like home,' Doris said quietly.

'Thank you,' Georgina said, and she hoped that Doris realised she was talking to her as well as to everyone else round the table.

Dinner was a rowdy affair, with Will telling them what little he could about his job – enough to mean that Georgina wasn't worrying about him – and Bea telling them about the play. Georgina chipped in with what she'd found out about the body under the floorboards.

'So you think this guy was a Jewish refugee from Vienna who used an English stage name,' Will said, 'and someone had a fight with him after the matinee performance, stabbed him fatally in the back, then wrapped him in a curtain and hid him underneath the floorboards in the room below the stage. That night, the theatre was bombed and, even after it was rebuilt and then restored, nobody found his body until Bert started scratching.'

'That's about it,' Georgina said. 'The evidence shows sharp trauma on Fred's skeleton, though I'd guess the murderer probably stabbed him in the kidneys as well and he bled out quickly, or maybe slit his throat.' She paused. 'The sad thing is that Fred had just got married. He had so much to look forward to.'

'So why did the other guy murder him?' Will asked.

'Obviously I don't have proof, but I do have a suspect. One of the cast. He'd lost his brother and his dad in the First World War, and he'd been invalided out of that war himself. My hunch is that he was driven by a mixture of professional jealousy, plus seeing Fred as the enemy. Certain bits of the press had whipped up people's anger against what they called "enemy aliens",' Georgina said. 'Perhaps he'd secretly been in love with Fred's new wife; or maybe he thought she should marry someone English rather than someone with a German name.'

'So what happens now?' Bea asked.

'I think Fred's wife had a baby. A son. I can't find a death record, so hopefully that means he's still alive. I need to find where he's living now,' Georgina said.

'Are you going to ask him for a DNA sample that you can match to the remains?' Colin asked.

'That's what I hope he'll agree to, but I'll have to play it by ear,' Georgina said.

'I'll help you with the search tomorrow morning, before the dress rehearsal,' Bea promised.

'Thanks, sweetheart,' Georgina said.

'Have you talked to Inspector Zhang?' Bea asked Colin.

He sighed. 'May I remind you that I'm not—'

'—allowed to discuss cases with people who aren't colleagues?' Georgina, Will and Bea chorused.

He gave them a rueful smile of acknowledgement. 'Obviously I say that to you a lot.'

'In fairness, probably because we ask you quite a lot,' Georgina said.

'I used to work with Mei, Bryn and Dougie, but this isn't my case,' he said.

'But Mum and I are involved in it,' Bea said. 'There's no reason why we can't speculate and watch your reaction... and work things out for ourselves.'

Colin groaned. 'Someone save me from an actor and a photographer who see too much.'

'Plus a scientist bound by the Official Secrets Act who likes analysing things,' Will said cheerfully. 'You don't really stand a chance, do you?'

'No,' Colin said wryly.

'All righty. What do we know so far? I've told Will what happened to me, so that's not a secret,' Bea said. 'Neil Faulkner was blackmailing people at the theatre, though we don't know who his sources were or how he found out about other people's secrets.'

'Maybe different people he worked with, over the years,' Will suggested.

'Maybe,' Bea agreed. 'We think he might have nudged people who were dithering about paying, making something happen to warn them of the consequences. Hence my broken wrist. We know about other accidents, too: Rebekah's food poisoning, John the carpenter's accident with the set, Elias nearly being beaned by a weight dropping from the flies, and I'm guessing that the broken bulbs were aimed at Leo the technician.'

'I'm saying nothing,' Colin said.

'Which we can interpret as Bea's guess being pretty much correct, or you would've argued with her,' Will said. 'Was there anyone else?'

'Not in the cast,' Colin said.

'Which means someone else at the theatre.' Bea's eyes narrowed. 'Sheena's been bellyaching about the cancelled performances, rather than just getting on with things and sorting them out, the way she normally does.'

'Who's Sheena?' Will asked.

'The finance and admin manager,' Bea explained.

'Do you think her behaviour's suspicious, Bea?' Georgina asked.

'I'm not sure. She didn't seem the moaning-and-groaning type when I first met her. She makes everyone fill in way too many forms, but she does it with a smile,' Bea said, 'and everyone gets paid on time. That isn't something that always happens.'

'Is anyone else acting differently, Bea?' Will asked.

Bea thought about it. 'Liza, the wardrobe mistress, has been a bit scratchy lately. But that might be because everyone else is being scratchy.' She wrinkled her nose. 'Mum, you were there the other day when Aliou went on and on about the play being unlucky. I think he'd almost persuaded everyone that there was a curse – not to mention the theatre's ghost.'

Colin shook his head. 'That's just a story. Ghosts don't exist. Memories and guilty consciences, yes, and evidence I can't see at a glance but a microscope or pathology technique can find for me. But not ghosts.'

'I agree. There's no scientific proof,' Will said.

'Yeah, right,' Doris drawled. 'The same as two positives don't make a negative.'

Georgina nodded in acknowledgement of Doris's views, even though the pun wanted to make her laugh and she really wished she could share Doris's existence with her children and Colin. Switching to a safer subject, she asked, 'So do you actually know how many people were blackmailed by Neil?'

'There are five that we know of,' Colin said. 'Don't ask me

what the issues were or who they are. All you need to know is that they involved secrets the people being blackmailed didn't want made public. Though at least one of them is going to face charges for something they did, possibly two,' he added with a grimace.

'Will they still be able to work on the show?' Bea asked. 'The thing is, a lot of the cast have more than one role in the play. There aren't any understudies – that's one of the reasons why we had to put the opening night on hold when Neil Faulkner died. Apart from the fact that the forensics team had to finish their work, Pete had to find another Banquo, because practically everyone else has a part on stage at the same time as him, and those who haven't are already doing two or three parts. Luckily the new cast member, Geoff, is getting on well with everyone.'

'Unlike Neil.' Georgina smiled at Will. 'Your dad would've put Neil on the "Wannabe Nick" list.'

'What's that?' Colin asked.

'Nick Bottom,' Georgina explained.

'*A Midsummer Night's Dream* – the one who thinks he can do every single part better than anyone else,' Colin said, 'and gets turned into an ass. Got it.'

'What was Neil doing with the money?' Will asked.

Colin groaned. 'I can't comment.'

'But it's traceable, right?' Georgina asked.

'To some degree. The team are looking into his financial and business affairs. Maybe something will come out of that,' Colin said.

'He was a horrible man. He made a lot of people worried and unhappy,' Bea said. 'I've noticed the atmosphere at the Regency is different, without him. People are less guarded and they're working better together. It's just a shame someone couldn't have stopped him without killing him. Nasty as he was, did he really deserve to die?'

'You're a nicer person than I am,' Will said. 'I would've been plotting pois—' He stopped. '*Metaphorically*,' he said to Colin.

Colin just smiled. 'I didn't hear what you just said. Because of course you know better than to try to murder someone.'

'I do,' Will agreed.

After dinner, Colin and Georgina took Bert for a late walk.

'That must've felt odd for you,' he said. 'Being with your children in London – and with me there instead of Stephen.' He paused. 'I hope Bea and Will realise I'm not trying to muscle in on their dad's place.'

'We all realise that. Besides, they like you very much,' Georgina said. 'It's not going to be an issue.'

Funny how that made him feel warm from the inside out. 'Good.'

'I know you weren't going to tell Bea or Will more than they already knew about the case,' she said. 'But remember I've talked to at least two of the people who were blackmailed, so I know a little bit more than they do.'

He groaned. 'I know where you're going with this, and it's not going to happen.'

'Five victims. Bea and the photos, plus Rebecca and the baby,' Georgina persisted. 'And I think the others are Elias, John the carpenter and Leo the technician. Remember, they were all involved in accidents.'

'Not Leo,' he said. 'The broken lights really were accidents.'

'So who's the fifth person who was blackmailed? Cast or crew?' When he didn't answer, she said, 'I just need to know how to protect Bea.'

'The other person won't be a problem for Bea,' he said. 'But the ones who are going to face charges – we're looking at a custodial sentence for at least one of them.'

'It's that serious?' Georgina's eyes widened. 'Would those people be a threat to anyone in the theatre?'

'Not over the issue they'll be charged for.' Elias had several speeding convictions, and the last one would've netted him a ban. Knowing this, he'd 'persuaded' his partner to take the points for him. Perverting the course of justice carried a custodial sentence for everyone involved, though Colin thought Elias's partner might be lucky and escape jail on the grounds that he put her under duress to take the points for him. 'But I wouldn't want anyone I care about dating one of them,' he added, wanting to be honest.

'I think you're worrying me more than you're reassuring me,' Georgina said dryly.

'Apart from this one person, who I admit would be top of my suspect list for Faulkner's murder, the others all think they were the only one Faulkner was blackmailing, and they're scared the revelations will damage the Regency's reputation as well as their own,' Colin said. 'I'm surprised they didn't connect their own near misses with those happening to other people, but I guess when you're frightened you tend to look inwards.'

'And they all paid him?'

'They all paid him,' Colin confirmed. 'Cash. We've gone through Faulkner's bank records, and it looks as if this isn't the first time he's done it. He's got quite a tidy sum stashed away. If he hadn't been killed, he would definitely have been looking at a jail sentence for blackmail.'

'The secrets he was threatening to expose – did he have records of them anywhere?'

'He had some evidence on his laptop, yes,' Colin said. 'But it's not going to be made public.'

'So Bea won't lose her job at the genealogy place?'

'No,' he reassured her. 'If Mei hasn't already had a quiet word with her ex, I'll do it, in my official capacity, to make sure he deletes any other copies of the photographs or hands them over to the police to be destroyed.'

'Thank you,' Georgina said. 'And I won't push you to tell me anything more.'

'Good,' he said. Sheena Campbell, the finance and admin manager, had admitted to skimming money from the accounts a few years back, to pay for her daughter's rehab from drugs; she'd intended to pay it back, but then Covid had happened and she'd had to falsify the accounts. John Riley, the carpenter, had stolen money to help with his brother's gambling problem. Both could end up with fines or even custodial sentences. Though Elias Petrus was the one who could cause real difficulties for the theatre; depending on when Elias's case was heard and how quickly he was given a custodial sentence, Peter would need to start looking for a new Macbeth. 'Actually,' Colin said, 'it's my turn to ask you an awkward question. I haven't been able to get hold of Harrison Taylor. He's not answering his phone, and he doesn't appear to be at the flat where all his documents say he lives.'

'He's not answering his phone to me either,' Georgina said. 'All I can do is keep trying and leaving messages asking him to call me.'

'I know you liked him and you want to think the best of him,' Colin said, 'but the longer the silence goes on, the more it worries me.'

'It worries me, too,' Georgina admitted. 'But I don't know what else we can do.'

'Wait and hope, I think,' Colin said, sliding his arm round her shoulders.

# SIXTEEN

The next morning, over breakfast, Georgina told Bea everything she knew about Robert Bailey. Bea logged in to her work apps and cross-referenced the details.

'I think I've found him,' she said. 'Robert Frederick Bailey, aged 82. He lives in Dunsted, a market town in Essex.' She wrote down a phone number and address on a sticky note, and handed it to Georgina. 'What are you going to say to him? You can hardly go straight in with the fact you found his dad's skeleton.'

'I was going to tell him that I've been doing some work on the history of the theatre and I believe he has a family connection to the Regency, so I wondered if I could talk to him,' Georgina said. 'If I can see him face-to-face, I'll be able to judge how and when to break the news of what happened to Fred.'

'Good plan,' Bea said. She glanced at her watch. 'I need to get my stuff together – we'll have to leave in about twenty minutes. Does Colin know where to meet us?'

'Yes – and what time,' Georgina said.

While Bea got ready, Georgina took a deep breath and called Robert Bailey's number.

'Am I speaking to Mr Robert Frederick Bailey?' she asked when he answered.

'I'm afraid I don't buy things over the phone,' he said.

Georgina smiled. 'Good. And I'm not selling. If you're the Mr Bailey I hope you are, my name's Georgina Drake – I'm a photographer, and I'm doing some work at the Regency Theatre in Islington.'

'Islington? My mum used to live there, before I was born,' he said. 'During the war.'

'It sounds as if you're the man I've been looking for. Just so you know I'm genuine, I think your mum's name was Esther Bailey, and she was a nurse at the hospital in Liverpool Road during the war,' Georgina said.

'Yes,' he said, sounding wary. 'How do you know that?'

'Because I've been researching some of the history of the theatre, Mr Bailey, and I'd love to talk to you about it. I'm pretty sure you have a strong family connection to it,' she said.

'Nobody in my family's ever been an actor – or written a play, as far as I know,' he said.

'Would you have time to meet me for a chat?' Georgina asked.

There was a pause, followed by a slightly doubtful, 'Well, I suppose so. How did you get my number?'

'My daughter works for a probate genealogy company,' Georgina said. 'She helped me to find you.'

'Oh.' He paused. 'Well, I suppose that's all right then. When do you want to talk to me?'

'I'm at the theatre this morning,' she said, 'but if there's a nice café near you, maybe I could drive over this afternoon, meet you there and buy you tea and scones?'

'So you're not expecting to come to my house?' he checked.

'Absolutely not. My daughter,' she said, 'would tell me never to invite a stranger to my house – and she'd say the same to you. As would I.'

He chuckled. 'My daughter would say the same! Well, I'm quite partial to the cheese scones at the Copper Kettle in the village. There's a little car park round the back, so you should be able to park all right. I'll see you there at half past three – Mrs Drake, is it?'

'Do call me Georgina,' she said. 'Thank you for agreeing to see me. Do you mind me bringing my partner? If it helps, Mr Bailey, he's a policeman.'

'That's fine. And you must call me Robert.' He paused. 'How will we know each other?'

'I'm guessing that you know the café well,' she said, 'so look for two strangers. I've got fair hair and Colin... well, he'd hate me saying this, but he looks a bit like Colin Firth as Mr Darcy.'

'Then I'll bring my daughter,' Robert said, 'because she's a big fan of *Pride and Prejudice*.'

Georgina laughed. She gave him her number, and he read it back out to her. 'I'll see you at half past three, Georgina,' he said.


Colin met Georgina and Bea outside the theatre at twenty to eleven. 'I'm looking forward to this,' he said with a smile. He made a fuss of Bert. 'We'll sit in the front row while Georgie takes photographs. And I promise to switch my phone off, not chatter and not rattle a crisp packet.'

Bea laughed. 'If only all the audience were that considerate!'

Georgina introduced him to Peter and the cast, then settled down in the front row with her camera. 'And this time hopefully the only dead bodies will be acted rather than real,' she said quietly to Colin. 'By the way, Bea helped me track down Fred's son. I'm going to meet him this afternoon for scones, tea and a chat. Want to come with me?'

'If it's all right with him,' Colin said. 'Sure.'

'He's bringing his daughter, I think,' she said. And there was something teasing in her smile that he couldn't quite work out.

He thoroughly enjoyed the performance, with Bert curled up at his feet; and he enjoyed watching Georgina at work, too, the way she moved quietly without distracting the actors and took a range of shots.

The tension in the air was palpable when the three Murderers despatched Banquo; remembering the way Georgina had described the next scene to him, he found himself holding his breath. Were they right in thinking that the killer had only targeted Neil Faulkner because of the blackmail – or had they miscalculated badly and there was a serial killer on the loose? In another moment, would there be another dead body under the stage?

But, as the stage lights came on again, it seemed that Geoff Kerr was very much alive in the room beneath the stage, and his ethereal 'ghost' taunted Macbeth at the feast table via the Pepper's Ghost. Even though Colin knew how the effect worked, thanks to Georgina, he was fascinated by it.

At the end of the performance, he stood up and clapped loudly. 'Bravo,' he said.

'Bravo,' Georgina said, joining in.

The cast gave a bow, all smiling.

'Bravo,' said two voices he recognised. He turned to see Dougie and Bryn.

'Well, if it isn't our Mr Darcy,' Bryn teased. 'Maybe that should be their next performance. You'd be a shoo-in for the starring role.'

'Very funny.' Colin shook their hands. 'Good to see you both.'

They all ended up in the pub across the road for lunch of the best paella Colin had ever tasted, and Bert sat nicely under the table waiting for his sausages to cool.

'You,' he told Bea, 'were amazing. I didn't know your dad,

but I know how I'd feel if I was watching my daughter, Cathy, giving a performance like yours on stage – so I reckon he'd be more than proud of you.'

Bea blinked back the tears. 'Colin, that's such a lovely thing to say.'

'And he's right, love,' Georgina added quietly. 'Your dad would've been roaring his approval.'

'I wish...' Bea shook her head. 'Ignore me.'

'I'm sure he knows,' Georgina said. 'And he'll be there in spirit on opening night.'

Her expression was suddenly very intense, and Colin thought about some of the things she'd said before now. Did Georgina believe in ghosts? Did it even matter? He slid his fingers round hers, under the table, and squeezed briefly, just to show his support. And the smile she gave him in return made his heart feel as if it had done an anatomically impossible backflip.

Mindful that they had an appointment with Robert Bailey, Colin and Georgina left while everyone else was still eating pudding, leaving money for their share of the bill with Bea. They took Bert back to Bea's house, then Colin drove them out of London and through the rolling Essex countryside to the small market town of Dunsted. The town was pretty, full of eighteenth-century houses painted cream, pink and pale blue, with bay windows and steeply pitched red-tiled roofs. There was a half-timbered market cross which led to a street of half-timbered houses, a flint-and-brick church with a tall steeple, and a cobbled market square.

'This place is gorgeous,' she said.

The Copper Kettle was in the middle of the market square, and Colin drove down the narrow street next to it to find a small car park behind the café, as Robert had described. Clearly the café was popular, because when they walked in there was only one spare table; but as Georgina glanced round, she saw a man waving at her. He was sitting next to a woman who looked close to Georgina's own age.

'Mr Bailey – Robert?' she asked when she and Colin had made their way over to the table.

'Yes. And this is my daughter, Angie,' he said, shaking Georgina's hand.

'This is Colin,' she said with a smile.

'Nice to meet you,' Colin said.

'Has anyone ever told you that you look like Mr Darcy?' Angie asked.

Colin groaned. 'Sadly, frequently.'

'And he can be just as grumpy,' Georgina teased.

Once they were all settled and had ordered tea and scones, Georgina said, 'Did your mum tell you much about your dad, Robert?'

'She never talked about him. I think it upset her too much. I assumed he died in the war, before I was born,' Robert said. 'We came back to Dunsted to live with my grandparents. I always got the impression that my grandfather hated my dad, though I didn't understand why. The one time I did ask, he shouted at me and my grandmother had to keep the peace. So it was easier not to ask anything.'

'I asked Nan, when I had to do a family tree at school and Dad couldn't fill in the blanks,' Angie said. 'She clammed up. But I always thought it was strange that we had the same surname as Nan's parents, and I only had one set of grandparents. I tried doing a bit of research on the internet, about ten years ago, but Dad's father isn't listed on his birth certificate so I couldn't really get anywhere. I assumed Nan called herself "Mrs" just to stop tongues wagging and said her husband had died in the Blitz in London. Dad said your daughter works as a genealogist, though, Georgina?'

'She does, when she's not acting,' Georgina said. 'That's my connection to the Regency; she's playing Lady Macbeth in their latest production, and I've been taking the photographs.'

'The Regency – isn't that where someone died, on stage in rehearsals?' Robert asked.

'Yes, but don't believe all the speculation you read in the press,' Colin said.

'Hang on. You said you think I'm connected to the theatre.' Robert looked first at Georgina, then at Colin. 'And *you're* a policeman. Am I related to the man who died?'

'No,' Colin said.

'He was young enough to be your son, technically.' Georgina paused. 'However, the last play performed at the Regency before it was bombed in 1940 was also *Macbeth*. And I think your dad was one of the actors in that performance.'

'But – how do you know?' Angie asked. 'Or was he a Mr Bailey and I missed it?'

'I'll leave Georgie to explain this. I haven't been involved in that side of the research,' Colin said.

'Your maternal grandfather's name was Robert – you're named after him,' Georgina said to Robert. 'But your middle name is Frederick, after your father. Though he was actually Friedrich rather than Frederick.'

'My father was *German*?' Robert blinked. 'Well, that would explain why my granddad hated him. He had a bad time in the First World War.'

'Friedrich Schmidt was an Austrian actor,' Georgina said. 'He was born in Vienna and he was Jewish. He came to England before the war started, as a refugee.' She took out her phone, brought up a file of photographs and handed the phone to Robert and Angie. 'The first two photos are the front and the back of the card from Friedrich's internment tribunal in 1939, with a character reference and his background.' She explained what she'd learned about 'enemy aliens' and tribunals.

Robert and Angie read the card in silence. 'Well, at least the owner and the director seem to have liked him,' Robert said.

'If you go to the next photograph,' Georgina said, 'that's the headshot taken from a theatre programme in 1938. He played Elyot in *Private Lives* at the Regency. He would've been in his early thirties at the time.'

Angie looked at the photograph, then at her father. 'I've got pictures of you with me sitting on your lap when I was small, and you look so much like him.' She looked at Georgina. 'So why isn't Dad's name Schmidt, or even Smith?'

'Your grandmother was a nurse. Back in those days, she would've had to give up work when she got married, or when she was pregnant and couldn't hide it,' Georgina explained. 'Plus there was a public backlash whipped up by certain newspapers against "enemy aliens" like Fred. I think she would've found it simpler to keep her English surname, and by law Fred wasn't allowed to change his name – though he used the stage name "Fred Smith".'

'Great-granddad Robert hated anything German,' Angie said. 'Probably because he fought in the First World War. But my great-grandmother, Mary-Ann, wasn't like that. Surely Nan could've told her the truth?'

'She knew, because she was the witness to Fred and Esther's wedding. They got married by special licence in St Mary's, Islington, a couple of weeks before it was blown up in the Blitz,' Georgina said. 'And I've got a copy of the register entry on the next photo.'

'This feels like being on that telly programme where they trace your family tree,' Robert said. 'I'm eighty-two years old, and this is the first time I've heard my father's real name or seen a picture of him. I had absolutely no idea.'

'Friedrich Schmidt. Fred Smith,' Angie said. 'I get why Nan never mentioned him in front of her dad, but why didn't she tell *you* about him, Dad? Why didn't she at least tell you that she'd married him and kept her name? And what actually happened to him?'

'That, I'm afraid, is the sad news,' Georgina said. 'He died during the war.'

'When the theatre was bombed?' Angie asked.

Georgina winced. 'I'm so sorry. There isn't a nice way to tell you. We found a skeleton under the floorboards in the room beneath the stage. My daughter and I have been trying to work out who he was, and we think he's your dad, Robert.'

'But why would he be under the floorboards? Surely if he was in the theatre when it was bombed, someone would've pulled him out?' Robert asked, frowning.

'My theory,' Georgina said, 'is that he had an argument with another actor. It got heated, and maybe the other guy didn't mean to kill Fred, but it happened and then he panicked. He wrapped Fred's body in a curtain and hid him under the floorboards – and then, when the theatre was bombed later that night, he thought maybe he'd got away with it. I can't prove that though, and I can't find the death record of the man I think's responsible either.'

'It's very likely,' Colin said, 'that your mum thought he'd been killed in the bombing that night, Robert. His lodgings were next door but one to hers. Apparently, that night, the Blitz was really bad in Islington. When he didn't return to his lodgings, she would have assumed he'd been killed.'

'And she came back to her parents to have me, because it was safer than staying in London,' Robert said. 'Maybe she thought everyone would judge Friedrich the same way her dad did, and it was just easier not to mention him. Though I wish she'd told me.'

'I'm sorry I've brought you upsetting news,' Georgina said.

'It's really upsetting to think he was killed by someone in a fight, but you've answered a question I never thought I'd get an answer to,' Robert said. 'And you've shown me what he looked like.' He paused. 'The body's definitely Friedrich Schmidt?'

'I'm pretty sure I've got enough documentary evidence to say yes,' Georgina said.

'What happens now? Do we bury him?' Angie asked.

'Unidentified remains are usually buried in an unmarked grave,' Colin said.

'But, with your help, I can prove for definite that the skeleton belongs to Fred,' Georgina said, 'and then you'll be able to bury him as you want to.'

'Of course we'll help. What do we need to do?' Angie asked immediately.

'If you can give me a DNA sample, Robert, we can compare it with DNA from Fred's bones,' Georgina said.

'I can organise the DNA kit, in connection with the case,' Colin said. 'But we thought you might like some time to think it over, first.'

'Would a DNA sample from me work?' Angie asked.

'If you're your father's biological daughter, yes,' Colin said.

'Then we'll both give samples,' Angie said. 'Just in case one doesn't work.'

'Can we see him?' Robert asked. 'And the theatre?'

'We'll need to identify the bones formally before you can see him,' Colin said. 'But then there's no problem.'

'And I can definitely organise you seeing the theatre. We can give you a proper tour,' Georgina said. 'The local heritage society bought it after the war and restored it, and then about twenty years ago Peter Newton took over the lease and restored it to how it was when it was originally built. Well, with the addition of comfy seating and proper electrics,' she added with a smile.

'We'd love that,' Angie said. 'If I give you my number, maybe you can arrange for the testing to be done and let me know when we can see the theatre?'

'Absolutely,' Georgina promised.

'The test results will take at least a couple of weeks,' Colin warned.

'We can wait,' Robert said. 'And it's so good to know more about where I come from. All these documents Georgina discovered – it's just amazing.'

'Give me your email,' Georgina said to Angie, 'and I'll send you all the information I have when I'm back with my laptop.'

'Friedrich Schmidt. My dad,' Robert said, looking at the photographs again. 'All these years, I wondered about him. I never thought I'd ever know his name, let alone see his face.' He smiled. 'I wish I'd had the chance to meet him. But I'm glad he didn't let my mum down. I'm glad I know the truth.'

# SEVENTEEN

Colin had arranged to see his ex-wife, Marianne, and his daughter, Cathy, that evening; Georgina was glad his relationship with them was starting to mend. She wasn't the least bit fussed that he hadn't asked her to meet Cathy, because it was still way too early for him to introduce her to his daughter. Will was due back in Salisbury for work, the following morning, but came round to share a takeaway for dinner after his course ended; Georgina thoroughly enjoyed the chance to spend time with her children.

There was still no word from Harrison, and his phone was still off. Georgina was starting to feel twitchy. Please don't let him have done anything rash, she begged silently.

On Tuesday, she called in to see her mum before heading to the theatre, and promised to take her to the opening night. When she got to the Regency, the building was buzzing with energy just before the school visit. The cast had arranged to perform a dozen key scenes from the play for a local school's Year Ten classes, including the Pepper's Ghost.

'We'll get them to talk about how they'd direct that scene,' Peter said. 'Would they have a "ghost" the way we do it, or would they have the actor playing Banquo wearing slightly different clothes to show that he was a ghost, or would they do it from the rest of the court's point of view and Macbeth is seeing things they can't? Or would they try something else entirely?'

Peter had asked Georgina to take photographs during the workshop. She knew that the parents of most of the class had given consent for their children's images to be used in the theatre's publicity shots; she'd asked if those who didn't have consent could wear small stickers to identify them, so they could still take part in the workshop but she could ensure they weren't in any photographs.

She was in the middle of taking the photographs when she noticed that one of the teachers was slumping in her seat, looking pale. Frowning, Georgina went over to her. 'Are you all right? Do you need me to get the First Aider?'

'No, no. I feel a bit shaky, but it's my own fault – we were told yesterday that we're having a school inspection at the end of the week, and we're all getting stressed. I took it out at the gym before work this morning, and I should've had some extra carbs to balance my blood sugar.' She rummaged in her bag and brought out a packet of jelly babies. 'Ignore me. I'll be all right in a few minutes. Four of these, and I'll soon be back to normal.'

Georgina glanced at the sweets. 'You're diabetic?'

The teacher nodded. 'Normally I manage it well, but it's been a bit of a summer.'

'You have my sympathy,' Georgina said. 'One of my friends at uni was diabetic, and we all got used to carrying jelly babies with us, just in case.'

The teacher smiled. 'I do the same with my friends and family. Even after years of being good with my control, I can get caught out. Stress doesn't help. I've been worried about Rebekah, with everything that's been happening here.' She gestured towards the stage.

'I'm Georgina Drake – I'm sort of the official theatre photographer, as my daughter's in the cast.'

'Oh, like Rebekah – she's my sister-in-law,' the teacher said. 'I'm Nalini Shaw.'

'Nice to meet you, Nalini,' Georgina said, keeping her tone light. She remembered now: Peter had said Rebekah's sister-in-law's class was coming for a workshop.

'Rebekah was the one who suggested the workshop for our school, knowing my Year Tens are doing the play for GCSE. I was thrilled for her when she got the part. My brother would rather she was a stay-at-home mum,' Nalini added, rolling her eyes, 'but I think she needs to act.'

And everything suddenly clicked into place.

Rebekah Khan was one of the four people who'd been on stage with Neil when he'd complained about being hit too hard. Mei's team had checked if anyone in the company was diabetic, but had they also checked everyone's family and friends? Or had Rebekah misdirected them?

And if Rebekah had taken some insulin from her sister-in-law, that would give her the means, the motive and the opportunity to kill the man who'd been blackmailing her...

'Are you sure you're all right, Nalini?' Georgina asked. 'Can I get you some water?'

'I'm feeling better already,' Nalini said with a smile. 'Sorry. I've held you up.'

'No problem,' Georgina said. 'Yell if you need anything.'

At the side of the stage, she texted Colin.

> Rebekah's sister-in-law Nalini Shaw is a teacher, here at theatre for workshop. *Is diabetic*

Her phone was on silent, but she felt the phone vibrate with his reply, a couple of minutes later, and checked the screen.

On way with Mei. Don't let either of them leave.

She went to find Peter. 'What time does the workshop end?' she asked quietly.

'In about twenty minutes,' he said. 'Do you need to go?'

'No, it's fine.' But twenty minutes might not be long enough, if Colin and Mei were held up by traffic. 'Can we get it to overrun by ten minutes or so?' she asked. 'If the kids and the teachers are really engaged, they might not notice the time. Can you get them to talk about staging, and ask Rebekah to say what it's like playing more than one role in a performance?'

He frowned. 'That's very specific. Why?'

'I can't say, right now,' she said. 'Just that Colin and Mei are on their way.'

His eyes widened. 'Oh, my God. Did Rebekah kill Neil?'

'I don't know,' Georgina said honestly. 'But Colin's asked us to keep Rebekah and her sister-in-law here. The police need a chat with them both.'

Peter closed his eyes briefly. 'If she's arrested, that means tomorrow night has to be cancelled as well. This is starting to feel like the last straw.' He exhaled heavily. 'OK, Georgie. I'll sort it. Thanks for – well, not being overdramatic.'

She patted his arm. 'I'm just sorry to bring you yet more tough news.'


Twenty minutes later, Colin and Mei walked into the auditorium. Georgina clearly hadn't heard them come in – she didn't always hear things behind her, especially when she was concentrating on her work – so he went over to her and placed his hand on hers.

She jumped, and blew out a breath.

'Sorry,' he said. 'I didn't mean to scare you.'

She nodded in acknowledgement.

'Which one's Nalini?' he asked.

'Third row,' she said.

Colin glanced over to the seats. There were three teachers, but only one was sitting in the third row, at the end. He gave Mei a nod to say he was ready, and she went into the wings, ready to arrest Rebekah as soon as the workshop ended, while he went to speak to Nalini.

He might need to caution her, but doing that in front of her class could make things complicated. Instead, he said quietly, 'Nalini Shaw? I'm Inspector Colin Bradshaw and I need to talk to you about something quite urgently. Could you ask your colleagues to cover your class for a while?'

'I... Yes, of course.'

She looked surprised. But was it possible that she was as good an actor as Rebekah?

'Can you give me any idea how long this will take?' she asked.

'Not really,' he said.

She had a brief word with her colleagues, while also calming down the children nearest to her who were asking what was happening, then came back to join him out of their earshot.

'Are you arresting me?' she asked. 'Do I need a solicitor?'

'I'm going to caution you formally,' he said, 'because I believe you might be involved in the death of Neil Faulkner and I need to talk to you.' He ran through the words he'd said so many times to suspects, explaining that she didn't have to say anything but it would harm her defence if she didn't mention something when questioned that she later relied on in court, and that anything she said could be given in evidence. He'd re-caution her before the interview. 'I'd like to take you to the station for an interview,' he said. 'You have a right to legal repre-sentation. It's up to you whether you're happy for the duty solic-itor to represent you, or if you'd like your own solicitor.'

'I don't have a clue what I'm supposed to have done wrong,'

she said. Then she glanced to the stage and her eyes widened in apparent shock. 'Is Rebekah being cautioned, too?'

'Yes.'

'Why? She hasn't done anything wrong.'

'I'm afraid I can't discuss that,' Colin said. 'You'll be travelling to the station in separate cars.'

'*Police* cars? I really hope none of the kids see this,' she said. 'And if they say anything to their parents, and the parents say anything to the school inspectors this week...' She rubbed a hand across her eyes. 'This is a *nightmare*.'

'I'm sorry, Ms Shaw,' he said. 'I did my best to caution you out of their hearing, and the cars are already here. If we go now, you shouldn't have an issue with them seeing anything.'

'Thank you for that,' she said.

'The quicker we get to the station, the quicker we can clear things up,' Colin reassured her.


Back at the station, he caught up with Mei.

'Rebekah told me everything in the car,' she said. 'We just need to take her official statement. She says that her sister-in-law isn't involved, but I'm not sure whether she's trying to protect her.'

How different this was to yesterday, Colin thought.

'Do you want to be in the interview with me?' Mei asked. 'She knows that Georgina's your partner, and that might relax her.'

'OK. This is your case rather than mine, so I'll follow your lead,' he said.

'Thanks.' She looked at him. 'I know you're officially on holiday, and you're really just lending a hand because of Georgie, but if I can get you seconded properly for the rest of the case, would that work for you?'

'Yes,' Colin said. 'We'll sort the paperwork later. We have

an interview to conduct, with a suspect who's already nervous. If we leave her much longer, she might not have the courage to talk to us.'

'True,' Mei said. 'Let's do this.'

'After you.' He gestured to the door of the interview room.

Mei made sure that Rebekah had some water, then introduced everyone for the tape and re-cautioned Rebekah.

'In your own words, tell us what happened,' she said. 'I know you've told me some of it before, but begin right at the start.'

'Neil Faulkner had been blackmailing me,' Rebekah said, and explained about the affair she'd had and the baby she'd lost. 'I have no idea how he found out about it, but he said if I didn't pay up he'd make sure everyone knew, and I'd lose the part because people would assume I'd had a termination and it'd be bad publicity for the theatre.'

'Why didn't you come to us?' Mei asked.

'I didn't think you'd be able to help. He'd release the information on the internet before you could stop him – and, once it's out there, it's out there for ever,' Rebekah said miserably. 'And if my husband found out... He'd never forgive me. He'd leave me and make sure he got custody of our son. I couldn't risk that.' She dragged in a breath. 'When I told Neil I wasn't going to pay, he put something in my sandwich that made me ill for a week.'

'How do you know he did it and it wasn't just that you'd bought something that was off?' Colin asked.

'Because he told me when I came back to work. That there would be more of the same, if I didn't pay – and he'd make sure everyone knew what I did.' She swallowed hard. 'I was desperate. The money he wanted was most of my earnings. How was I going to explain that to my husband?'

'So what did you do?' Mei asked.

'Nalini's a diabetic. I've seen her before when she's had a

hypo – her blood sugar drops and she feels terrible. And I thought maybe that would be enough to make Neil back off. But none of this is Nalini's fault,' Rebekah added, sounding desperate. 'She didn't know anything about it.'

'What happened?' Colin asked.

'I took a vial of insulin and a syringe from her bathroom. The needle's really short, so I managed to hide the syringe in my sleeve. There's a scene where the three Murderers are meant to kill Banquo on stage – we have retractable daggers. I slid the syringe into my palm, and when I hit him I pushed the insulin into him.' She shivered. 'He wasn't supposed to die. I thought it'd make him feel dizzy and faint, and he might mess up the scene when he went through the trapdoor to the room under the stage – it's a Pepper's Ghost which puts his reflection on the stage,' she explained. 'I didn't expect him to die. I didn't *mean* him to die. I just wanted to scare him.' She frowned. 'Anyway, I thought he died from being stabbed? When Leo tried to give him first aid, there was all this blood – and that definitely wasn't because I gave him insulin.'

There were two problems, Colin thought. Firstly, Rebekah had just admitted intent to harm; secondly, they still weren't sure whether the insulin or the stabbing had killed Neil Faulkner.

'How did you manage to give him the syringe when you already had a dagger in your hand?' Mei asked.

'The dagger's retractable, and the haft is slightly shorter than the syringe. I held the syringe and the dagger at the same time; I pressed the button to retract the dagger, and then I could push the needle through his jerkin and push the plunger on the syringe,' Rebekah said.

'And what happened then?' Colin asked.

'He complained someone had hit him too hard. I was panicking that the insulin might work quicker than I'd thought it would. We all apologised and Pete – the director – made us do the scene again,' Rebekah said. 'At the end of the scene, the lights went down and we went into the wings to change costumes – Elias plays Macbeth and Bea plays Lady Macbeth.'

'What did you do with the syringe?' Mei asked.

'I hid it in my costume. And when we all went home I wrapped it so nobody would get hurt by the needle, and put it in the bin.'

'What did you think when the lights went on in the room under the stage and Neil Faulkner had collapsed?' Colin asked.

'I panicked that I might have given him too much insulin,' Rebekah said. 'But then Leo started talking about blood, and it was obvious Neil had been stabbed. That's what killed him, isn't it?' Her dark eyes were pleading. 'Not me. I'm not a killer. I just wanted to frighten him so he'd back off and leave me alone. I wanted to make him feel a bit unwell, the way he made me feel, so he knew what it felt like and would just *stop*.'

Colin and Mei looked at each other; although they both sympathised with Rebekah's position, she'd at the very least caused actual bodily harm. 'I'm sorry, Rebekah,' Colin said gently. 'You tried to harm Neil Faulkner, and we're going to have to charge you.'

'But I didn't kill him!' Rebekah's face was full of horror. 'It wasn't me!'

The opening night of *Macbeth*, Colin thought, was going to have to move. Again.

But, even though they had Rebekah in custody, and a full admission about what she'd done with the insulin, there was still doubt over whether the insulin or the stab wound had killed Neil. And they still had a potential killer on the loose. A killer who'd be very jittery indeed, by now...

'So where are we at with this case?' Colin asked.

'We know who Neil was blackmailing: Beatrice Drake with

intimate photographs, Rebekah Khan over an affair and a baby, Sheena Campbell over skimming money from the accounts, Elias Petrus over coercing his partner to take his points for a speeding offence, and John Riley over stealing goods and fencing them to pay his brother's gambling debts,' Mei said. 'What we don't know is whether the insulin or the stabbing was the main cause of death, who stabbed him, or what they used. They all had the motive to kill him.'

'I think we can exclude Rebekah,' Colin said, 'because she's admitted to administering the insulin and the amount she says she gave him wouldn't have been enough to kill. She wouldn't have had time to stab him with anything else, and didn't you say that forensics didn't find any blood spatter on the stage?'

'Only from fake blood,' Mei said. 'We've checked all the daggers that were being used on the stage, as well as the spares, and they're all retractable – and blunt. Although Beatrice and Elias were on the stage, I can't see how they could have stabbed him. Someone would've seen the blood.' She frowned. 'Elias was surly when I talked to him, but I don't think he would've stabbed Faulkner in secret on the stage. I think if he'd snapped, he would've been more likely to hit his blackmailer – he's got enough strength that a single punch would've been enough to kill – or strangle him.'

'I agree. He would've wanted Faulkner to know who killed him,' Colin said. 'Could John or Sheena have had the opportunity to stab him?'

'When?' Mei asked. 'The only time Neil could've been stabbed was when he was on the stage. Dougie and Bryn have been testing the trapdoor, and they say there's not enough room for a second person to have been waiting for him in the trapdoor, or as he went through it. He needed to be in position to play the ghost scene within the sixty seconds it took for Elias and Beatrice to change their costumes. Leo had the signal, turned the light on, and that's when everyone saw Neil collapsed.'

'And we're absolutely sure Leo didn't have a motive to kill him?'

'We haven't uncovered any connections between Leo and Neil's victims, so I can't see a motive for him trying to get revenge for someone else,' Mei said.

'Was anyone else in the room below the stage with Leo?' Colin asked. 'Is there a reason why Sheena or John might have been there?'

'John's the more likely of the two – he might have had to make some adjustments to the trapdoor or the scenery below the stage – but neither of them were mentioned in any of the witness statements,' Mei said. 'Though we can interview him again, see if he changes his story.'

'We're missing something,' Colin said. 'But what?'

# EIGHTEEN

'Morning, Georgie.' Mandy in the box office smiled at Georgina as she and Bert walked in. 'Before you dash off somewhere, I have some post for you.'

'Post, for me?' Georgina was surprised. Of the people who knew she was in London at the moment, most of them knew she was staying with Bea and all of them knew her mobile phone number. Who on earth would write to her here, at the Regency?

Mandy handed over a square cream-coloured envelope.

'Thank you,' Georgina said. The address was handwritten, and the envelope was postmarked London. She didn't recognise the handwriting at all. Frowning, she opened it, to discover that the front of the card was a photograph of The Beatles' *Abbey Road* album.

A shiver of foreboding ran down her spine. The person she associated with that album had had his phone switched off for days – and he hadn't returned a single one of her calls.

Had Harrison written to her instead of talking to her? But why would he do that?

She found a quiet seat in a corner of the foyer, sat down and opened the card. Bert shuffled closer to her, as if sensing that she was out of sorts and might need comfort.

*My dear Georgina*

*It was a delight to meet you and Bert, the other day.*

*I've had a while to think about things, and I decided it was time to confront Irene again.*

Oh, no. Oh, no, no, *no*, Georgina thought, and the card shook slightly in her hand as she read on. Please don't let Harrison have done anything rash. Please don't let him be the one who killed Irene.

*She recognised me. Sneered at my hair, as she always did. Told me I was weak and pathetic. And I suppose she has a point, because I've let her get away with it for all these years, haven't I?*

*I told her I knew what she'd done to Doris. I knew she'd killed the love of my life – pushed her down the stairs, watched her hit her head, and left her to die.*

*She said she didn't care. That Doris was no better than she should be – and that's not true.*

*If she'd shown any sign of remorse, I would've let it be. But she didn't. How could I let that woman live any longer, poisoning everything she looks at? Loneliness isn't enough of a sentence. I had thought about pushing her down the stairs at the nursing home, so she died in the same way Doris did, but even though I hated her I couldn't be so cruel.*

*In my profession, you meet a lot of people. If you need something, there's always a friend of a friend of a friend who can get it for you. So I injected her with insulin at the back of her neck, just by her hairline. It was kinder than she deserved, but at least it was an ending.*

*Your suggestion for me to help young musicians was a good one. My will leaves everything to a trust fund, to give bursaries to young musicians at my old school, and to those who train as English teachers, like Doris planned to do.*

*I'm sorry if I've dragged you into anything difficult, and I'd like you to hand this to the police so I can make it clear to them that you had absolutely nothing to do with what I've done. You were kind to me when I needed it, and you reminded me how impor-tant love is. I'm grateful to you for that.*

*I'm going to join Doris now. Finally finishing the job I started more than half a century ago. I've been too long without her. And I hope I leave the world having done some good, as well as ridding it of Irene's poison.*

*With kindest regards*

*Harrison Taylor*

'No!' Georgina shouted. '*No!*'

Bert whimpered and licked her hand.

Frantically, she grabbed her phone from her bag and tried Harrison's phone number. The recorded message that had been her only answer for days mocked her yet again: 'The person you are trying to call is unavailable. Please try again later.'

She didn't have a clue where to find him. 'Later' might be too late. There had to be a way to stop him doing something drastic, if he hadn't done it already. There just *had* to.

'Georgie? Has something happened?' Mandy asked, coming out into the foyer.

'I... I don't know. I hope not.' Georgina's vision blurred, and she realised that she was crying.

And how the hell was she going to explain any of this to Doris?

This was all her fault. If she'd just left everything well alone, Harrison would still be in London. He'd still be having flowers put on Doris's grave on the fourteenth of every month. But no. She'd found him, she'd told him what Irene had done, and she'd brought a good man nothing but pain and suffering he didn't deserve.

Bert whined and moved closer.

'Georgie?' Mandy said again.

'I need to call Colin.' She gulped, took a snap of what Harrison had written, and made the call. Please don't let him be in a meeting or have switched his phone to silent. Please let him answer. *Please*.

'Georgie? What's wrong?' Colin asked when he answered.

'You need to get someone over to where Harrison Taylor lives,' she said. 'Urgently. He's written me a letter. It's...' The words 'a suicide note' stuck in her throat, and she gave a sob.

'Where are you?' Colin asked.

'The Regency. Don't worry about me.' She sent the photo across to him with the caption:

read this *now*.

'You need to find *Harrison*. Right now. Before something terrible happens.'

'Christ,' Colin said, clearly scanning the words as he talked to her. 'OK. I'm on it. I'll call you and tell you what's happening as soon as I can.'

'Mum? Mum, what's happened?' Bea rushed into the foyer

– clearly Mandy or someone else in the theatre had gone to find her and told her something was wrong – and put her arms round Georgina.

Georgina couldn't speak. She gestured to the card.

'Can I read it?' Bea asked.

Georgina nodded.

Bea glanced through it swiftly, then gasped. 'Oh, my God!'

'I just hope Colin can find him.' Georgina's voice wobbled. 'Before it's too late.'

And Bert threw back his head to give the most mournful howl she'd ever heard.


'He can't have killed her. He can't. The stupid, *stupid* man,' Doris fumed. 'I wish I'd let you tell him about me, now. I could've told him just to let that woman live out her miserable last years as she was. Loneliness was enough to punish her. I could've told him to find someone to love him, to find the good things in life and that way he'd still be close to me. Why did he have to kill that horrible woman? Why? It didn't achieve *anything*!'

'I know,' said Georgina, walking Bert through Canonbury Gardens towards the canal. She'd insisted she was fine, even though she wasn't, because she needed to talk to Doris – and to do that she needed to be on her own. Anything else would involve explanations that were too difficult. Hence the extra walk with Bert.

'He's not a killer! Trev's – Harrison's,' Doris corrected herself crossly, 'the gentlest man I ever knew. All he wanted was me and his music. Why the hell couldn't he...?' Her voice faded.

'Doris?'

'I don't want him dying alone and frightened and in pain,' Doris said quietly. 'I wanted him to live, really *live*, and to make the best of each day. To find the joy.'

'He suffered from depression and he'd spent years trying to conquer his challenges. Maybe it was finally too much for him,' Georgina said. 'If anything, it's my fault. I should have just left things as they were. If I hadn't stirred up his feelings, he wouldn't have killed Irene and he wouldn't be in danger now.'

'You were trying to help me,' Doris said. 'And I appreciate that.'

'I haven't helped you, though, have I? My interfering has ended up with one person being killed and another...' Georgina shuddered, feeling as though she were drowning in guilt. 'I just hope Colin finds Harrison in time. Surely he must be at Harrison's place by now. Why hasn't he called me?'

'I don't know. But I've got a bad feeling about this,' Doris said.

'Me too,' Georgina admitted.

Walking with Bert wasn't helping, the way it usually did when she was worried or upset. And there wasn't anything else she or Doris could say. Defeated, Georgina gave in, turned round and took her dog back to the theatre.

Just as she arrived outside the Regency, she saw Colin's car pull up. He climbed out, came over to her and wrapped his arms round her.

'Was Harrison at his home?' Georgina asked, her stomach clenched tight with fear.

'No.' He held her more tightly. 'I'm so sorry, Georgie. The Marine Support Unit contacted us when I was on my way to his flat. His body washed up near Limehouse this morning. He'd been in the water at least a day, they think.'

She couldn't bear to think of Harrison slipping into the water, his white hair spreading out like waterweed as he sank into the darkness of the Thames. 'Oh, God. If I hadn't tracked him down, he'd still be alive.'

'You don't know that,' Colin said gently. 'It still might've happened if you'd never met. From what you've told me, he'd missed Doris badly for all those years, and maybe he felt he'd waited long enough to be with her again. It's very sad – but it's not your fault, Georgie.'

'It feels like it's my fault.' She shivered. 'I don't care about Irene. She was a nasty piece of work and nobody's going to miss her. But I care about Harrison. He was nice, Colin. Sweet and funny, and he clearly loved Doris so much.'

'I know.'

'I don't think he has any family, unless there's a distant cousin or something. I'll talk to Jack and see if we can bury him with Doris. Organising his funeral is the very least I can do.' She dragged in a breath, feeling guilty and miserable. 'That poor, poor man.'

Colin stroked her hair. 'I'm sorry.'

But this wasn't about her. She needed to put someone else's feelings first. What might Doris want to do? Would she want to see him? 'Can I see him?' she asked.

'That's not a good idea,' Colin said gently. 'The river's not kind to people. I don't think he'd want you to see him like he is now.'

'I don't want to see him,' Doris said softly. 'I want to remember him as he was when I last saw him. His beautiful hair, and the way you and Bert made him smile. But thank you for offering to organise his funeral and talk to Jack. I'd like him to be with me.'

'Will there need to be an inquest?' Georgina asked.

'Yes, but it won't be a long inquiry, and you'll be able to bury him fairly soon,' Colin said. 'The police surgeon can confirm death by drowning, and Harrison's letter to you will establish that on the balance of probabilities he intended to cause himself harm.'

She noticed what he'd left out. *After killing Irene.* 'It's so sad,' she said.

'It is,' Colin agreed. 'And I've got some bad news for Peter, too. He's about to lose a chunk of his cast.'

'Seriously?' Georgina pulled back and looked at him in horror.

'I already told you, some of the people Faulkner black-mailed did something illegal, things they'll have to face up to,' he said. 'Plus Rebekah's admitted to giving him insulin, which counts as grievous bodily harm.'

Not murder, Georgina noticed. 'So it wasn't the insulin that killed him?'

'It was a contributing factor. It was rapid-acting insulin, which might have made him feel dizzy as his blood sugar dropped, and he was less likely to have been able to fend off the stabbing. Maybe he didn't cry out when he was stabbed because he was too groggy to think straight,' Colin said. 'It wasn't anything to do with the stage daggers, but we still haven't found the murder weapon.'

'What did the pathologist tell you about it?' she asked. 'I've hung around theatres long enough in my time. If you can share what you know, I might have some useful ideas of what it might be.'

'It was a straight edge rather than serrated,' he said. 'And it was very narrow, maybe ten centimetres long.'

'A screwdriver?' She thought of John the carpenter. But she'd liked him. He hadn't seemed like the sort of man who could stab another person.

He shook his head. 'The wound was flat rather than circular.'

'A chisel?'

'Too thick.'

She ran through a stage carpenter's typical kit in her head. 'Not a hacksaw blade – that would bend too easily. A pen knife, or maybe a vegetable paring knife?' she suggested.

'It's a similar sort of thickness, but not as broad as that across the flat bit, and with a very sharp tip,' Colin said. 'Either the killer had enough medical knowledge to know exactly how and where to place the knife, or they were very lucky, because the blade went parallel between Faulkner's fourth and fifth ribs and into his right ventricle.'

'What about a retractable utility knife?' she asked, still thinking of a stagehand's kit.

'Too short, and too wide,' Colin said. 'I'd better go and tell Peter the bad news. And then Mei and I have some arrests to make.' He dropped a kiss on her forehead. 'I'm so sorry about Harrison.'

Not as sorry as she was. 'I'll see you later,' Georgina said.

Right now, she really needed to talk to Doris. She and Bert headed away from the theatre again. 'Doris?' she asked softly.

'I'm here.' But Doris's voice sounded choked.

'I'm so sorry,' Georgina said.

'Me too.'

'I never meant this to happen.'

'I know. And It's such a waste. I wish Harrison could've lived the life we wanted – I wish we both could've lived it,' Doris said. 'If it had been the other way round, and he'd been the one to die too young, I would've been miserable without him. I would never have forgotten him, but I like to think I'd do what you've done. Carry on and make the best of it. Don't let the love and the light drain away.'

'I don't think he could help the way he felt,' Georgina said. 'Depression clouds your thinking. He was musical, and a lot of creative types seem to battle depression.' She blinked away the tears. 'If only he'd returned my call, maybe I could've talked him out of it. *All* of it.' The murder and the suicide. Not for Irene's sake, but for Harrison's.

'We can't do anything for him right now,' Doris said. 'But we can do something for the theatre. We need to find the killer.'

# NINETEEN

'We've failed to work out who it is from the likely suspects,' Georgina said. 'Maybe we need to try it from the other way round and work it out from the weapon – what it was and who was most likely to have used it. We know Rebekah was responsible for the insulin, so who could've been involved in the stabbing?'

'Let's look at what we know about the weapon,' Doris said.

'It's a narrow, flat blade with a non-serrated edge and sharp tip,' Georgina said. 'Colin says it's narrower than a paring knife or a pen knife, and anyway a pen knife's tip isn't usually that sharp because it often doubles as a screwdriver.'

'Are there any knives that might fit the profile in the staff kitchen?' Doris asked.

'I'll check that when we go back to the theatre,' Georgina promised. 'But I'm also thinking about where the blow actually fell. Colin said whoever did it either knew the right place to aim for or it was a lucky hit, because the knife went parallel between the ribs. I know a couple of the actors and backstage staff have done first-aider training, but I'm fairly sure the training doesn't involve how to kill someone by stabbing. Plus, if that person wasn't being blackmailed by Faulkner, why would they want to kill him?'

'What does the internet say about stabbing someone in the heart?' Doris asked.

'I don't think any websites would be allowed to give advice on that,' Georgina said. 'But there might be case studies, say from an emergency department, aimed at medical students. How to treat someone who'd been stabbed – and you'd need to know how they were stabbed before you could treat someone effectively.' She did a quick search on her phone and found a website that gave exactly the sort of case studies she needed. 'According to this, the most likely way for a stabbing to reach the heart is if someone stabs a blade upwards under the xiphoid process and towards the left shoulder blade.'

'What's the xiphoid process?' Doris asked.

Georgina looked up another page. 'It's the cartilaginous bit at the bottom of the sternum. Apparently if the assailant stabs downwards, the knife's likely to bounce off the ribs. But this one was a parallel thrust.' She frowned. 'Let's think about the chore-ography of the fight scene. Rebekah, as the First Murderer, had her right hand up with her fingers round the grip of the dagger. She was close to Neil, so if the blade in her hand had been real instead of retractable it would've struck him...'

'...in the area between the fourth and fifth rib,' Doris finished. 'What does the website say?'

'A blade going through that space would hit the heart,' Georgina confirmed. 'We know the puncture wound from the insulin was in a similar place. So somebody of a height similar to Rebekah's, who was right-handed and standing close to Neil, could have delivered the fatal blow.' She paused. 'Using a blade that was narrow and straight-edged with a very sharp tip.'

And she could think of a blade that fitted that description exactly.

She'd check the kitchen, first, but she had a feeling that the knives would be the wrong shape. Colin had taught her that if someone committed murder they would have the means, motive and opportunity. There was someone in the theatre who definitely had the means and would've had the opportunity to murder Neil; but did that person have a motive?

'Come in,' Peter called when Colin knocked on his door.

As Colin and Mei walked through the door and Colin closed it behind him, Peter Newton looked up from his desk, and his expression turned wary. 'Are you both here in an official capacity?'

'Yes. I'm sorry, Peter. It's not good news. We've got a number of arrests to make,' Colin said, 'and I'm afraid that's going to make life hard for you, because you'll need to replace some of your cast.'

'You've found the murderer?' Peter asked.

'Not quite. Not unless one of them admits to it, anyway,' Mei said.

Colin grimaced. 'We're telling you this first as a courtesy, but we need you to keep this to yourself until we've made the arrests.'

'Of course,' Peter said.

'Rebekah Khan admitted giving Neil Faulkner the insulin, so she'll be charged for grievous bodily harm,' Mei said.

'But we know now the man was blackmailing her! And she didn't know it would kill him. She thought it would just make him ill,' Peter protested.

'Her solicitor may be able to make a plea for mitigation,' Colin said. 'She was trying to stop the criminal actions of a man who had already caused bodily harm to her, with the food poisoning, and mental distress by extorting money from her.'

'My sympathies are with Rebekah rather than Neil, I'm afraid,' Peter said.

'I can understand that, but the law has to be impartial,' Mei said gently. 'It's a first offence and there's possible mitigation, but she still might get a custodial sentence.'

'So I'll probably need another First Murderer and Second Witch,' Peter said. 'Is there anyone else?'

'Elias Petrus. He'll be charged with perverting the course of justice, and I'm afraid that's a definite custodial sentence,' Colin said.

Peter stared at them, looking shocked. 'What the hell did he do?'

'He put pressure on his wife to take his speeding conviction, to avoid getting a driving ban,' Mei said. 'There have been enough cases in the news in recent years where someone persuades another to take their speeding points to avoid getting a driving ban, and both of them end up in prison for it. He must've known he wouldn't get away with it.'

'*Idiot*,' Pete said, shaking his head. 'Anything else?'

'The other things won't affect the casting, but they'll affect the running of the theatre,' Mei said. 'John Riley, the carpenter – in his last job, pre-Covid, he stole money and goods that he sold to raise money. Not for himself; he was trying to help his brother, who was in trouble with money lenders for gambling debts. He's a first-time offender, so he might be lucky and just get a suspended sentence. And his brother is apparently getting help for his gambling addiction.'

'I suppose at least one good thing's come out of the mess, then,' Peter said.

'I'm afraid the next one might be more unexpected,' Colin said. 'And more upsetting. Sheena Campbell – on the grounds of theft from her employer.'

'My finance and admin manager?' Peter stared at him as if he had two heads. 'No way. Sheena's one of the most honest and upright people I know. She'd never steal from me.'

'She's already admitted to skimming the accounts,' Colin said quietly.

'I don't believe you,' Peter said. 'Why would she do that? She's been with the Regency for years.'

'Sorry,' Mei said. 'I know this is difficult for you.'

'Difficult?' He blew out a breath. 'We've been struggling financially, and she knows it. She's been as worried as I have. Why would she make it worse by pocketing money? And she's a friend as well as a colleague. She knows I would've tried to help her if she'd told me she was in trouble.' Peter shook her head. 'She's had a few problems with her daughter – the girl's easily led and she got in with the wrong crowd, started doing weed and then harder stuff – but I would've said Sheena was the most stable...' He broke off, clearly having seen the pity in Colin's expression. 'Why did she do it?'

'To pay for her daughter's rehab,' Mei said.

'Oh, God. It feels as if the world's turned upside down,' Peter said, bracing himself against his desk. 'Three weeks ago, if you'd asked me, I'd have told you we had a good team here and a success on our hands. Now, one of my cast is dead, two might be going to jail, the theatre's finances are on a knife-edge, I don't have a clue how I'm going to sort it all out, and now you're telling me the person I relied on for all the admin side has been taking money?' He shook his head. 'I just can't...'

'If it helps, Sheena didn't intend to permanently deprive you of the money,' Colin said. 'She says she always meant to pay it back. Just she hasn't been able to, because her daughter's rehab cost more than she was expecting.'

Peter sighed. 'She's worked with me for years. I can't abandon her. I'll stand up for her in court and say she's always been honest before, and I've always been able to rely on her.' He shook his head, as if trying to clear it. 'But I'm not sure what's going to happen now. What if I refuse to press charges? I don't want her to go to court. She's got enough on her plate.' He closed his eyes. 'On the other hand, how am I ever going to be able to trust her again?'

'Revamp your procedures, I guess,' Mei said. 'Make sure she's not the only person signing something off, in future.'

'Is there anyone else I need to know about?' Peter asked, opening his eyes again and looking as if he was bracing himself for more bad news.

'Bea Drake.' Colin cleared his throat. 'That's a personal matter and it's nothing she did wrong; it was someone behaving rather less than honourably towards her. I think she'll be a bit more careful about who she trusts in future.'

'Poor kid. And Neil knew all these things? But how did he find them out?' Peter shook his head. 'I still can't get over him blackmailing people. And what kind of manager am I, when I didn't have a clue any of this was happening under my nose?'

'I gather Neil wasn't very popular with the rest of the actors and crew,' Mei said.

'No, he wasn't,' Peter admitted.

'Out of interest,' Colin asked, 'why did you cast him as Banquo?'

Peter grimaced. 'It's not been a great few years for the arts.' He rolled his eyes. 'Now I know the state of our own finances wasn't helped by what Sheena did. Anyway, Neil offered to buy into the company. He didn't want to manage or direct, just share the profits and have a part in the play. Stupidly, I didn't look the gift horse in the mouth. I saw someone who'd been working in the business for years – someone I thought loved the theatre as much as I did and wanted the Regency to succeed.'

'Maybe that was what all the money in his account was for,' Mei said. 'Clearly he's been blackmailing people for years, because he's amassed quite a sum.'

'My judgement,' Peter said, 'was astonishingly poor. And now I have to face the consequences. Without an actor in the title role, we can't put on the show.' He shook his head. 'The worst of it is, I'm not just letting the audience, the cast and the crew down, I'm letting the theatre down. Once I've refunded all the tickets, the theatre will be in debt. Even if I sell everything I own to clear those debts, I can't afford to run the place anymore. I'll have to let someone else take over the lease.'

'Can I be rude and ask how much?' Colin asked.

Peter named a sum that made him wince.

'I have a feeling,' Colin said, 'that this might've been Neil Faulkner's plan all along. Not to be your partner, but to have the whole thing. He had more than enough money to buy you out.'

'I should've gone to a loan shark,' Peter said. 'At least then I'd be the only one affected. I can't believe I trusted him. How stupid am I?'

'I'm sorry,' Mei said.

'So am I,' Colin said. 'Do you know where they all are?'

'John will probably be backstage, Sheena will be in her office and the others will be rehearsing,' Peter said with a sigh. 'Actually, I'll get everyone to gather in the auditorium. I need to tell everyone that we're closing.'

# TWENTY

Colin had said that he and Mei were going to make arrests. Elias and Rebekah might be remanded in custody, in which case Peter would have to put off opening night yet again. Apart from the strain on the cast, getting themselves psyched up to start the show and then slumping when it was cancelled again, it was a strain on the theatre's finances. The more tickets they had to refund, the more likely it was that the Regency would run out of money before the show could start.

Georgina didn't want her daughter to lose her chance of playing Lady Macbeth in a production that she'd seen for herself was excellent and would be a hit.

The only way round this was to persuade the murderer to admit the truth.

Firstly – for her own peace of mind – she checked the drawers in the staff kitchen. The bread knife was serrated; the paring knife was too broad; and none of the other knives had a sharp tip.

'I think this proves it,' she said quietly.

'You're going to tell Colin?' Doris asked.

'He's busy – either filling Pete in on the situation or making arrests,' Georgina said. 'I need to persuade the murderer to talk to him.'

'This is someone who stabbed a man to death. Georgie, it's too risky,' Doris said.

'She's not going to stab *me*. I'm not a threat to her,' Georgina said.

'Don't go alone,' Doris warned. 'You need someone from the police with you.'

'No, I don't. Anyway, I'm not alone. I have Bert. And, more importantly, I have you,' Georgina said.

And then she went backstage.

She found her quarry with a mending pile.

'Hey, Liza. I'm about to do a coffee run. Can I get you one?' she asked the wardrobe mistress.

Liza smiled at her. 'That'd be really kind, Georgie. Thanks.' She made a fuss of Bert, who wagged his tail at her. 'We definitely need a full-time backstage dog in the Regency. I'm going to miss this one when you go back to Norfolk. I don't suppose you'd consider letting us adopt him?' She scratched the top of his head, and Bert's tail swished harder.

How could someone so *nice* be a murderer? Georgina wondered. Could she have got it wrong? Especially as Bert seemed to like Liza...

'Afraid not. I'll bring him with me whenever I come to London,' Georgina said, 'but he loves it in the country – and I'd hate to be without him.'

'Then I need to persuade Pete to let us go to Battersea and adopt a theatre mascot,' Liza said with a smile.

'You can only try! I'll be back in a tick with your coffee,' Georgina said. 'Black, no sugar, isn't it?'

'That's right. Bless you, Georgie.'

When Georgina returned, with Bert beside her, Liza was still busy with her mending. 'I'm going to have to watch the next dress rehearsal closely,' she said, 'so I can work out exactly what they're doing to strain these seams, and then I can reinforce them in the right places.'

'Actors.' Georgina rolled her eyes. 'By the way, I meant to say thank you for pinning up Bea's shirt when she ripped it at the weekend.'

'It wasn't her fault. If the press were a bit less pushy, she wouldn't have slipped and torn her shirt,' Liza said. 'The last thing she needs is another bang to her wrist while she's still healing, poor love.'

Georgina was convinced of Liza's sincerity. From what she'd seen of the wardrobe mistress, Liza was *nice*. She mothered the Regency's actors in the same way that Georgina had looked out for Stephen's actors, noticing which ones looked as if they hadn't had a hot meal in a week and needed a bit of looking after.

Which made it all the harder to understand how someone like Liza could actually murder anyone. Even if the victim was as much of a snake as Neil Faulkner had turned out to be.

'Bea appreciated your help,' Georgina said.

'I would've done some running repairs rather than pinning it up,' Liza continued, 'but I couldn't find my scissors.'

And that was precisely why Georgina suspected that Liza was the murderer. 'You don't use snips?' The two small, sharp triangular blades, which were on the end of the legs of a contraption which looked like a pair of tongs with a spring connecting the legs halfway down, were in the kit of most wardrobe mistresses Georgina knew.

'Over the last year, I've developed a touch of arthritis,' Liza said. 'I find scissors easier to use, nowadays.'

'I know what you mean. It's the same with my embroidery scissors. Titanium sharp-tipped scissors – oh, and a daylight lamp. They're the best things I've ever bought for cross-stitch,' Georgina said, wanting to establish a shared connection of sewing with Liza and get the older woman to trust her. Except the length of the blades Colin had mentioned were twice as long as the blades on her own embroidery scissors. Long, narrow scissors – just like the ones she remembered seeing Liza using to repair a costume while Georgina had been taking the actors' headshots.

'Those daylight lamps are so good, aren't they? Sadly, you can't use one backstage when you're doing repairs in the middle of a show,' Liza said. 'I wear my head-torch round my neck, because it's easier to see what I'm doing – but half the time I have to switch it to a red light, so the audience can't see it.'

'Did you ever find your scissors?' Georgina asked casually.

Liza shrugged and spread her hands. 'It's a complete mystery where they went. I always keep them in my kit – and that's always round my waist when I'm working. Nobody asked me to borrow them, and nobody apart from me would use them anyway.'

Crunch time.

Georgina was about to lie. And Liza's reaction would tell her if her suspicions were true. But she hadn't bargained on Liza having a pair of sharp fabric shears on her table.

Then again, fabric shears had thicker blades, and the tip wasn't the kind of fine point that would slice easily into skin...

Steeling herself, and preparing to fling her mug of hot coffee at the other woman if Liza made a grab for the fabric shears, Georgina said, 'It's amazing what the police can find when they go through the rubbish bins. Especially if the pathologist told them what kind of blade to look for.'

Liza's eyes widened. With interest or alarm? Georgina wondered.

'Oh?' Liza said, but it was clearly an effort for her to sound casual.

'The forensics team Colin works with has this special spray that shows up blood, even when people think they've bleached it from an area,' Georgina added. 'Plus the team has these new infra-red cameras that can show up all kinds of trace evidence, including tiny blood spots on dark clothing.'

The blood drained from Liza's face.

'And,' Georgina said quietly, 'the police are making some arrests even as we speak. Pete might have to close the theatre for good.'

Liza frowned. 'But why? Neil Faulkner's not here to cause trouble anymore.'

'He doesn't have to be here to cause trouble,' Georgina said. 'What he did is already enough to cause problems.'

'Did you know he was blackmailing people?' A tear spilled over Liza's lashes. 'It's not fair. Pete works so hard. He doesn't deserve this.'

So *that* was her motive, Georgina thought. Protecting Peter.

'I think,' Georgina said, thinking fast, 'that the murderer needs to confess. Because otherwise the evidence might point to Pete.'

This could go one of two ways. Either Liza would feel she had nothing left to lose and would grab the fabric shears – and Georgina would have to hope that she could scream loudly enough to alert the actors on the stage and in the wings, and that the hot coffee would help her fight off Liza for long enough for other people to get here. Or else Liza would realise that this was the end and give in gracefully.

She didn't think that Liza was the violent sort, even though the wardrobe mistress had stabbed Neil Faulkner fatally. But maybe she'd rushed into this and Doris was right: she should've told Colin what she was thinking and let him deal with it.

Please don't let her have got this wrong.

To Georgina's relief, Liza covered her face with her hands. 'Oh, God. What am I going to do?'

'What happened, Liza?' Georgina asked gently.

Liza shook her head. 'That *bloody* man. He ruined every-thing. Everything Pete's worked so hard for.' She swallowed hard. 'I heard him talking to one of the other actors, saying if they didn't pay up they'd regret it – he had friends in the press, and if he wouldn't pay Neil to keep it quiet, then the press would pay him for what he knew.' She shivered. 'I knew things were a bit sticky at the theatre – we really needed the show to be a success, and we didn't need all that extra trouble. In the dress rehearsal, when he came through the trapdoor and I had to do his make-up, I told him I knew what he was up to, and if he didn't stop I'd shop him to the police.'

'What did he say?'

'He laughed at me,' Liza said. 'Who'd take any notice of a someone who was just paid to sort out make-up and clothes, he said. I ignored him, because he was obviously trying to get a rise out of me, and I said the police would take notice.' She dragged in a breath. 'There was a tear in his costume. You know what it's like in Wardrobe – you always have a few needles ready-threaded with black or white cotton for emergency repairs. I'd just fixed the tear and snipped off the thread when he told me that if I made trouble for him, he'd tell... He'd tell Pete I was in love with him.'

'Are you in love with Pete?' Georgina asked.

Liza nodded. 'I have been, for years, but he's never noticed me as anything but Liza from Wardrobe, the one who reminds him to eat and brings him a mug of tea or a sandwich every so often. Every time I try to get the nerve up to ask him out for dinner, I chicken out because I don't want to make things awkward at work.'

'He's a nice guy,' Georgina said. 'He might say no, but he'd never make you feel bad.'

'I know.' Another tear dripped down Liza's face. 'I hated to think of Neil Faulkner sliming his way into Pete's office and telling him some sleazy story or other, laughing at me. I told him to shut up.' She dragged in a breath. 'That was when he said he could tell me things about Pete, things that would make me despise him. And I know he was lying. Pete's a good man, he really is – he's helped so many kids get a foot on the ladder, given so much of his time to the theatre. I couldn't bear Neil's nasty, spiteful lies. It made me so angry, I punched him – and I forgot I was holding my scissors.' There were tears in her eyes. 'I didn't mean to kill him. But then my scissors were sticking out of his chest and he was making this weird gurgling noise.'

'What did you do?' Georgina asked.

'I pulled the scissors out. He staggered, and then he collapsed. I panicked, and I ran. Because I always wear black at work' – so she wouldn't be visible to the audience, Georgina knew – 'I knew the blood wouldn't show on my clothes. But I've hardly slept, since – every time I close my eyes, I see his face and hear that gurgle.'

*Sleep no more! /Macbeth does murder sleep, the innocent sleep,/ Sleep that knits up the ravell'd sleeve of care...* The lines slid into Georgina's head.

Except Neil Faulkner hadn't been innocent. He'd caused a lot of misery.

'Liza, you need help,' Georgina said gently. 'Right now you're tired and you're *incredibly* stressed.'

Liza nodded.

'Come with me,' Georgina said. 'We can go and see my part-ner, Colin, and then you can tell him what you've told me.'

'That I killed Neil Faulkner? I'll be locked up for years and years – I might even die of old age in prison,' Liza said. 'And Pete...' Another tear slid down her face.

'I think Pete regrets the day he ever set eyes on Neil Faulkn-er,' Georgina said. 'Come and talk to Colin. You didn't mean to kill Neil. It was an accident. I think every member of the company will have sympathy with you, and there are plenty of people who'll give you a character reference. Come with me,' she urged gently.

And finally Liza nodded and stood up.

# TWENTY-ONE

It was bad enough, arresting Sheena and John in the theatre office and backstage; Colin felt worse still when they had to walk into the rehearsal to arrest Elias and Rebekah. Particularly as Peter was waiting in the auditorium with the rest of the staff.

'Before you go,' Peter said, 'I have an announcement to make. I'm very sorry, everyone, but as of today the Regency Theatre is closed and the Scottish Play is cancelled. With us losing two more actors and two of the wider crew, we're not going to be able to open the show tomorrow night. It'll take weeks for us to get replacements and rehearse back up to scratch – and by then we'll be out of money.'

There were calls of, 'No!' and, 'Oh, my God!' Everyone on the stage with Colin looked shocked, and then utterly desolate.

'I'm only sorry I couldn't give you the chance you deserved to shine. I will of course be happy to give references to anyone who needs one. I'll try my best to pay you for this week, but...' Peter shook his head, looking as if all the burdens of the world were on his shoulders. 'I'm sorry.'

Georgina came onto the stage with her arm round Liza's

shoulders and Bert on her other side. 'Wait. There has to be another way, Pete.'

'With the best will in the world, Georgie, these last few weeks have seen one disaster after another,' Peter said. 'It's time to cut our losses.'

'I have something to say,' Liza said. 'I'm sorry. Some of this is because of me.' She took a deep breath. 'I killed Neil Faulkner. I didn't mean to do it. I overheard him threatening you, Aliou, and I was sure he was trying to blackmail other people in the cast, too – because they never stop at one, do they? They get greedy. At the dress rehearsal, when he came through the trapdoor, I told him I was going to the police.'

Colin couldn't quite believe what he was hearing. 'Why didn't you come to us?' he asked.

'Because he laughed at me. He said nobody would listen to me.'

Just like nobody had listened to Harrison Taylor when he'd said that his mother had killed his girlfriend, Colin thought.

'He said if I made trouble for him, he'd make trouble for me.' She looked directly at Peter. 'It doesn't matter anymore, because I know I'll go to prison for what I did. But he was going to tell you that I've been in love with you for years.' She dragged in a breath. 'I'm sorry.'

'Liza – I had no idea you felt that way,' Peter said quietly.

'It's all right. I don't expect you to love me back. I know you see me as just part of Wardrobe. But then he said... he said he could tell me stuff about you. Things that would make me change my mind about you. And I knew he was lying, trying to manipulate me. I was so angry, I thumped him.'

But thumping the man hadn't killed him, Colin thought.

'It was like a red mist had come over me. I forgot I was holding my scissors when I hit him. And then he made a funny noise.' She was shaking. 'I hear it every time I close my eyes,' she whispered. 'I see him fall.'

'But surely Leo would've seen or heard you stab him,' Aliou said. 'He was only the other side of the room.'

Everyone turned to look at Leo, whose face went bright red. 'I didn't see or hear anything. I was focusing on the screen that shows what's happening on stage, so I could make sure to turn the light on at the right time for the Pepper's Ghost. I heard the trap close, yes, because it makes a creak and I kept meaning to ask John to sort it out, but I didn't hear a fight.'

'You know everyone backstage dresses in black, to make sure the audience doesn't see us,' Liza said. 'And I had my torch switched to red light. Leo wouldn't have seen me.'

'What happened to your scissors?' Colin asked.

'They were sticking out of Neil's ribs. I twisted them and pulled them out. Then I wrapped them in some spare cloth and threw them away,' Liza said. 'I'm sorry. I... You can take me away and lock me up, now. But don't shut the theatre, Pete. I stopped Neil Faulkner blackmailing people, and I'm going to pay the price for it – but if you shut the theatre, it'll all have been for nothing.'

Her words were met with complete silence; everyone looked too stunned to take in what had just happened.

Quietly, Colin gave the police caution to Liza, to make her aware that she had the right to silence but it would harm her defence if she didn't mention something that she later relied on in court, and anything she said could be used in evidence.

'Aliou, can you come with us, too, please?' he asked. 'We need to talk to you about Neil Faulkner and the blackmail.'

'Do I need a solicitor?' Aliou asked.

'You have the right to legal representation,' Colin said. 'If that's what you'd like, we can arrange for the duty solicitor to attend, or you can instruct your own solicitor.'

'I...' Aliou sighed. 'The duty solicitor will be fine.' He looked at Peter. 'I agree with Liza. Don't close the theatre. We're a team. We can sort this out between us.'

'Seconded,' Bea said.

'Thirded,' Anjali said.

'Fourthed,' said the actor playing Lennox.

'Fifthed,' said Jake.

'Sixthed to tenthed, on behalf of backstage,' the lighting director said.

'Eleventhed to fourteenthed, on behalf of Reception, the box office and support staff,' Mandy said.

There were more choruses of support after Mandy, and it reminded Colin a bit of the 'I am Spartacus' scene in the old movie. It seemed that all the crew and cast were backing Peter Newton.

'I think,' Georgina said quietly, 'your team wants to get this show on the road, Pete. Ring around the agents, and we'll start brainstorming how we can get more money in. This isn't all on you. We're a team.'

Colin was going to have a word with Georgina later about putting herself in danger. But right at that moment he was proud of her, because it looked as if she was going to be the leading light in rescuing the theatre.

'Am I in for a lecture?' Georgina asked that evening, in Bea's kitchen.

'What do you think? You went after a murderer *on your own*,' Colin said. 'How dangerous was that?'

'I wasn't on my own.' She coughed. 'Bert was with me.'

'Stop splitting hairs. You went to see someone when you worked out she'd killed Neil Faulkner with a pair of scissors. What was to stop Liza doing exactly the same to you?'

Georgina shook her head. 'I wasn't a threat, the way Neil was.'

'How did you work out it was her?' Colin asked, curiosity just about winning over all his other emotions.

'I worked backwards from the weapon. I checked the drawer in the kitchen, but the blades were the wrong shape. When I thought about it, what you described sounded quite like my embroidery scissors, but longer,' Georgina said. 'And I remembered that Liza told Bea she'd lost her scissors. Then I looked back at the fight scene. You said that the puncture wound from the insulin was near the stab. The First Murderer was standing right in front of Banquo when she "stabbed" him – so that meant whoever stabbed him would also have been standing close, and was around Rebekah's height – oh, and right-handed. If you're doing costume repairs while the actor's still in said costume, you'll be standing as close to them as Rebekah was. And Liza's about the same height as Rebekah. I just put it all together.'

'And what if she'd stabbed you?'

'I knew she wouldn't,' Georgina said. 'The way she is with the actors here – it's like I used to be with Stephen's cast. You notice the young ones who need a bit of a confidence boost or a decent meal, and you sort it out quietly without any fuss. Everyone here loves Liza. Plus I sew: I have things in common with her. We talked about stitching, daylight lamps and scissors. We talked about Bea's cast. Liza made a fuss of Bert.'

'And she killed Neil Faulkner,' Colin reminded her.

'If she told you what she told me,' Georgina said quietly, 'you'll know she didn't do it on purpose. Neil deliberately taunted her and made her so angry that she forgot she was holding her scissors when she thumped him. She didn't set out to stab him. It's that "ooh" moment of anger when you clench your fists. And it was sheer bad luck that the point of the scissors went between his ribs and into his heart – she isn't one of the theatre's First Aiders, and if she'd stabbed him a couple of millimetres higher the scissors would've bounced off a rib.' She grimaced. 'Poor Liza. She's feeling as guilty as Macbeth did after he stabbed Duncan.'

'Whatever you say, she could have stabbed *you*,' Colin said. 'I took her backstage to pick up her bag before I took her to the station, and there was a massive pair of scissors on the table.'

'Fabric shears. Which have a much thicker blade than her other scissors, and don't have a sharp tip,' Georgina pointed out. 'I assure you, Liza was never going to stab me.' She paused. 'And you might also have noticed two mugs of coffee on the table. I admit I was holding mine the whole time while we were talking. Just in case I needed to distract her.'

'Got you,' Colin said. 'Even so, please don't ever do anything as reckless as that again. I was in the building. You could've come and got me.'

'You were busy.'

He glared at her. 'Not *that* busy.'

Bea came into the kitchen. 'Hi, Colin. Come to tell Mum off?'

'For being incredibly reckless? Yes.'

Bea just laughed. 'And you think she'll listen?'

'Oi. I am *here*, you know,' Georgina said.

Bea kissed her cheek. 'I know. Will you stay for dinner, Colin?'

'Thanks for the offer, but I'd better not,' he said. 'I'm heading back to Norfolk. I just wanted to make your mum promise she'll never go after a murderer on her own ever again.'

'You can try,' Bea said, 'but telling her what to do isn't the way to get her to do it.'

'What is?' Colin asked.

Bea grinned. 'You make her think that it's her idea in the first place. Or you guilt her into it. Ask Sybbie how she got her to adopt Bert.'

'You,' Georgina said, 'as my daughter, are supposed to take my side, not give away my secrets.'

'Given that I owe you for both of my jobs, right now, you've got anything from me you ask for,' Bea said.

'So Peter's not going to close the theatre or sell up?' Colin asked.

'No. Mum had this genius idea,' Bea said.

'It wasn't an *original* idea,' Georgina pointed out.

'But it's still a good one. The press officer's working on a release at the moment, explaining why the Regency has to cancel opening night yet again,' Bea said. 'And at the same time we're opening a fundraiser – getting people to sponsor us. Not a Friends programme – we've got one of those already, and we're unlikely to get new corporate sponsors with the way the economy is right now – but an adoption thing.'

'Adoption?' Colin asked, surprised.

'The way zoos do – if you pay a certain amount of money then, together with a few other people, you can "adopt" a lion for a year. Museums are doing it, too,' Georgina said. 'You offer people the chance to adopt an object, and the price varies with size and importance. We'll get people to adopt costumes and props.'

'But what would people get out of adopting a prop?' Colin asked, completely at a loss.

'A digital certificate, their name on the theatre website, a photograph, and regular updates on what the theatre's doing. So the landlord of a pub called the King's Head might adopt Henry V's crown, or a funeral director might adopt Yorick's skull,' Georgina said. 'They could have a framed picture on the wall.'

'It's the sort of gift you buy for people who have everything,' Bea added. 'Someone who really loves *The Wizard of Oz* might want to adopt the ruby slippers. And if you go from a silver adoption to a gold, you'll get extra perks – a programme or play-bill from that show signed by all the cast, or a meet-and-greet, or an invitation to a question-and-answer session with the director and some of the actors after a performance. We're still working it out, but it's going to be really good for the theatre.'

'I'm glad,' Colin said.

'What's happening to the people you arrested?' Georgina asked.

'Elias and John have been released on bail, pending their court appearance. Peter refused to press charges on Sheena. Given the nature of the charges, Rebekah and Liza are remaining in custody until their appearance in the magistrates' court, which will be tomorrow,' Colin said. 'Aliou's been released pending further investigation. After that, I can't tell you – it depends on whether they plead guilty or not, and what kind of sentence they're likely to receive. The magistrates will decide if it goes to Crown Court, and whether they wait for trial in custody or on bail.' He looked at Georgina. 'Are you staying in London?'

'For a couple more days,' Georgina said. 'But I won't be needed here much longer. And, to be honest, I'm missing Norfolk and so is Bert. I'll be home soon.'

# TWENTY-TWO

A month later, Georgina and Jack were standing in the churchyard at Dunsted, with Robert Bailey, his daughter, Angie, and his cousin Pauline, as Fred Smith's body was interred next to Esther's. They all threw a red rose into the grave and the vicar said a prayer. They paused for a moment of silence; all they could hear was birdsong.

'I'm sorry I never got the chance to know you, Dad,' Robert said quietly. 'But I'm glad you're with Mum, now, where you belong.'

After the graveside service, the five of them headed to the local pub for lunch.

'Thank you for helping push through the DNA results, Colin,' Robert said. 'I have to admit, even though Georgie had all that documentary evidence, it wasn't until I held the DNA results in my hand and saw proof of the genetic link that I was finally convinced.'

'The sad thing is that I knew about it, years ago,' said Pauline, Robert's cousin. 'When Auntie Essie was still alive. I'm ten years younger than Robbie – just as my mum was ten years

younger than his mum – and I can remember hearing Mum and
Auntie Essie talking one night. I must've been about twelve at
the time. You'd left home by then, Robbie. They thought I was
asleep, but I wasn't, and I remember them talking about
Robbie's dad. I always assumed that nobody ever talked about
him because he was German, and Granddad Robert was *really*
anti-German, even years and years after the war.'

'So you knew Fred had married Esther?' Georgina asked.

Pauline nodded. 'My mum – Muriel – was her bridesmaid
up in London, and apparently Nan went to the wedding as
well. Even the Matron, and she wasn't supposed to know about
the wedding because you weren't meant to work if you were
married.'

'That's true,' Georgina said. 'I think that's one of the reasons
why she kept the name Bailey. So she could pretend she wasn't
married, if she had to.'

'That, and she could hardly have changed her name to a
German name, not during the war. There would've been bricks
through her windows,' Pauline agreed. 'Though Mum said
everyone liked Fred, and she reckoned even Granddad Robert
would've come round if he'd actually met him. That night, they
were speculating about why Fred had gone missing when she
was pregnant with you, Robbie. Mum thought he'd probably
been caught in a bomb blast and there just wasn't enough of
him left to find, afterwards, but Auntie Essie was always scared
that one of the other actors might have done him in.'

'He *did* do Fred in,' Doris said. 'We know that.'

'Did Esther say why she thought one of the actors had killed
him? Or who she thought it was?' Georgina asked.

'Partly jealousy, because Fred was really good at acting, and
partly because Fred had a German name. One guy in particular
had picked on Fred a few times, hit him hard enough that
Wardrobe used to have to cover the bruises on his face before a
show, but Fred refused to fight back. Some of the rest of the cast

stepped in to stop the fight, and the director warned the guy that he'd have to let him go if he didn't stop picking on Fred.' Pauline shrugged. 'Which I suppose made him resent Fred even more. He called Fred a coward for not fighting back, but Fred always said they were on the same side and he hated Hitler as much as anyone in England. But I suppose if you're really stuck in your ways, you don't tend to listen.'

'Such a shame,' Georgina said.

'It's a pity Mum wasn't well enough to come to the funeral today,' Pauline said. 'She would've enjoyed chatting to you about the old days. She's ninety-seven, now, but she's still got all her marbles.'

'Do you think if I gave you a list of the other actors in the company, she'd be able to take a look and see if she recognised any names?' Georgina asked. Because that would be the final proof, and bring closure to the case.

'I'm sure she'd love to help,' Pauline said with a smile.


Back in Norfolk, Georgina went through her files and emailed a list of the cast to Pauline.

Later that evening, Robert called her. 'Auntie Muriel looked through those names and she recognised one instantly. She said it was Eric Daubeney.'

'He's the one I thought it was,' Georgina said. 'When your dad was sent to the internment camp in Liverpool, Eric took over his roles; when Fred came back, Eric went back to the lesser roles. He probably resented that as well.'

'He'd be long dead by now, so he'll never face justice,' Robert said. 'I don't want to know any more about him. But I'll look up all my dad's reviews in the newspapers of the time. I'm just so pleased to know he was a good man and I can be proud of him.'

'You absolutely can be proud of him,' Georgina agreed with

a smile. 'And I'll look forward to seeing you, Angie and Pauline on opening night at the Regency – a couple of hours before curtain up, so I can take you round backstage and introduce you to the cast.'

'And Fred and Esther are looking forward to seeing their boy in his dad's theatre – even though Fred won't be on the stage,' Doris added quietly.


Two days later, Georgina and Colin attended another funeral, this time in Little Wenborough. The coroner gave a verdict of suicide for Harrison, whose body was released to Georgina and Jack as the nearest he had to family.

Jack had suggested that they bury Harrison next to Doris, and insisted on going halves with Georgina on the costs of the funeral, the wake and the changes to the headstone.

The funeral was quiet, with Jack, Tracey, Georgina and Colin the main mourners, and a scattering of people from the village who remembered Harrison in the days when he was known as Trevor.

Georgina had asked Jack which hymns had been used for Doris's funeral, so Harrison could have the same ones: 'Jerusalem', and 'Lord of All Hopefulness'. At the end of the service, Harrison's coffin left the church to the strains of 'My Sweet Lord', which had Georgina struggling to hold back her tears.

'It still feels a bit odd to think of him as Harrison, even though I know he changed his name by deed poll. In my head, I think he'll always be Trev,' Jack said.

'I know what you mean, but Harrison suited him. We walked over the Abbey Road zebra crossing together, and he looked just like a white-haired version of George Harrison,' Georgina said.

'Doris would've loved that,' Jack said. 'I wish they'd had their time together. And it's horrible to think that woman got away with what she did to my sister for all those years.'

'Though she did pay a price,' Georgina said. 'Harrison refused to have anything to do with her. She was alone for a great deal of her life.'

'Which is what she deserved. But at least Tre— *Harrison*,' Jack corrected himself, 'is with Doris now. They're together again.'


The Regency Theatre's woes and their adoption campaign caused a sensation in the press, and the response was so good that their production of *Macbeth* finally got its opening night, as well as being able to rebook the first six weeks that they'd had to cancel.

Georgina was in the middle of the front row, with Colin on one side, her mother on the other and Will next to her mother. Sybbie and Bernard had come up from Little Wenborough; Cesca, her husband, Giles, Jodie and Young Tom had also joined them. Robert, his daughter and his cousin had thoroughly enjoyed their tour of the theatre earlier, given by Georgina and Peter, and Doris had whispered, 'Fred and Esther say their boy's grown into a fine man.'

'So how much of the cast is original?' Sybbie asked Georgina, leaning across Colin.

'Most of it,' Georgina said. 'Banquo was the first one to be replaced' – she didn't need to remind everyone that Neil had been murdered – 'but Geoff's a better actor as well as a much nicer person. Macbeth and the First Murderer are both new, too, and they've fitted in well with the cast.'

'What happened to the people who played them?' Will asked.

'Rebekah got six months for GBH, and Elias got a year for perverting the course of justice,' Colin said. 'Though his wife's sentence was suspended, because he coerced her into taking the points for his speeding fine.'

'What about Liza?' Cesca asked. 'The one who actually killed the blackmailer?'

'She's in custody, awaiting her trial,' Colin said. 'Her lawyer's hoping for a verdict of involuntary manslaughter rather than murder.'

'Pete visits her every week,' Georgina said. 'He's got someone temporary helping with Wardrobe, but he says she'll have her job back as soon as it's all sorted.' And she really hoped it worked out for them. Liza had made a terrible mistake, but she would never harm Peter.

The lights in the auditorium went down, a slow drumbeat sounded, dry ice blew across the stage, and everyone was silent and watching as the three witches walked on. Even though Georgina had seen several rehearsals with the new cast, as well as taking photographs of the dress rehearsal, the play still felt fresh and vibrant for her. She heard gasps and sniffs in the audi-torium in the scene where Bea folded the baby clothes, and almost burst with pride at how well her daughter coaxed emotion out of the audience.

At the end of the play, there was a standing ovation. Georgina glanced behind her, and every single person was on their feet and clapping wildly. Bea was glowing.

And suddenly the theatre was silent. Georgina could swear that she could hear Stephen's voice. 'Our girl was amazing tonight. She'll definitely be the Beatrice of her generation and I'll be applauding her all the way.' There was a pause. 'I do love nothing in the world so well as you.'

Words he'd quoted to her so many times over the years. He'd even told her that every time he played Benedick, when he spoke that line he thought of her, and that was why it was so convincing on stage.

'Be happy, my love,' he whispered. 'He's a good man. Live well and be happy.'

'I will,' Georgina promised, and the silence lifted to bring back the sound of applause.

# A LETTER FROM THE AUTHOR

Huge thanks for reading *The Body Under the Stage*; I hope you were hooked on Georgina, Doris and Colin's journey. If you want to join other readers in hearing all about my new releases and bonus content, you can sign up for my newsletter!

www.stormpublishing.co/kate-hardy

If you enjoyed this book and could spare a few moments to leave a review that would be hugely appreciated. Even a short review can make all the difference in encouraging a reader to discover my books for the first time. Thank you so much!

This series was hugely influenced by three things. Firstly, I grew up in a haunted house in a small market town in Norfolk, so I've always been drawn to slightly spooky stories. (I did research it when I wrote a book on researching house history, but I couldn't find any documentary evidence for the tale of the jealous miller who murdered his wife. However, I also don't have explanations for various spooky things that happened at the house – including the anecdote in *The Body at Rookery Barn* about Sybbie's dogs, which happened in real life with our Labradors and a tennis ball.) Secondly, I read Daphne du Maurier's short story 'The Blue Lenses' while I was a student, and... I can't explain this properly without giving spoilers, so I'll say it's to do with how you see people. Thirdly, I'm deaf; after I had my first hearing aid fitted, once I'd got over the thrill of hearing birdsong for the first time in years, my author brain started ticking. The du Maurier story gave me a 'what if' moment: what if you heard something through your hearing aids that wasn't what you were supposed to hear? (The obvious one would be someone's thoughts; but that's where my childhood home came in.) It took a few years for the idea to come to the top of my head and refuse to go away, but what if you could hear what my heroine Georgina ends up hearing?

And so, Georgina Drake ends up living in a haunted house in a small market town in Norfolk...

*The Body Under the Stage* comes from my love of theatre – all my spare cash has always gone on books, music and theatre tickets! I highly recommend the tours at the Georgian Theatre in Richmond and the Theatre Royal in Bury St Edmunds. They're both beautiful buildings and the tours are fascinating.

The nicest thing about having a modern and a cold case in each book in the series is that I can explore different bits of history that fascinate me. I wanted the cold case to be linked to the theatre and toyed with the idea of the Restoration, but then decided the London Blitz would suit me better as a way of hiding Fred's murder. My mum's parents were both in the Navy during the war, and while I was researching some family history, I came across the story of the internment camps and the *Arandora Star*. It made me wonder what London was like during the war if you weren't English – and what happened if you fell in love with someone who was English? And what if someone else wanted you out of the way?

Little Wenborough isn't a real place, but the name is a mash-up of the town where I grew up and the river where I walk my dogs in the morning. But Norfolk is an amazing place to live. Huge skies (incredible sunrises and sunsets), wide beaches (aka my best place to think, and the Editpawial Assistants are always up for a trip there), and more ancient churches than anywhere else in the country (watch this space!).

Thanks again for being part of this amazing journey with me and I hope you'll stay in touch – I have so many more stories and ideas to entertain you with!

All best

Kate Hardy

facebook.com/katehardyromanceauthor
x.com/katehardyauthor
instagram.com/katehardyauthor

# ACKNOWLEDGEMENTS

I'd like to thank Oliver Rhodes and Kathryn Taussig for taking a chance on my slightly unusual take on a crime series; Emily Gowers for being an absolute dream of an editor – incisive, thoughtful and a wonderful collaborator as well as being great fun; and Shirley and Maddy for picking up the bits I missed! I've loved every second of working on this book with you.

Gerard Brooks has been a particular star with location research, coming with me to visit the Georgian theatres at Richmond and Bury St Edmunds.

Special thanks to my family and friends who cheer-led the first Georgina Drake book, made useful suggestions about theatres/cake/ghosts, and are there through the highs and lows of publishing: in particular Nicki Brooks, Jackie Chubb, Siobhàn Coward, Sheila Crighton, Liz Fielding, Sandra Forder, Philippa Gell, Rosie Hendry, Rachel Hore, Jenni Keer, Lizzie Lamb, Clare Marchant, Jo Rendell-Dodd, Fiona Robertson, Rachael Stewart, Michelle Styles, Heidi-Jo Swain, Katy Watson, Ian Wilfred, Susan Wilson, Jan Wooller and Caroline Woolnough. (And apologies if I've missed anyone!)

A big shout-out to my friend Suzanne Bell for answering questions about the wardrobe department – any errors are mine.

Extra-special thanks to Gerard, Chris and Chloe Brooks, who've always been my greatest supporters; to Chrissy and Rich Camp, for always believing in me and being the best uncle and aunt ever; and to Archie and Dexter, my beloved Editpawial Assistants, for keeping my feet warm, reminding me when it's time for walkies and lunch, and putting up with me photographing them to keep my social media ticking over while I'm on deadline.

And, last but very much not least, thank you, dear reader, for choosing my book. I hope you enjoy reading it as much as I enjoyed writing it.

Printed in Great Britain
by Amazon